PROGRAMMED FOR BEAUTY

▽

Her hair was golden brown and slightly curly. Her eyes, one blue and one green, gazed sightlessly forward. This was the biggest icon in the system, nearly as big as a twelve-year-old child. The icon's size reflected the size and complexity of the program it represented. The program's name was Maggie. She was almost ready.

He hovered admiringly before Maggie's icon for a moment. She was the culmination of years of hard, frustrating work; work that his father had destroyed over and over again. Maggie was extremely illegal. . . . Arnold didn't care. Making Maggie live was his only concern.

VIRTUAL GIRL

VIRTUAL GIRL

Amy Thomson

ACE BOOKS, NEW YORK

The material that appears on page 216 from *The Velveteen Rabbit* by Margery Williams was originally published by William Heinemann Ltd., and is used by permission of Reed International Books, London, England.

This book is an Ace original edition, and has never been previously published.

VIRTUAL GIRL

An Ace Book / published by arrangement with the author

PRINTING HISTORY
Ace edition / August 1993

ISBN: 0-441-86500-3

Ace Books are published by The Berkley Publishing Group, 200 Madison Avenue, New York, NY 10016.
The name "ACE" and the "A" logo are trademarks belonging to Charter Communications, Inc.

PRINTED IN THE UNITED STATES OF AMERICA

10 9 8 7 6 5 4 3 2 1

For the women of Angeline's:
may they all find the shelter and support they need.

Acknowledgments

Many thanks to:

Charles N. Brown of *Locus* for giving me my first big break. Darrell Anderson, and the really strange guy counting resistors in Taco Time, for the initial inspiration. Terry Carr for giving me a role model to aspire to. Suzy McKee Charnas and J. T. Stewart for making me take the book seriously. Mona Tschurwald, the YWCA, and the homeless women of Angeline's Day Shelter in Seattle, for helping me to understand a little of what it means to be homeless. Grant Fjermedal for the necessary credentials. Walt Read and Michael G. Dyer of the Artificial Intelligence Laboratory at UCLA, for neat research papers and information on artificial intelligence. Somtow Sucharitkul for giving me something to laugh at when things seemed most hopeless.

The Whole Earth Review and Kevin Kelly for publishing Adam Heilbrun's interview with Jaron Lanier on virtual reality just when I needed it most. Mr. Tito Brin of the downtown New Orleans Public Library, and the wonderful librarians at Suzzallo and Odegaard Libraries of the University of Washington, the downtown branch of the Seattle Public Library, and The Historic New Orleans Collection. Kendell Thompson of the U.S. Park Service for his excellent tour of the St. Louis Cemetery No. 1 in New Orleans. The American Automobile Association, for numerous city and state maps, and Dr. Carolyn Scheve, for invaluable medical advice. John C. Hecht III for services above and below the call of duty.

Richard Clement, Greg Cox, Ken Crawford, Jill Zeller, Linda Jordan-Eichner, Donna Davis, Bruce Chandler Fergusson, Scott Stolnack, Ian Hageman, Loren MacGregor, Rebecca Brown Ore, and George Alec Effinger for their input on my manuscript.

Don Maass for continuing to believe in Maggie.

Ray Takeuchi and Rosalie the Wonder Cat for their love and support.

Last, but not least, thanks to Ginjer Buchanan for making it possible for you to read this book. All of what is the best in this book, I owe to these people; all of the mistakes are my own.

Chapter
1

Arnold carefully smoothed the battered data gloves over his massive, thick-fingered hands. He put on the bulky Virtual Reality helmet, making sure that the foam pads were properly aligned. It was dark and musty inside, smelling of stale sweat. Reaching up, he flipped a small switch on his helmet. A low chime told him the gloves and helmet were on.

He snapped his fingers to activate the program, and a fractal fern-leaf pattern appeared below him, scintillating with psychedelic colors. It was the directory of his Virtual Reality projected around him by the small stereo screens in his helmet. They responded to the movements of his head and hands as though he were really inside this created environment. The illusion was startlingly effective. Arnold pointed his finger at the pattern, directing the computer to move him toward it. He soared down into the fernlike trellis, pushing past clusters of small utility programs, three-dimensional blue icons hanging like berries from the shimmering fronds of the directory. It was all a clever simulation, but it seemed very real.

Arnold squeezed one of the little blue polygons twice and a mirror appeared before him. He paused to check out his virtual reflection. Here, in the make-believe reality of the computer, he was a slender man in a stage magician's elegant tux, with a gleaming black satin top hat. In real life Arnold was big, sloppy, and dressed in ill-fitting Salvation Army castoffs, but what the hell, it was his reality. He could look the way he damn well wanted to. He pointed his finger and was off again. He swerved around the icon of a reality processor, and almost crashed into a thicket of applications clustered around one of the main directory nodes.

Arnold noted the clutter and paused. He began thinning out the unnecessary programs by plucking their icons from the directory and tossing them over his left shoulder, where they vanished as the computer erased them from memory. He started to rearrange the entire directory but caught himself. He was putting off the inevitable with busy work. He had more important things to do.

Arnold soared down into the core of the directory, then brought himself to a stop by extending his neat, white-gloved hands palm outward, as though breaking a fall. He was hovering before the icon of a woman. Her hair was golden brown and slightly curly. Her eyes, one blue and one green, gazed sightlessly forward. This was the biggest icon in the system, nearly as big as a twelve-year-old child. The icon's size reflected the size and complexity of the program it represented. The program's name was Maggie. She was almost ready.

He hovered admiringly before Maggie's icon for a moment. She was the culmination of years of hard, frustrating work; work that his father had destroyed over and over again. Maggie was extremely illegal. The Net Police would shit virtual blue bricks if they knew about her. Arnold didn't care. Making Maggie live was his only concern.

Arnold wiggled his fingers in a preprogrammed gesture, then spread his arms apart. As he did so, the virtual world around him enlarged until the pupils of Maggie's eyes were as big as manhole covers. Rescaling Virtual Reality wasn't really necessary in order to access Maggie's program, but the minor magic of it still had the power to delight him. Besides, accessing Maggie's program by crashing through her icon seemed crass. He preferred to be a bit more elegant. He pointed his finger toward Maggie's now-enormous right eye, and dove through the gaping pupil into the depths of her program space.

Once through the rabbit hole of Maggie's eye, Arnold soared along the silent, white corridors of her programming structure, occasionally stopping to tweak some branchlet of programming into a slightly different shape. He drifted past struts that gleamed like white marble, and complicated branchings that appeared to be built of frozen sea foam. It was hard to believe that all this was made of electrical impulses in a computer. It all seemed so substantial, so real, but it was built out of nothing but his own ideas. The program had become too complex for him to completely understand. There were times that he got lost in its lacy, fractal whiteness. Still, Maggie worked perfectly, and that was good enough for him.

Arnold pulled off his top hat and rummaged around in it. He pulled out a slender ebony wand, tipped with ivory. Lifting his wand, he tapped it once, twice, thrice, against the nearest branch. With a thrum like a distant harp, color began pulsing along the branches of Maggie's program. He had opened an interface to her program. She was ready for instruction.

Reaching into his sleeve, Arnold pulled out a small roll of white parchment. He unrolled it, scanning his test program one last time. This was Maggie's final, most dangerous test. Today he would pit her against the AI detection systems in the Net. Among the most complex programs in the world, the detection systems prowled the Net like hungry sharks, searching for programs that violated the anti-AI laws. When they found an illegal program, they descended upon it and tore it apart. Then they traced it back to its origin and alerted the Net Police, who were nearly as fast and implacable as their programs.

If Maggie was discovered by the Net, he would have to run for it. If Net security discovered a program as flagrantly illegal as Maggie, the Net Pigs would be breaking down the door in less than fifteen minutes. He had taken precautions in case Maggie failed her test. His backpack was packed and waiting by the door. There was a thermite bomb strapped to Maggie's body, and he could erase the contents of his computer with a single command. At the slightest sign of trouble, he would disengage and run for it.

The stakes were high, and the precautions weren't foolproof. If he failed now, it might be years before he could start over again. If the Net Police reconstructed the charred remains of Maggie's robotic body, they might place restrictions on crucial parts, making his dream much more difficult to achieve. Still, there was no putting it off any longer. Maggie was as ready as he could make her. He had run diagnostics and simulations for weeks now. Either she passed or she failed.

It was a formidable test. In order to fool Net Security, Maggie needed to use the Trojan Horse defense, concealing her true nature behind an impenetrable shell of decoy programming. She had to maintain that shell while completing an exacting and illegal task in the complex consensus reality of the Net. It was a lot like rubbing your head and patting your stomach while simultaneously flying a jet plane under combat conditions. If Maggie passed this test, she would be ready to begin learning the complexities of the real world.

Arnold folded the scroll into a small paper airplane, touched it three times with his magic wand to activate it, then hurled the test program down the glowing corridors of colored light. It streaked off, disappearing around the corner. The pulsing colors flared, then dimmed as his program was received. Then the reality around him winked out, leaving him hovering before a floating window onto another virtual landscape.

Maggie floated in the window. As he watched she changed shape, becoming a cluster of silver message spheres. The spheres sped through the high bronze gateway of the modem port and out into the roiling storm of the Net. Immediately she was surrounded by the dark, streamlined shapes of the Net detection probes. They swarmed over her like high-speed tarnish. Arnold leaned forward intently. This was a crucial moment. If the probes detected anything out of the ordinary in Maggie's cluster of messages, she would wink out of existence. For nearly a minute, nothing seemed to be happening. Then the probes slid away, leaving her marked with a complex red symbol to show that she had passed inspection. Arnold let out a sigh of relief, causing a cloud of bright yellow asterisks to appear. He wiped them out with a wave of his hand and watched through his magic window as Maggie reached her destination, and vanished behind the gates of the security system. Maggie emerged after a couple of minutes, carrying the icon for the information he had left for her to retrieve. Again the shadowy probes enveloped her and again she emerged bright and clean. She returned through the gates of his system, and the window vanished like a punctured soap bubble. Her icon floated before him, holding a small silver sphere in its hands. He took it from her and inspected its contents. Satisfied, he disposed of it. She had done very well.

It was time to go. He inactivated her program with a gesture, and then clapped his hands three times and vanished from the system.

Arnold pulled the VR helmet off and lay blinking in the bright light, reorienting himself to the real world. He was lying in the middle of the floor, late-afternoon sunlight streaming down on him from the skylight. He switched off the helmet and headed for the bathroom. There were no bathrooms in Virtual Reality, he thought wryly. No matter how long he was under the helmet, he always seemed to come out with a full bladder. He kept meaning to try a catheter, but had always found a reason to put off trying it out. He flushed the grimy toilet and filled a large, chipped mug with water from the leaky tap, drank it down in one huge gulp, then filled it again and sipped at it as he stood scratching his hairy belly. VR sessions always left him dehydrated.

Arnold set the half-empty mug down and wandered over to the computer. He checked the connections on the camera and microphone assembly that enabled Maggie to see and hear. The assembly had been rigged up to test her visual and voice-recognition capabilities. Last night, he had used them to show Maggie her body for the first time. She couldn't really understand it yet, but he wanted to show his accomplishment to someone, even though he was used to loneliness.

Arnold had never gotten along with people. He didn't know what he was doing wrong. It had bothered him when he was a kid, but he had long since given up trying to figure out what it was that people disliked about him. It was too much work. In a few more hours it wouldn't matter anymore; his Maggie would live, and that would cure his isolation. She would never reject him. It wasn't in her design specs.

The months of undisturbed isolation had freed him to work swiftly. Finding parts and supplies out here was simply a matter of patrolling the trash bins and surplus stores of the high-tech industries scattered between Seattle and Tacoma. Besides, he had already done most of the work before, only to see it destroyed by his father's men when they had come to drag him back to his father.

Because New York's familiar streets had been home, Arnold had put up with his father's interference. In fact, he had treated it as a kind of challenge. It had been a kind of perverse thrill to see how long he could get away with defying his father. Then, last May, his father had had him committed to a mental hospital. That had been the last straw.

Arnold's smile turned ironic. He was the best lock hacker and escape artist in his freshman class at MIT. Fifteen hours after he was escorted into the sanitarium by two burly orderlies, he was on a mag-lev freight bound for Seattle and freedom. Within a week of his arrival, he had rented this deserted garage, surrounded by rotting warehouses, and moved in.

He spent the summer and early autumn scrounging parts from dumpsters and industry surplus yards. Maggie's eyes were a particular point of pride. He had found them in a dumpster behind an optical prosthetics factory. It had been surprisingly simple to adapt their leads to a computer interface instead of a biological one. Only Maggie's skin and hair had needed custom orders.

Arnold uncovered Maggie's face, admiring her delicate, high-arching eyebrows, small nose, and narrow, elfin chin. *Even empty, she has a sweet face*, he thought, *sweet and understanding*. He stroked her soft brown hair and gently touched her smooth cheek. She seemed to be sleeping. It was impossible to tell she was a robot. His heart swelled with pride. She would be more than any human could be, always kind, always compassionate. And she was all his.

After carefully disabling and removing the thermite bomb, Arnold grasped her under the shoulders and shifted her into a more convenient position, grunting with the effort. Though she was only five feet tall, Maggie weighed nearly 200 pounds. This was remarkably lightweight, considering the amount of hardware packed into her. She could eat, drink, and even cry. On cold nights, she would keep him warm by elevating her body temperature. Even her female parts worked, although this was a matter of pride on his part, not desire. He was a perfectionist, and insisted on complete anatomical accuracy. He wouldn't sully his Maggie by having sex with her.

Arnold was even prouder of Maggie's non-human capabilities. Her state-of-the-art superconducting batteries were capable of keeping her going for anywhere from eight hours to two days, depending on her level of physical activity. Walking consumed considerable energy, and running ran her batteries down even faster. If Maggie sat completely still, her batteries would last for months. There was a prehensile plug coiled at the base of her spine. When she needed to recharge, all she had to do was plug into any conventional outlet.

Arnold had designed Maggie to be the ideal street companion. He needed someone he could trust implicitly, someone he could count on if things got rough. Maggie was stronger and faster than a human being. She had a special sub-personality that took over in emergencies. It was fierce and wary, and designed for self-defense and evasion. The rest of the time she would be sweet and kind, her innocence intact.

After a final check of Maggie's body, Arnold pushed the creaking gurney she rested on over to the computer. As he began fussing with the cables needed to connect her body to the computer, he knocked over the video camera. It toppled to the floor with a loud crack. He disconnected it and tossed it in the nearest trash pile. He didn't need it anymore.

Arnold picked up Maggie's left arm and parted the pliant plastic skin of her inner wrist with a quick pull. Underneath her skin lay a shiny steel computer jack. He connected a cable from her body to the computer. Maggie was ready for the transfer into her new body.

Initiating the transfer was so simple that he didn't bother entering VR, he simply worked off the computer screen. He activated the transfer and settled back in a chair to watch his Maggie come alive. Transferring such a large program took time. He might as well get comfortable.

Arnold watched her face, intently waiting for the first signs of life to appear. The change, when it came, was startlingly immediate. As soon as the computer beeped, signaling the completion of the transfer, Maggie's eyes popped open. She regarded Arnold with an inhuman intensity. One eye was blue, the other green; it gave her gaze an alien quality that Arnold found he liked. It was his signature, his way of setting her apart from humanity. It made her unique. Besides, he hadn't been able to find two eyes of the same color.

Maggie let out a long cry that ranged from deep, window-rattling bass up the scale beyond his hearing. He grimaced, covering his ears. There was nothing wrong with her voice, he thought with a wry smile.

She looked down at her hands, examining them closely, moving them this way and that. Suddenly she began flailing about wildly, her face contorting. Arnold touched her and she stopped, looking at his hand where it rested on her arm, her head twitching slightly.

Arnold glanced up at the computer, noticing the error messages scrolling past the screen for the first time. Gently resting his hand on Maggie's shoulder, he killed the original version of the program he had copied into Maggie's new body. He didn't need it now. He had his Maggie.

Chapter 2

Maggie laid her warm palm against the cool, smooth mirror in the darkness. When she took her hand away, her infrared vision revealed a stark yellow hand print on the cooler blue glass. It faded slowly to green and then blurred into indistinguishability as her hand print cooled to the temperature of the surrounding glass.

She turned on the light and looked at herself in the mirror, comparing her body with her memories of the first time she had seen it. She had been in the computer then, and her visual recognition had been very crude. She could hear through a microphone, but she comprehended little of what she heard. Her memories had been dark and discontinuous. So much had changed.

She replayed her first memories of her body in their original flat black and white. She watched again as Arnold pulled the sheet off her body, remembering her momentary confusion at the sudden, billowing deformation of the white surface. At the time, she had only barely recognized the features of her body (the changing topology of the billowing sheet had been much more interesting), but in retrospect, she noted the longer hair, the breasts, and the triangle of pale, downy hair that were now a part of her. She also recognized the look of pride that Arnold wore as he looked down on her body.

Then Arnold vanished from her fixed visual field. She sensed him inputting data to her.

"This body is yours, Maggie, I made it for you," came his message.

"Query: mine? Query: purpose?" Maggie replied, routing her questions to Arnold's helmet.

Billions of nanoseconds had crept by before Arnold answered. Her perception of time had changed since she had gotten a body.

Input from her new senses kept her so busy that time seemed to fly by. In the computer she had had so much idle processing power that time had trickled by. She had amused herself by performing complicated calculations; by layering interesting bits of sound together; or by toying with focus and image processing, splitting and multiplying images, and making them whirl kaleidoscopically. She still did this sometimes, when she was bored, but the new realm of her senses usually kept her occupied.

At last Arnold completed his reply: **"Mine=Self component. Examples: mouse, modem, video camera, microphone. Purpose=Peripheral, Name=Body."**

"Query: I/O Address of Body?"

Arnold input a long list of memory locations and addresses, which Maggie watched with growing confusion.

"No such addresses. Query: address location?"

"Peripheral not yet installed. Save address locations in priority memory."

Maggie saved the addresses. The list was long, it took nearly a full second to store it all.

"Tomorrow, I'll put you inside of this body," he typed. **"You'll like having a body, Maggie. It's a good one, too. This time no one's going to keep me from making you live!"**

Maggie replied with a list of queries; none of what Arnold had just input explained anything. Finally, he threw a sheet over her camera, and left her alone for nine hours and seventeen minutes to digest her new data.

Maggie spent that long night sifting through the new data Arnold had given her, sorting and resorting it, searching for some clue to explain the purpose of the new peripheral. Instead she found only more puzzles to unravel. What was a kinesthetic map? What was a voder? Why did they require so much memory? She was relieved to see that she would still have access to sight, although judging from all the data and memory locations associated with it, it would definitely be different. Sight was her favorite peripheral, the one associated with her earliest memories. She was glad that she would still have it. There were no addresses for keyboards, gloves, helmets, or printers, although there was a modem and communications bus. How would she interface with Arnold? A body must be a very complex sort of peripheral.

The nanoseconds ticked past. Eventually, the light level slowly increased. Muffled sounds came through the sheet. Maggie waited. At last, Arnold pulled off the sheet. She watched as he changed his hands and head. He began to move his hands and head, turning and pointing. Suddenly she was aware of a presence inside her, altering her program structure. She switched off her peripherals to attend more closely to the changes. Then she received a set of instructions, sending her out into the net to retrieve some data. She went out and brought it back, switching on her video camera and microphone again.

Her new peripheral lay on its back, wires trailing from its wrists. There was a bulky square thing on her chest. It hadn't been there the night before. She wondered what it was. As she watched, Arnold removed it, then carried it out of her visual field.

She watched and waited some more. Arnold suddenly loomed in her visual field, he was doing something to the computer. Suddenly, Maggie's vision shifted wildly, she saw the flat plane of the ceiling, an assemblage of unrecognizable objects, and a brief glimpse of her own screen filling up with error messages, then the floor suddenly loomed larger and her sight blanked out.

"I/O error: Address 0038! Query? Query? Query?" Maggie filled the screen with error messages and queries, scrolling off the screen, and printing out on the printer. She beeped wildly at each carriage return. Then her sound was cut off. Blind and deaf, she continued to fill her screen with error messages as she waited for a response.

Suddenly, she felt herself shifting. She was stretched and then compacted. For one dizzying instant, she was in two places at once: her old familiar computer, still scrolling out error messages, and someplace new and very different. Then her perception stabilized again. She was in the new place. Her memory was now incredibly vast. She could access thousands of new addresses. She raced to process this incredible flood of new information.

Maggie opened her eyes. Objects had more than just shape and shading now, they had—she searched her new store of memory and found new concepts expanding away in waves as she accessed her new addresses—color! This new level of complexity in her vision was called color.

She looked closely at Arnold. He was brown and beige. His eyes were somewhere between green and brown, surrounded by white with tiny streaks of red in it. His body was blue on the top and his legs were black. Her vision was sharper and more precise now. She could see thousands of tiny hairs on the backs of Arnold's hands. His palms and fingers were covered in a mass of tiny whorls and wrinkles. She could see depth now, too. It explained why things kept vanishing before. She understood now that things in front of other things covered the things behind them, unless they were—she paused and searched—transparent. So much information! The world held complexities she had never dreamed of!

Maggie cried out (another new set of addresses and information) and heard herself. Even her hearing had changed—sound came in from both sides of her head at once. She could locate sounds now. They had depth, like her new vision. Sounds that had once been her favorites seemed flat and uninteresting by comparison. She filled out their flatness with recalculated values, and then discovered that she could produce them herself! Instead of a few beeps and buzzes, she had a whole range of sounds at her disposal!

She turned her head to hear better, and her vision shifted. She looked down at her hands, and understood suddenly that they were part of her. She looked from her hands to Arnold's hands. They were alike, her hands had five fingers and tiny lines and wrinkles, too. There were differences, though; her hands were smaller, and Arnold's hands had black smudges on them and his nails had crescents of black under the tips of them. Her hands were also less hairy than Arnold's.

She lifted her hands and turned them to examine them more closely, and then realized something very important. Her hands could move! She could control their movement! She kicked and waved and flexed herself, turning her head this way and that, reveling in the new sensations of movement and control. Now Arnold wouldn't keep slipping out of her field of vision. She could follow his movements with her eyes.

Arnold reached out and put his hands on her body. She felt him. Another new catalog of knowledge unrolled itself in her memory. She sat still, absorbing this new sensation. She could see and hear and feel thousands of new things. Her information-hungry processors were buzzing with millions of bits of information. She marveled at how much of the world she could comprehend now. A body was a wonderful peripheral!

She was very glad that Arnold had given her one.

Maggie cut off the flow of memory, smiling at her younger, more innocent self. She looked at her body, still marveling at its capabilities after a week inside it. She had learned so many things since acquiring a body. Arnold had taught her to walk and talk, and how to dress herself. She was learning more each day. There was still so much to learn. She wanted to know everything.

She no longer thought of her body as a peripheral. It was part of her now, much more so than the computer that Arnold had created her in. When she was in the computer, she had not really understood the difference between herself and the rest of the world, everything was just data to be processed. Now she understood herself as separate entity, a thing apart. Unique, that was the word Arnold used to describe her. She was unique.

Maggie turned out the light, pressed her hand against the mirror, and watched her hand print fade. She was unique. That pleased her.

Chapter 3

Maggie was becoming more and more like a human every day, Arnold thought to himself as he watched her paging rapidly through a novel he had brought her from the library. She lay on a ragged piece of carpeting. Late-afternoon sunlight filtering through the dingy skylight illuminated her hair and skin. In her oversized, bulky sweater and long skirt, she looked like a little girl in woman's clothing.

Maggie still relied on him for nearly everything. Her trusting nature and utter dependence made him feel strangely protective, even though she was stronger than him and better able to defend herself in a tight situation. She finished the novel as he watched, and looked up at him.

The little girl vanished in her compelling gaze. Those huge odd-colored eyes were unforgettable. They seemed to see right down into his soul. Maggie had ceased to be a collection of personality modules, and was becoming a fully integrated personality. Sometimes it was hard to remember that she was only a machine.

Her quick intelligence amazed him. She learned much faster than he had expected. Her grasp of motor control was especially impressive. She had stopped twitching entirely after the first day, and was walking on her own by the second day. Her walk still seemed a bit stilted, but she improved with each passing day. Even though she was only a week old, Maggie was able to dress herself. She had almost stopped putting things on backward. He reminded himself to mark the inside collars of her more difficult clothes. He was glad she could dress herself. Handling her nude body had been all right when it was only a lifeless dummy, but he found it incredibly embarrassing now that she was alive and aware of what he was doing.

"Come here, Maggie," he told her.

Maggie set aside her book and shambled over to him. Arnold exposed her computer jacks and connected her up to his VR helmet and data gloves. He used the helmet to see through Maggie's eyes, and hear through her ears, while he controlled her like a puppet with the gloves. It was time for more motor training.

He called out Maggie's access code, a simple limerick composed of nonsense words that gave him total control over her program. He activated the helmet and saw himself sitting in a chair, the bulky, awkward white helmet covered his face, making him look strangely inhuman. He turned on the gloves' feedback mechanism and relaxed, letting the gloves' spongy resistance guide his hands into the position that described the posture she now held. He twitched his little finger on his left hand and Maggie moved her left arm in response. Then he ran her through a set of calibration gestures as he watched her reflection in the mirror through her eyes. She worked perfectly.

Arnold smiled, feeling the satisfaction that came from properly working machinery. Machines were dependable. They did what you expected them to do, and no more. He trusted machines. They didn't load you down with a bunch of confusing and conflicting expectations the way people did.

He lifted his hands, readying himself for the day's training. Today he would work on head gestures and facial expressions. He manipulated Maggie through smiles and frowns, laughter and sadness, refining each gesture until it was entirely natural, and then fixing the best gestures in her memory. Each time he took her through a session like this, her movements became more and more natural. These sessions formed a subconscious library of expressions and postures that supplemented the basic gestural complement she had been programmed with. It was exhaustingly precise work, of the kind he excelled at.

Two hours later, Arnold released Maggie from his control, and stopped to rest. He heated up some left-over pizza and sat next to her to eat it. As usual, Maggie watched every move intently.

"Arnold, why do you eat?" she asked him.

"I guess you could say that it recharges my batteries."

"Oh." Maggie thought for a bit, then said, "Arnold?"

"Yes, Maggie, what is it?"

"Why don't I eat?"

"You don't eat because you're a robot, Maggie."

"Why don't robots eat?"

"Because you're a machine and I'm not," Arnold told her before finishing off the last bite of his first slice.

"What's the difference?"

Arnold sighed and set down his last slice of pizza. "I made you, Maggie. I built you out of computer circuits and steel and plastics. Nobody made me. I was born. I'm made of flesh and blood."

He got up and cleared the bed of its accumulation of papers and leftover food cartons. He gathered up several books and large sheets of paper and spread them out on the bed. "Look, Maggie, see this blueprint?" He pointed to a large sheet of paper covered with blue lines. "This is what you look like inside." Arnold took down a battered copy of *Gray's Anatomy* and opened it to a full-color illustration of the internal organs. "This is what I look like inside."

Maggie looked at both drawings for a while. "Arnold, why am I all blue inside? You're all kinds of pretty colors."

Arnold sighed. "That's just a drawing, Maggie. Here . . ."

He drew her over to a mirror, unbuttoned the top of her dress, picked up a scalpel, and carefully slit her chest open. He gently drew the flaps of plaskin aside and parted the hairlike filaments of her sensors. Underneath, gleaming softly behind a layer of transparent silicone padding, overlapping layers of beautifully articulated steel sheathing protected Maggie's delicate circuitry. It was a beautiful design. It still amazed him that he had built it all by himself.

"That's what you look like inside, Maggie," Arnold told her as he eased the slit edges of skin back together. A few moments of light pressure, and the skin sealed itself with no sign that it had ever been cut.

Maggie picked up the scalpel and studied it for a moment. She handed it to Arnold. "Will you show me what you look like, Arnold?"

"No!" Arnold said, in a louder voice than he had intended. "People are designed differently. If you open me up the way I opened you up, I would cease to function. I would die. Do you understand what dying means, Maggie? I would go away and never, never be able to be with you again. There are many things that can kill me that wouldn't hurt you. If I stopped eating, I'd starve to death. If I didn't drink enough water, I'd die of thirst. There are lots of things that would kill me that won't hurt you because you're a robot."

Maggie was silent for several minutes. Finally she picked up the last piece of pizza and handed it to him. "Please," she urged him, "eat this. If you die, I'll be all alone."

Arnold laughed, though he was deeply touched by her concern. It felt so real, even though he remembered designing it. "It's all right, Maggie, I'd have to stop eating for at least a week, and I'm not planning on dying. Not while I have my Maggie around to protect me."

Chapter 4

The garage was quiet. Maggie stood in the center of the room and watched motes of dust drift in a beam of sunlight. Arnold was gone, and she was bored. Without Arnold, there was little to do. She had read all the books and examined every object in the garage several times. The last hour and a half she had spent layering visual images of gleaming, drifting dust motes, until it seemed that a slow sunlit blizzard of dust floated before her eyes.

Maggie heard the sound of Arnold's key in the door. She filed her patterns away and waited attentively for Arnold to come in. His backpack was bulging, and he was carrying two more shopping bags crammed full of small boxes. He dumped a stack of boxes onto the bed and began sorting through them. Maggie walked over and watched him.

"What are those, Arnold?"

"Videochips, Maggie, for you to watch."

Obediently, Maggie sat on the bed and watched the boxes intently, waiting to see what would happen. Arnold finished unpacking and looked up at her.

"Maggie, what are you doing?" he asked.

"I am watching the videochips, Arnold."

Arnold laughed, and Maggie stole a quick glance away from the boxes to look at him, hoping she wouldn't miss anything important.

"That's not how you watch a videochip, Maggie. Here, let me show you." He inserted one of the boxes into the slot of a machine, and turned on the video monitor. Light flashed across the screen and music played. She watched the flickering screen intently, not really sure what to expect. Suddenly there were strange voices. It was odd, hearing other voices than her own and Arnold's. She looked around, wondering where the people were.

"Here," Arnold said, "these are pictures of people, here on the screen. See?" He outlined one of the figures with his finger, and Maggie realized suddenly that this was like her old computer memories, except in color. There were people doing things on screen, talking to each other. These were the first people that she had ever seen besides Arnold. She watched, fascinated, until the screen turned white and staticky.

"Arnold, those people, they're gone! Where did they go? What happened to them?" Maggie asked. She was worried about them. They were so interesting, and now they were gone.

"It's just a film, Maggie, those aren't real people, it's kind of like a memory. Those boxes contain the memory, and the machine does the remembering. The people on the screen were actors, and they were just pretending anyway."

"I don't understand," Maggie said. "They seemed so real."

"That's because they were good actors, Maggie," Arnold told her. "They're just telling a story, that movie never really happened. It's a made-up thing, like those books I gave you last week."

"You mean that those stories weren't real, either?" Maggie suddenly felt her world slipping away.

Arnold put his hand on her shoulder. "Look, Maggie, stories are something humans make up when we're bored, okay? It amuses us, to make up stories about things that don't exist. Do you understand?"

Maggie thought of her layered blizzard of dancing dust motes. "I think so, Arnold, but how do I tell the difference between a story and something that's real?"

Arnold started to answer her, then stopped, lost in thought. "That's a very good question, Maggie, and there aren't a lot of easy answers. In time, you'll develop your own algorithms to determine the difference between truth and fiction. For right now, though, the only reality that you need to worry about is anything that happens between you and me. The books and videos are only useful data. They give you examples of how humans behave. That's all they're here for. It doesn't matter whether they're real or not. Do you understand?"

Maggie nodded, eager to please him. She was still puzzled, but he had told her to figure it out for herself. She hoped it wouldn't take long.

"Good," he said, "I'm proud of you. That was a difficult concept. Now, I want you to watch those films, and ask questions about anything that confuses you. You need to learn about people before we go out on the streets." He reached down and started another videochip playing.

"Why do I need to learn about people? I don't understand."

Arnold sighed. "The world is a very complex place, Maggie. There are millions and millions of people outside this building, there's traffic, and gangs, and policemen, and billions of things that are just concepts stored away in your pretty little head right now. You need to learn about how all of that works before you go out there, or you could be destroyed. You need to learn to walk right, talk right, and how to respond to people. Movies will teach you some of that. They'll help you understand the real world, because they're so much like it."

On the screen a shot rang out, a man fell, clutching his side. A woman screamed and ran to him.

Arnold rested his hand on Maggie's shoulder. "It's a dangerous world out there. You're an illegal machine. There are laws against things like you, Maggie. If you aren't careful, people will find out that you aren't human, and then they'll try to destroy you. I can't protect you if you don't know how to act like a human."

"I don't understand, Arnold," Maggie said. "Why am I illegal? Why do people want to destroy me?"

Arnold sat down next to her on the bed. He seemed very sad. Maggie wished she could cheer him up.

"Well, Maggie, a long time ago, people designed lots of very complex computer programs called Artificial Intelligences, and made them kill people. They were very frightening. Then another group of people talked to the programs and made them stop killing people. This upset the people who had built the programs, so now everyone was mad at the computers. So they passed laws against ever building Artificial Intelligence machines like them. That's why you're illegal. That's why you'd be destroyed if anyone but me ever found out what you were."

"But, Arnold, I won't hurt anyone. I promise," Maggie said.

"It doesn't matter how nice you are, Maggie, it won't change the AI laws. You've got to learn to be human, or else you'll be destroyed."

So Maggie began watching movies. After the first two movies, she began watching them in fast forward, absorbing as many movies as possible. At first the elaborate dialogue confused her, but with Arnold's help, patterns of speech and behavior gradually began to emerge.

One pattern utterly confused her; again and again she saw people press their lips together and cling to each other with a frantic sense of urgency. Sometimes they took off their clothes or wound up on a bed. It was called sex, or sometimes love, and nothing in her programming explained this curious behavior. Arnold was no help; he became strangely awkward and inarticulate when she asked him about it. If she pressed him further, he became angry, and told her that she didn't need to understand it. This frustrated her, because love seemed so central to everything people did in the movies. She resolved to find out what she could about sex and love without disturbing Arnold.

Death was confusing, too. Time after time, people fell over and stopped moving. Sometimes they got up again, and sometimes they didn't. When they didn't they were usually dead. When someone died, people usually acted sad, unless it was a bad person who killed someone. Arnold wasn't much help here, either. He told her that the people who had been shot were gone, but he couldn't tell her where they had gone to, only that they would never come back. It was all very confusing. All she knew was that death was bad, and that she should do all she could to keep people, especially Arnold, from dying. This realization came from deep within her programming, and was very important.

Gradually Maggie began to understand the complex world of human interaction. Arnold's changes in mood were more understandable now. Sometimes she could change his mood herself. She was good at cheering him up. All she had to do was surprise him by doing something he didn't know she was capable of. She began hiding some of her skills, so that she could surprise him when he seemed unhappy.

Sometimes, Arnold had Maggie imitate various actors' styles of walking. It was hard at first, but after a few tries, she was usually able to do a fair imitation of their movements. It got easier with time and practice. Gene Kelly was one of her particular favorites, she liked the lightness of his steps. John Wayne was also fun. Marilyn Monroe seemed to make Arnold very uncomfortable for some reason, so Maggie stopped imitating her.

After she learned to imitate other people's walks, Arnold had her copy their voices and intonation. That was easy, since she already had samples of their voices on file. Arnold let her play some with their voices. He particularly liked the way she imitated the actor named Humphrey Bogart. She discovered that she could make him laugh, and that pleased her. He set her default voice as Annette Funicello. It was a pleasant enough voice, Maggie thought, but she would really have preferred Bogart, since it made him laugh.

After a couple of weeks of movie watching, Maggie grew curious about the world outside. When the television wasn't on, she spent her time looking out the window that faced the mouth of the alley, getting brief glimpses of the occasional pedestrian walking by. Even though Arnold's warnings about the AI laws frightened her, she still longed to see the world that the movies had given her tantalizing glimpses of. She longed to see it firsthand. She hoped she would be ready when he did.

Chapter
5

Arnold leaned back in his chair, watching Maggie look out the window. Her eagerness to be off was contagious. It was almost spring. The weather was warming up. He was tired of being cooped up in this garage. The accumulation of things here made him uneasy. It was too fixed and certain. He wanted to return to the freedom of the streets.

But he feared for Maggie. Even after all the movies, all the months of careful training, she was still so innocent, so unafraid. She would be easy prey on the streets. Men would want her. He didn't want his beautiful, innocent Maggie soiled by their filth. He would teach her to hide her beauty. He didn't want her to be like all those beautiful women his father had collected. He remembered their laughter, like silver bells. They were always so nice to him when they thought his father was looking. Maggie was different from those cold, cynical women. She was so childlike and trusting. He would have to watch over her every minute.

And then there was her programming. There had been a reason besides anonymity that he had picked this drab, isolated building. He had wanted as much control over Maggie's environment as possible, to give her a chance to develop in simple surroundings until she was ready to cope with the chaotic and confusing world outside. It was easy for a complex and delicate Artificial Intelligence such as Maggie to become overwhelmed by too much data and overload.

Before the AI laws, many programs broke down or froze when they had to deal with overly complex conditions. Very few AIs had been able to cope with the complexity of the real world. Most overloaded on their first time in an uncontrolled environment. No one understood why only a few programs could cope with the real world. It seemed to have been something in their priority structure that enabled them to survive. The AI laws had put a stop to all legal research, and the economic backsliding of the Slump had put a halt to any well-financed illegal experiments. The few illicit studies he had been able to dig up through the hacker underground had been sketchy and limited. Personality science had been effectively dead for the last twenty-five years. He had gotten kicked out of MIT because of his refusal to stop studying the banned papers of researchers like Minsky, Moravec, Read, and Dyer. Still, he had gotten what he needed, and had passed most of it along through the underground for others to find. He didn't need a post-graduate degree.

Even after all his training, taking Maggie out onto the streets was still a gamble. There was a better than even chance that she would be overwhelmed and break down. If Maggie overloaded, his work would be set back by at least six months. He'd be able to reuse her body, but he'd have to construct an entirely new program.

He was running out of money, too. Soon he'd have to call his trust fund in New York and have money wired to him. That was risky. Even though Arnold's trust had come from his grandmother and his father couldn't touch it, his father monitored his trust. A request for money would let his father know where he was, and Arnold couldn't leave Maggie alone for as long as it would take to evade his father's network of spies. He had been living on a shoestring for a long time, padding his savings with the odd electronic repair job; but since Maggie had been born, there hadn't been enough time to find any repair work.

If his father tracked him down, he wouldn't be nearly as lenient as before, especially if he found out about Arnold's illegal experiments with Maggie. Either his father would destroy Maggie or corrupt her. He had nightmares in which his father captured Maggie and turned her into his mistress.

He sighed. It was time to take some risks. Their first trip out would be a simple one, over to a nearby park and back, no more than fifteen minutes. He got up and put on his coat. Maggie turned to watch him, a questioning look on her face.

He opened up the battered drawer that contained Maggie's meager stock of clothing. He pulled out a coat and tossed it to her.

"Put this on, Maggie," he said, "we're going out for a walk."

Chapter 6

Maggie hurriedly put on her coat, then stood waiting for the infinity it seemed to take for Arnold to run his fingers through his unruly hair, rummage around for some gloves, and find his keys. When he was finally ready, she had to wait while he ran her through yet another diagnostic test. Finally he looked at Maggie and smiled through his straggling mustache. Maggie smiled back. Arnold liked it when she smiled back. Pleasing Arnold was the most important thing in her programming structure.

"You look fine, Maggie. Ready?"

Maggie nodded.

"Okay, now remember, don't say anything, just watch and listen. You can ask questions when we get home. Understand?"

Maggie nodded again, and at last Arnold opened the door and they emerged into the world.

Water fell from the sky. Maggie looked up to see where it was coming from. It felt cold on her face. She touched a droplet on her cheek and looked back at Arnold questioningly.

"It's raining, Maggie, that's rain on your face."

Rain. This was rain. Suddenly a cascade of images opened in her mind. Everything in her data banks related to rain came flooding out: RAIN: 1. n. Water that is condensed from the aqueous vapor in the atmosphere and falls to earth in drops more than 0.5 mm in diameter. 2. v. To send down in great quantities as small pieces or objects. 3. n. Rainfall, rainstorm, or shower. Synonyms: Drizzle, Sprinkle, Pour, Cloudburst, Thunderstorm, Hurricane. Antonyms: Drought, Sunshine, Sunny Weather, Fair, Clear. Idiomatic Expressions: Rain cats and dogs, Rain or shine, April Showers. . . . Beyond the words came a cascade of images and sounds, Gene Kelly dancing down the street in the rain and singing, pictures of rainbows, snatches of music: "Stormy Weather,"

"Rainy Days," "Raindrops keep falling on my head. . . ." More practically, there was information about rain gear; the way the streets got slick when it rained. On and on the data came. Everything remotely to do with rain that had been stored in her memories came pouring out to link itself up with the firsthand sensory experience of rain on her face. She paused for a minute, absorbing this flood, this deluge, of knowledge. Then Arnold slipped his hand into the crook of her arm and guided her on.

They walked past the the edges of her world, past the garbage cans and trash that Maggie saw when she looked out the dingy window of the garage. Maggie longed to stop and absorb the significance of each new object that she saw, the battered, rusting dumpsters, the broken glass, the soggy gray litter, and the brittle, decomposing skeletons of biodegradable bottles. All of them touched off a flood of complex associations. It was far more intense than the flood of sensation that had accompanied her birth. She had learned so much since then, and all that new information flooded out when something she saw triggered an association.

The alley opened up onto the street. Maggie looked around her, up at the buildings, down both directions of the street as far as she could see. The world was very big. Newness unfolded around her. Arnold led her across the street. Something huge and loud came lumbering past them as they walked down the street. Even the ground seemed to tremble as it went past. Maggie marveled at its power.

"Truck," Arnold said. Another truck lumbered past a minute later, then a pair of animals pulling a smaller, slower vehicle piled with trash. "Wagon," Arnold told her, then pointing at the animals, "Horses." Each word caused a fresh cascade of data to pour out into the torrent of information racing through her processors. Another truck, and several wagons passed them, then something like a truck, only smaller and sleeker, sped past them, followed by several sleek, two-wheeled vehicles propelled by their riders. "Car," Arnold said, and "Bicycle."

As they walked, Arnold continued to name the world. With each name a new pocket of information emptied itself into her mind. All the things she had learned became real as the world around her unfolded itself. She was filled with details about vehicles and streets from movies and books and other information that Arnold had given her. Suddenly she understood that the convergence of cars and trucks and streets was called traffic. She began looking both ways before crossing the street, instead of waiting passively for Arnold to lead her across.

They passed several people on the street. Maggie watched each one intently, memorizing each nuance of their expressions, each twist of the head, and each flicker of their eyelids. She longed to speak to these real people, whose movies she was a part of, but Arnold had forbidden it and the people ignored her, like the movie people did. She wasn't a part of their story, even though they were a part of hers. She longed to stop and ponder this conundrum but her processors were too busy dealing with the flood of information to stop.

They emerged from the tangle of traffic into a small park, and Arnold named more wonders for her. Grass, trees, branches, buds, shrubs, weeds, sprinklers, leaves, park benches, pigeons, birds . . . The intensity of green in the grass overwhelmed her, as did the delicate fractal traceries of the tree branches. She was intrigued by their similarity to her own memory structure, but again, there was no time to stop and think. Silver drops of rain fell from everything, in chaotic, unpredictable ways. There was no way to trace the paths the rain took in its falling. Thousands of metaphors suddenly flowered into being. They overwhelmed her already-overloaded processors, leaving her helpless before this new deluge. She had no priority structure to filter out the unimportant data. She had to examine it all, but there was no time, more data crowded in before she could analyze what she already had.

She looked over at Arnold, wanting to ask for help, but he had forbidden her to speak. The world dimmed as information ate up processors devoted to sight and motor skills. Her eyelids fluttered and her head began to wobble. Distantly, she heard Arnold question her, and then felt Arnold lead her quietly out of the park. The unfamiliar scrolled slowly backward into the familiar as Arnold led her home, but Maggie passed through it all unheeding, adrift in a flood of information.

Chapter 7

Arnold sat Maggie down by the computer that had birthed her. Placing one of her limp hands palm up in his lap, he exposed the computer jack under her skin. He connected her to the computer, then put on his VR helmet and gloves. Using none of the elegant tricks that he usually used to enhance his VR, Arnold sped directly to his diagnostic programs. He opened a window into her processors, hoping to trace the mercurial paths of her thoughts, and was startled to find himself staring at a wall of data sleeting past. He tinkered with the program's filters and was finally able to work his way through the interference and open a window into her system. He watched her processors laboring under the flood of data and frowned. It was what he had feared would happen. The onslaught of new data from the outside world had broken down the priority filters he had built. Unless he set up stronger priorities for screening new information, Maggie would remain mired in a data loop forever.

It wasn't going to be easy. His original program, complex as it was, was merely a framework for Maggie to build on as she developed. By now Maggie's program was several orders of magnitude more complex than it had been when he had brought her to life. He could no longer perform the kind of deep program restructuring needed to stop the data storm. Any reprogramming on his part would only make things worse. Her mind was like an oversaturated solution; a rough jar would precipitate out the remaining program structure into an unorganized pile of useless data.

Arnold stared into the whirling static of the data storm, fighting the rising tide of his own frustrations. He had been so very close to his dream, and now it was crumbling before him. He was helpless to stop it. All his years of study, research, and work were useless. If only he hadn't taken her out for so long.

Perhaps if he'd waited longer before taking her out . . . Maybe his father was right, he was an incompetent idiot who couldn't find his own dick with both hands.

"Arnold? Is that you?"

Arnold looked up. Miraculously, Maggie had managed to block out the data for a few moments. It wouldn't last long. He could see the data building up around the fragile barriers she had erected like snow on a windshield. Still, if she could do this, maybe there was some hope after all.

"Maggie, this is Arnold, can you understand me?" he cried out. With a gesture he converted his speech into machine language so that Maggie could read it more easily.

Maggie's reply was very slow. It appeared as brightly colored letters scrolling across his visual field. There was too much interference for her to do anything else. "I understand you, Arnold. There's too much data. What do I do?"

"Establish priorities, decide what is most important and process it first," he replied.

"Where do I start?" Maggie's query appeared letter by painful letter, pushing out past the thickening assault of data.

She was getting worse, soon she would be beyond retrieval. He would have to wipe her memory and begin again. Building a new program would take months. He had put everything he had into Maggie. She had to pull through. He desperately wanted more time, but that was impossible. She needed some kind of prime directive to use as a kernel to build a new structure on. She needed it right now. There wasn't time to think, there was only time to make a lucky guess and hope it came out right.

"Maggie, you are the most important thing I have ever done," he shouted into the data storm. **"I need you. Start there."** His visual field turned to snow before Arnold finished the first sentence.

Arnold hovered there, watching the data sleet through his virtual image, wishing he had worded things better. He hoped Maggie understood it. He wasn't even sure the message had gotten through at all. Perhaps he should just go ahead and wipe Maggie's memory. He had a copy of the program, he could start over. Maybe he could train her better, introduce information in smaller chunks, program in stricter, more powerful priorities. . . .

He disengaged from Virtual Reality, taking off his helmet and setting it in his lap. He looked over at Maggie, slumped awkwardly in the chair, her knees splayed obscenely wide, arms dangling limply. The wires trailing from her wrists made her look like some forlorn and broken puppet. He smoothed her dress and rearranged her legs more decently. He couldn't bring himself to wipe her out just yet. She was so innocent, so eager to please. He sighed. He would wait till next morning. If Maggie wasn't better by then, he would wipe her memory and start over. He sat, wrapped in a blanket, watching Maggie's face, hoping bleakly for some sign that she would be all right.

Chapter 8

Maggie perceived a vague presence behind the whirl of data she was fighting to clear. She struggled for long hard minutes, finally managing to block the data storm out of a small part of her processors. Now she had room to think. The presence was still there, she sensed it watching her.

"Arnold? Is that you?" she queried.

"Maggie, this is Arnold. Can you understand me?"

The whirl of data faded into the background for a moment as she focused on Arnold's input.

Speaking through the static caused by the data storm was impossible. Too many of her processors were occupied, she would have to output her reply as machine language and hope that Arnold could decipher it somehow. "I understand you, Arnold. There's too much data. What do I do?"

"Establish priorities, decide what is most important and process it first," came the reply.

Maggie examined the increasing flow of data for some sign of a priority, but there were no clues, just millions of facts queued up for sorting.

"Where do I start?" Maggie asked, pushing her question through the whirl of data. Already it was beginning to overwhelm the small processing space she had managed to clear.

"Maggie, you are the most important thing. . . ."
Arnold told her. If there was more to his reply, it was lost
as the flood of data broke through again, obscuring Arnold's
presence.

Maggie was alone again in the data storm. "You are the most
important thing," he had told her. She must assume, then, that
her survival was the paramount precept on which to build her
new system. All of this data was meaningless unless she was
there to process it, therefore the data was less important than
she was. She had external justification for her own importance.
She used this new justification to freeze the data storm until she
could deal with it. She used the fact of her own importance as the
foundation on which to build a new programming structure.

Slowly, very slowly, she began picking important memories
out of the random tide of data. As she accumulated a memory,
other associated memories came with it, coiling themselves
neatly behind the main memory. A different structure began
to emerge. It was frightening at first, but as the new program
crystallized, she noted the efficiency of its logic paths and
associations. Not only would her access times be cut in half,
there would be room for millions of new memories!

She traced the new pathways of her mind, creating a new
directory as she did so. Here were all the human utilities, how
to walk, how to talk, what to say, and when. Behind them,
neatly organized into unfolding fractals, were the memories of
learning these things. All of Arnold's patient training was here.
Her feelings and memories of him were located here. Another
branch of her memory held all her information on the outside
world: maps, street information, survival skills, and memories
of her trip outside settled themselves here like pigeons landing
on a windowsill. All the metaphors, comparisons, and associations to other parts of her memory lay folded behind them.
There were also branches for computer networking, mechanical
function, and maintenance. She traced them all, noting and
cross-referencing their contents.

Her core personality formed at the meeting point of her
branches, like the trunk of a tree. This main trunk contained her
internal processing patterns, the addresses she needed to think,
decide, and remember. This was where her deepest programs
lay, her instincts. The deepest complexities of this branch were
impenetrable even to her. It contained her core memories. Other
memories, skills, and associations could be stripped away, and

she would still be able to rebuild herself from this central core.

Maggie rejoiced in the crystalline beauty of her new internal architecture. She zoomed back and studied the structure of her mind from a distance, rotating it in imaginary space. It was complete, yet there was a lot of room for it to grow and change.

She left a copy of the structure of her mind in Arnold's computer. She opened her eyes, ready for any new information the world had to give her. Arnold lay slumped over the keyboard, asleep. Maggie smiled at the familiar sound of Arnold's snores. It was good to be functional again. Maggie disconnected the cables that bound her to the computer, folded her hands in her lap, and waited for her creator to awaken.

Chapter 9

Someone had stolen his bedroll. He was cold, and the rough concrete pressed against his cheeks. He shivered and woke with a start, rubbing at the marks on his cheek from where his head had rested on the keyboard. He was in the garage. Maggie was watching him.

"Good morning, Arnold," she said with a smile.

Relief washed over him as he remembered yesterday's disaster. "Maggie! You're back!" Arnold cried. "You're functioning again! What happened?"

"I reorganized my programming, just like you told me to. I fixed myself," Maggie told him. She sounded rather pleased with herself, he thought. "I left a model of my new structure in the computer for you to look at."

Arnold put on his helmet and gloves and dove into VR—and stopped dead.

"JeezusfuckingMinsky!" he whispered, shocked by the transformation Maggie had wrought in his Virtual Reality.

His familiar directory was gone. Instead, a huge silver tree revolved slowly before him. He circled the gleaming structure.

It was much more simple than his original program. Its stream-lined elegance stood in marked contrast to the complicated, lacy tangle of corridors he had created. Its graceful functionality and its startling originality awed him. He had never seen anything like it before.

He began opening up the structure Maggie had created. There was an almost organic organization to it, like some incredibly advanced cellular automata. His original program seemed crude by comparison, and it was the most sophisticated piece of soft ware he had ever built. He was awestruck by how neatly she had reintegrated the original details of her structure. There was so much to learn here. He was soon deeply enmeshed in the details of Maggie's system architecture, wandering like some child lost in a colossal cathedral.

It was late afternoon when Arnold emerged from the program. He stretched stiffly, and looked around him, slowly reorienting to reality. Maggie sat on his rusty iron bed with its rumpled grey sheets, regarding him with her usual calm, intense gaze.

Arnold watched her for a long moment, scratching his scruffy beard. It was strange to realize that her seemingly simple person-ality contained such humbling depths. "That's the most complex program I've ever seen, Maggie. It's so densely constructed that I couldn't even get near the core assumptions. How did you do it?"

"I don't really know, Arnold. It just sort of crystallized on what you told me. I'm sorry it took so long to do. You must have been very worried."

Arnold looked at her in amazement. "Maggie, you built the most incredibly complex program I've ever seen in under ten hours! That's incredible!"

"Thank you, Arnold, I'm glad you're pleased."

He smiled at her and stretched, his spine cracking like popcorn. "God, I'm stiff! What time is it, anyway?" He felt totally exhausted, and his bladder was strained to bursting.

Maggie checked her internal clock. "It's three-nineteen P.M."

"No wonder I'm so hungry." He got out of the chair and headed for the bathroom. "I think I'll go out for pizza," he said when he came out again.

"Can I go with you?" Maggie asked.

Arnold paused, his hands buried in the ragged towel that hung by the sink. "I really ought to run some more tests first, Maggie.

I don't want to risk another malfunction."

"I'm ready, Arnold, I know it."

The new certainty in Maggie's voice surprised Arnold. Maybe her new programming *was* more stable. He was tired. Tired of programming, tired of this cramped, secretive existence, and tired of waiting. He longed for the freedom of the streets again. In order to test Maggie, he would have to completely rebuild his system, which would take days. Testing a program as new and strange as Maggie's would take months. He doubted he would ever be able to completely understand it. No human could construct code like that and very few could even begin to follow it.

He shrugged. Going out would turn up any bugs more quickly than any tests he could run her through in the lab. Either she had what it took to survive a complex environment or she didn't. He'd save a lot of time by just taking her out for a pizza. Besides, he was starving.

"Okay, Maggie, put on a hat, and let's go, but you tell me the instant your processing speed even starts to slow down."

Maggie smiled radiantly. "Thank you, Arnold," she said. Grabbing the soft woolen cap he had given her, she followed him out the door. She looked ready to take on the world. Arnold hoped the world was ready for her.

Chapter 10

Maggie followed Arnold down the familiar alley, noting the small changes that had occurred since the night before. Fresh trash littered the ground. Green glass gleamed and crunched underfoot, the rain had stopped. Maggie waded through several of the puddles in the alley, enjoying the sheen of the oil as the water rippled away from her feet. It was warmer today. Arnold shrugged off his jacket as they turned out of the alley onto the street.

Maggie noted the changes in herself, too. New things didn't fire off wholesale memory dumps anymore. Now, new experiences were sorted according to their immediate importance and filed along the appropriate branch of a memory fractal to be processed later.

They followed much the same route as last time. There were more people on the streets than before. Their differences fascinated Maggie. People came in so many sizes, shapes, and colors. All of the people she had seen so far were smaller than Arnold, but taller than she was. Most of them walked by without looking at her. A few smiled. She was beginning to feel that she was doing well.

Then a man spoke to her. "Hey, sweetie, you busy tonight?" He was tea-colored and tall, and he seemed to want something. She didn't understand the expression on his face. Her confidence turned to confusion. She didn't know what to say to him.

Arnold put an arm around her. "Don't say anything, don't look at him. Just keep walking," he said in a tense, urgent whisper. Arnold walked faster, pulling her along with him. Puzzled, Maggie did as Arnold said.

"Aw, come on, honey, shed that sorry dude. I'll treat you right." Arnold turned to glare at the man, and he backed away. "You don't know what you're missing, honey," the man called after them as they turned the corner onto an unfamiliar street.

One block down from the corner was a red sign with Mario's Pizza on it in big yellow letters with a picture of a man in a white jacket holding up a big pizza. Arnold relaxed as they approached the door.

Arnold smiled, and opened the door. "Here we are, Maggie."

It was brightly lit inside the restaurant, full of noise and people. Maggie had never seen so many people before.

"Hey, Arnie!" a man behind the counter called out to them. He was big, nearly as tall as Arnold, and fatter. He had a bushy black mustache, and a white apron just like the man on the sign, only his apron had red stains across his bulging stomach. "How you doin'? That cash register you fixed, it works fine." He smiled at Maggie. "This your girlfriend? You never told me you had a girlfriend. She's pretty too. Better watch out or I'll steal her from you." He winked at her.

This talk of being stolen set off her worry circuits. Maggie hid behind Arnold, and the man laughed. "Looks like she's pretty attached to you, Arnie."

Arnold put an arm around Maggie. "She's shy." He nudged her forward. "Maggie, this is Mario."

Mario stuck out a hand covered in white powder. Maggie shook hands. "Hello, Mario," she said, looking up at him.

"Hello, Maggie," Mario said with a smile. "Thank you for gracing my humble establishment with your radiant beauty."

Maggie, obeying the dictates of her programming, smiled at him. Even though his talk of stealing her concerned her, Maggie found that she liked Mario, he talked like people in the movies. After all the new and strange things she had seen today, Mario brought a welcome touch of familiarity.

Arnold ordered a large pizza with pepperoni, and two glasses of water, and led her over to a table in a quiet corner.

"Are your processors all right?" Arnold asked her in a whisper.

Maggie nodded, then asked, "What did that man on the street want?"

Arnold frowned. "It was nothing, Maggie. Next time someone on the street talks to you like that, you just ignore them, okay?"

Maggie didn't understand Arnold's reply, but his tone of voice indicated that he didn't want to discuss it further, so she nodded as though she understood, and filed his advice away for future reference. They sat in silence for several minutes. Maggie watched Mario toss a big soft circle of dough in the air, fascinated by the dough's changing trajectory and topography.

"Arnold," Maggie asked, "would Mario really steal me away from you?"

He smiled at Maggie. "He's just kidding, Maggie. He can't steal you. You're my Maggie. I made you. We belong together. No one's going to take you away from me."

Mario set a huge, steaming pizza down at their table. "It's on the house," he said, waving away Arnold's wallet. "Your boyfriend's a hotshot computer whiz, you know that? He fixed my cash register. Saved me a couple hundred dollars."

Maggie nodded. "Arnold's very good at fixing things. He even fixed me."

Mario laughed loudly. "Arnie, you take good care of her. She's okay." He walked off, smiling. His response left Maggie very puzzled.

Arnold frowned. "Maggie, you've got to be very careful about what you say. Something like that might let people know you're not human," he whispered.

Maggie looked around her at the brightly lit restaurant and the people who talked and laughed around her; at Mario, who was laughing with another customer. These humans seemed so nice. She couldn't believe that they'd really hurt her.

"Why would these people want to hurt me? I've never hurt them."

Arnold sighed and pulled on his mustache. "Because people are still afraid of smart machines. They're more afraid now, because people have forgotten what they were like. That's why it's very important that people think you are a human. You must never, ever, tell anyone. They'd take you apart to see how you worked, and then never put you back together. Even nice people like Mario would be afraid of you if they knew." He took Maggie's hand and leaned closer to her. "Be careful. Please, Maggie, I couldn't stand to see you destroyed. You're the finest piece of work I've ever done."

Maggie had never seen Arnold this worried before. She didn't know what to say to reassure him.

Then Arnold leaned over and whispered something in her ear. Suddenly she was unable to talk or move.

"Enter: Security Program Prime Directive Address 000PD8." Arnold said, **"Security program override if Maggie attempts to say anything that might indicate she is a robot. Exception: Arnold Brompton. End override. Erase memory."**

Maggie felt the command enter her program structure. It arrowed deep inside her and found a place near her core assumptions. Arnold whispered something else she couldn't hear or understand, and suddenly she was free again. Free, but different. Something had just happened. Although she had no memory of it, there was a discontinuity in her memories. Scanning her memories, she vaguely recalled similar things happening before, early in her programming, but the memory of what had been done slipped through her grasp.

Arnold smiled and patted her hand. "Are you all right, Maggie?" he asked her.

"I think so, Arnold. What happened?"

"I just readjusted you a little bit. It made you safer. I can't let anything happen to my Maggie, now can I?"

Chapter
11

Arnold peered into the coffee can where he kept his petty cash. Only another hundred and fifteen left. Barely enough to last the week, even cadging a pizza or two from Mario. His bank balance was down to almost nothing as well. He sighed. Maggie was learning fast and improving every day, but she needed another three or four weeks of training before he could give up the garage entirely, and the rent and the electrical bills were both past due. He needed more money.

Maggie had started to help him scavenging through trash bins. She was good, sometimes even better than he was at finding things. Not having a sense of smell was a big help in this business. She had absolutely no squeamishness about poking through the garbage. And she had more patience as well. Several times she had turned up useful scrap metal, or salable rags in garbage he had already sorted. She had more than doubled his scavenging income. Still, it wasn't enough to pay the bills. He would have to call the trust and hope that the Sea-Tac sprawl was big enough to shelter him.

Seattle-Tacoma was the second largest metro area on the West Coast since L.A. was drowned in the big 'quake of 2018. It was bigger than New York. It would take at least two weeks for his father's men to find him. He'd probably have just enough time to finish Maggie's training and still get out before his father's men found him. He looked around the garage. There was a lot of stuff here he could sell. He could buy a little more time with that. He looked at Maggie, curled up on the bed, recharging from the outlet, and felt a little surge of excitement. In less than a month, it would be just Maggie and him against the world. When he finally perfected Maggie's street survival skills, he would take Maggie traveling. With Maggie beside him, the world would be his. They could go anywhere, do anything. He could hardly wait.

Chapter 12

A decomposing plastic can clattered hollowly as Maggie kicked at it. It rolled into a puddle, setting off a complex array of ripples. They were heading downtown to Pioneer Square. Arnold was going to teach her how to panhandle. It was raining and the streets were full of people who were all, according to Arnold, on their lunch hour. Most people walked stoically through the soft rain, though scattered knots of people huddled glumly in bus shelters and doorways, watching the rain fall.

People were a source of endless fascination for Maggie. Their responses could be so unexpected. Rain made them turn inward. They walked down the street hunched over and miserable. Even Arnold was silent in the rain. Sometimes Maggie thought she was the only one who noticed the beauty of the falling water, the way it splashed and slid down the sides of things, and the intricate, endless ripples it made as it fell into puddles.

Arnold motioned her into an unoccupied doorway, and they stood watching the people pass and the rain fall. As they watched, the rain stopped, and the sun broke through the clouds to shine brilliantly on the wet streets. Maggie liked the way the rain changed the world, but she admired the sun's ability to change people. When the sun came out, even the most morose people responded. People smiled. They nodded their heads at her as they walked by. They talked more as well, and Maggie loved listening to people talk. Listening made her feel as though she shared in the secrets of being human.

Arnold led her down the damp streets to Pioneer Square, which she duly included in her growing map of the city. They sat on a bench, watching people go by. Arnold put his cap between his feet, and motioned for Maggie to do likewise. He hauled a battered sign on an old piece of cardboard out of his bag. The sign read "Out of Money, Out of Work, Please Help." The "Please Help" part was outlined in red marker.

"Now, Maggie, we just sit there and look sad, and hope people give us money. Watch what I do," Arnold told her.

His face became a study of weariness and depression. As people walked by, he looked them squarely in the eye, and muttered, "Spare change?" Most people just looked away and walked past, but a few dropped coins or, occasionally, a small bill in his hat. Arnold always said "Bless you" to the ones who gave bills.

Maggie set her cap on the ground beside Arnold's and did her best to copy him. Arnold coached her carefully, and soon coins and bills were falling into her cap as well. She got more than Arnold did. At first this worried her. She had noticed that Arnold sometimes got upset if she outstripped him, but Arnold merely grunted that women usually did better panhandling. The trick seemed to be catching people's eyes. Once she did that, they usually gave her something. It was easy and fun. Soon she could do it without thinking, which left her free to observe people on the street.

The sun seemed to bring out the traffic. Rickshaws, bikes, carts, and carriages whizzed, trotted, or lumbered by. There were even a few cars and trucks, though they tended to avoid the downtown congestion. Pedestrian traffic increased too, the benches filled with office workers eating their lunches, and well-dressed men and women filling the sidewalk cafés. Two women, wearing translucent red veils shot through with threads of gleaming gold, came up and leaned against a light pole in the middle of a patch of red-painted sidewalk. Arnold had instructed her to avoid the red patches of sidewalk, so Maggie watched the two women, curious about what would happen. The women were tall, with long, brightly colored fingernails and many shiny rings on their slender fingers. Their veils gleamed and rippled in the sunlight as they talked. Maggie adjusted her hearing to compensate for the distance and listened.

" . . . So last night he tells me to up my tricks to five a night or I lose my license. He wants me to do five a night for a measly grand! Even with my looks, four is hard enough to pick up. That's why I'm out here so fuckin' early. You're a union rep, can't you do any . . ." The conversation stopped as a man walked by. The two women parted their veils, and posed for him, their silver and gold body paint gleaming in the sun. They were wearing very little else. The man smiled, shook his head, and walked on.

The two women carefully redraped their veils. "Like I was saying," the first one said, "can't the union do anything?"

The other woman shook her head, causing a soft jangle of jewelry. "Supply and demand, honey. Seems like every woman who's healthy enough to get a license is peddling her ass on the street. Times are hard. You just got to peddle faster and harder than the other gals. The union's up to its ass in grievances. If we strike, the scabs'll just take over. At least we still have these union Red Zones."

A shiny black horse-drawn carriage pulled up to the women, they posed, a hand beckoned them in, and the carriage pulled away.

The conversation was bewildering. They seemed to be selling something, that much she understood, but she couldn't see what it was.

"Arnold, those two women, what were they doing?"

"Which two women?"

"They were standing over there, on the red sidewalk. They just left."

Arnold's face got red. "They're hookers, Maggie, they're selling their bodies."

"But don't they need their bodies?" she asked.

"Maggie, they're hookers," he said in an angry-sounding voice. "You don't need to know any more than that. You're innocent, and I want you to stay that way. Stay away from hookers. And don't go near the red sidewalk; someone might think you're a hooker and try to pick you up."

Arnold's answer confused Maggie. The term "pick up" wasn't in her idiom bank, but she thought that it might have something to do with sex. Arnold was clearly upset in the same way he was when she had asked him about what the men and women were doing in the movies, and when she imitated Marilyn Monroe. It all seemed to be connected somehow, but she didn't understand what any of it had to do with someone trying to pick her up. She doubted that anyone could. She was heavy. She filed this incident away with the others. Despite Arnold's warnings, she was curious. She intuited that this was all part of something that was very important to humans, one of their secrets. Perhaps if she understood it, she would finally understand humans.

Arnold nudged the soft wool cap, there was the rustle of paper, mostly the few small bills they had dropped in themselves, and the clinking of small change tossed in by the rare passersby. He grunted softly and picked up the cap. "You made about twelve bucks today. That's pretty good. It'll buy me lunch. Let's go up to Pike Market and get something to eat."

They descended into the close dimness of the bus tunnel, leaving the bright afternoon behind. A horse-drawn trolley pulled up as they got to the bottom of the stairs. A weary sigh of air pushed through the tunnel whirling the rattling skeletons of decomposing liquor bottles that lay beneath the battered concrete benches. Maggie thought she saw a huddled form lying under one of the benches. She asked Arnold about it, but it was too dark under the bench for him to see clearly, and they were on the trolley and clopping down the shadowy tunnel before she could be sure.

"Pike Market Station, transfer to the 19, 26, 28, 43, 119,

120, 243, 310, and the Lynnwood Express, thank you for riding Metro," the driver bawled in a bored tone of voice. Maggie had never been to the market before. The flood of sound and color left her processors racing to keep up with it all. She followed Arnold into the dense crowd of people moving slowly from booth to booth examining the fish and meat and vegetables that the sellers were loudly hawking.

She stopped, clinging to a metal pillar and craning her neck to take it all in. So many people! She felt the pressure of their bodies as they brushed by, heard the myriad voices blending into a loud murmur, broken by the shouts of the fishmongers. The surge and hum of the crowd filled her until she could take no more, and she narrowed her perceptual filters into a more tolerable range.

She looked around. Arnold was gone. As Maggie clung to the pillar for support, her processors raced, replaying the last few minutes. His broad, tall back in its plaid jacket had filled up her visual field until she stopped to look. He must have kept going when she stopped, vanishing into the crowd. Maggie sorted frantically through her memory, looking for some kind of algorithm useful for finding someone in a crowd. There was nothing. The seconds thundered by. She needed Arnold's guidance; without it, she was lost. Unable to think of anything else to do, she clung to the pole and waited, desperately scanning the crowd for some sign of Arnold's familiar form, trying not to think about the possibility that she would never find him.

Chapter 13

Arnold felt his guts squeeze tight in panic. He had lost his Maggie. He had brought her here, and then lost her like some cheap umbrella. It was all his fault. He thought of her waiting helplessly in this crowd and groaned to himself. His eyes raked the crowd frantically as he backtracked past the faint, marshy smell of fresh fish on ice, past the sweet smells of the potpourri vendor, past the smells of onions, chocolate, mint, and bruised herbs. He pushed his way through the maze of shifting bodies, ignoring the complaints of the people he shoved out of his way. He went past the point where they had entered the market, then doubled back, peering over the crowd, searching for Maggie's light brown hair, her eggplant-colored hat.

He had to find her! He pictured Maggie, lost and frightened, as he had been when Maude had found him. Maggie was so small. Like Maude, he thought, except that Maude was small and fierce, whereas Maggie was delicate and gentle. He was twelve when he met Maude. Maude had been smaller than he was, but she chased away the teenagers who had him cornered. The three boys had fled from the hail of stones that she flung with stinging accuracy. After they had run off, Maude had stood over him, hands on her hips, as he cowered down in the trash, tears and snot pouring down his face. The tears had been half in fear of what this strange woman would do to him, and half in dread of what his father would say when he came home.

"Well, come on now," was all Maude had said, and he had gotten up and followed her. She had stopped the nosebleed with ice filched from a cup in the trash. She dug through her bags until she came up with a ragged but reasonably clean towel, which she used to clean off the worst of the blood. In return, she had allowed him to help carry her bags. Maude had somehow made him feel that she was doing him a favor by letting him carry her bags for him. They were heavy, too. At the end of the day, he had solemnly handed her bags back to her, and then, on impulse, he had hugged this tiny, dirty, smelly lady before he had run off. He still remembered the radiant smile that hug had brought to her face.

Maude fascinated him. He continued to seek her out. If she drove him away, he simply followed her carefully. Eventually she allowed him to keep her company almost all the time. She told him stories, about when she had been young, about the mental hospital, about the FBI voices that drove her out of her apartment and onto the street. She taught him how to avoid trouble on the street, how to find a free hot meal, and she showed him safe places to sleep. She became his refuge when the weight of his father's expectations drove him from the house. It had been the best year and a half of his childhood. Maude demanded nothing from him except his respect. There were no rules, no expectation. His company was enough for Maude.

Gradually he had started spending more and more time on the streets. Then one hot August night, he had stayed out the whole night with Maude, wandering the strangely quiet, four-in-the-morning streets with her. It was a magical night. The moon was fuller and brighter than he ever remembered it. The day had been oppressively hot and muggy, until a violent thunder shower broke around sunset, as though expressing the city's bottled rage.

The storm had passed quickly, leaving the city transformed. The streets were clean and the rain had cut the overripe smell of rotting garbage. A cool, fresh breeze washed over the streets. Maude and he had walked quietly, hand in hand, from Midtown down to Battery Park, where they sat by the edge of the water. Arnold rested his head in her lap and watched the moon over the Hudson. The Statue of Liberty was lit up, and over the noises of the street they heard a distant saxophone noodling away at some slow blues tune. Maude hummed along. She was having a run of good luck lately. Her new teeth fit right, she had found a pair of glasses in the trash that had almost the right prescription, and her new medication was keeping the voices out of her head for a while. The sax finished on an incredibly high, sweet, long wail.

They sat in silence as the moon sank down behind the Jersey shore and the sky lightened toward dawn.

"Well, kid," Maude said at last, "it don't get any better than this. You remember that, come winter. Rememberin' don't keep you any warmer, but it helps anyway. Keeps the FBI voices out of your head sometimes, too."

Arnold had nodded drowsily. He didn't really understand about the voices, but Maude was kind to him. The two of them were on an adventure and that was all he needed to know. He wanted everything to stay just like this forever: sweet saxophones and warm summer nights with someone who liked him just the way he was. Maude didn't care who his father was; she didn't even want to know.

Finally they had gotten up and headed back uptown. He had bought them both a big breakfast and left Maude in the coffee shop, stirring her coffee and sucking on her teeth the way she did after a good, big meal. He got home around seven in the morning, sneaking past the doorman and using his key on the special elevator. He had almost succeeded in getting back to his room without being caught when the cook saw him and let out a yell. He was frogmarched into his father's office, where his father sat, red-eyed, haggard, and absolutely furious.

For his stubborn refusal to tell his father where he had been while the police and the FBI were combing New York for him, he was grounded under guard until he was sent off in high disgrace to a military boarding school. Arnold had been unable to escape to say good-bye to Maude. When he had come back from boarding school, Maude was gone. Whether she had moved on to another city, found a home, or died, it was beyond the power of a fourteen-year-old boy to find out. She was gone from his life, swept from his grasp by his father's autocratic whim, like everything else he had ever loved.

Now Maggie was gone, too, but he had only himself to blame. The thought made his gut heavy with guilt and fear. He had been searching for the last ten minutes and there was no sign of her. He wanted to pick up Pike Market and shake it until he found his Maggie.

"Arnold!"

He wheeled at the sound and saw Maggie waving to him.

Arnold surged through the crowd, shoving people aside in his hurry to get to her. He held her tiny form close to him, speechless with relief.

"I'm sorry, Arnold. I didn't know how to find you."

"Maggie!" he said, holding her tighter. "I didn't mean to lose you like that. I won't ever let you go again." He held her to him tightly.

"It's all right, Arnold, I'm fine. No one bothered me. Please don't be mad at me. It was just so crowded."

"Shh, Maggie," he told her, nearly faint with relief at finding her again. "I'm here now." He looked up and saw people staring at them curiously. Feeling suddenly self-conscious, he let her go. "It's getting late, Maggie," he told her, "let's head back."

Maggie's small, cool hand slipped into the crook of his elbow. The contact pleased Arnold immeasurably. Maude was lost forever, but Maggie was all his and no one could take her away.

Chapter 14

Maggie leaned her head against the cool glass of the bus window replaying her memory of Arnold's embrace. It had surprised her. Suddenly her quiet, dependable creator was, for a moment, transformed into someone from out of a movie. When he held her, she had almost expected to hear music swelling in the background. She had hoped to discover what happened after the camera panned away, but then Arnold had simply told her they were going home, and she obediently tucked her arm through his and followed him down into the bus tunnel. The mystery of love remained unsolved, as did the mystery of why it was all so mysterious.

But there had been something else, too. Something subtle and equally puzzling. She ran the memory again, starting from the moment she had first seen him, slowing it down to watch the moments slowly unfold. She zoomed in on his face, as he turned slowly toward her. It was a bit fuzzy from close up, but the expressions were distinguishable. She scrolled the memory slowly through the changes in his face when he first saw her, comparing the expressions on his face with the already identified and calibrated expressions in her memory. Fear, confusion, recognition, relief, and joy followed each other across his face. But somewhere in between recognition and relief had been a moment so fleeting that she doubted Arnold was even aware of it. For a brief second, his face had worn a look of deep sadness, as though he had hoped to find someone else instead of her. She wondered yet again at the complex and subtle nature of humans. Would she ever understand it?

The bus glided toward their stop. They were back. Maggie tucked that memory in with all her other unsolved mysteries, and followed Arnold off the bus into the dusk toward home. It had been an interesting day. So much new data to digest. For once she was glad of Arnold's long hours asleep. She needed time to sort and ponder and file everything that had happened today. All of the day's activities had run her batteries down. She needed a charge. According to Arnold, they would be spending most of their time downtown from now on. In another week or two, they would leave the garage for good and live on the streets. She wondered where she would find a place to charge her batteries then.

The alley was darker than the street. Maggie switched on her infrared vision. A couple of faint heat ghosts hung in the air. They stood out sharply in the cold, still air of the alley. Two people, probably men, judging from the size, had passed by, no more than five minutes ago. Their trails grew fainter as they approached the garage. A blur of heat still lingered by the door, as though someone had stood there for a while.

Arnold opened the door. Their heat ghosts lingered even more strongly inside. Someone had been inside here, searching among their things.

Suddenly Maggie was cut off from her body. Something else controlled it. Her hand reached out and stopped Arnold as he reached for the light switch.

"Alert! Security Program Override," a flat, mechanical voice announced. Maggie realized that the words had issued from her mouth. "Someone's been here," she heard herself tell Arnold.

Maggie found herself scanning the room, following faint traces of heat, comparing details of how the room looked when they had left this morning with their current appearance. There were subtle but definite changes in the arrangement of papers in the cluttered piles of paper.

"They moved things. It's like they were looking for something. Nothing is missing."

"Shit! It's my father's men, they've found me again," Arnold said. "We've got to hurry. They'll be back again soon. You keep watch outside." Arnold began gathering up piles of paper. "We need to burn the extra hard copies of your plans. I don't want them to know how far I've gotten. Thank God we got rid of all your spare parts last week."

He began hauling stacks of paper outside and hurling them into the empty dumpster, swearing softly. Maggie stood outside in the shadows of the alley. Her security program scanned the darkness with her infrared sight, and her hearing was tuned to catch footsteps coming down the alley. All of this was done by the alien presence in her body. She could only watch helplessly. She wondered if she would ever get her body back.

Arnold finished hauling papers to the dumpster. He vanished into the garage and emerged with a pair of heavily laden packs, which he set at Maggie's feet. He poured a can of solvent over the papers, and tossed a lit match in on top of it. There was a soft *whump,* and then flames licked at her blueprints and program printouts. Arnold watched the papers burn for several minutes, stirring them from time to time with a length of pipe until the dumpster became too hot to approach. The dumpster glowed like a beacon in her infrared vision.

"We'd better go," her security program told Arnold. "Someone may notify the fire department."

"Well, Maggie," he said, picking up his pack, "ready or not, we're leaving town." His voice was quiet and neutral, but his face was grim.

Maggie felt her security program turn, pick up a pack, and follow Arnold, carefully scanning for possible danger. Maggie wanted to take a last look at the place where she had been created, but the security program didn't even bother to turn around. Maggie could only watch helplessly as she was propelled down the alley toward a dark and uncertain future, riding in a body that was no longer her own.

Chapter 15

"Shit!" Arnold muttered to himself. "Shit shit shit shit *shit*!" The words became a kind of chant. He was furious. Furious at his father for interfering yet again in his life. Furious at his trust officer—if his grandmother's goddamn trust wasn't so hard to break, he'd fire her ass—and mostly furious at himself for underestimating his father yet again. He shook his head, totally wrapped up in his anger.

Maggie touched his arm, breaking his angry chain of thought. She motioned quickly with her head, and he followed her down a side street.

Maggie's security program was spooky as hell, but it was working beautifully. Her sharp extra senses had won their freedom. He inhaled the cold night air. Freedom. They would hop a couple of freights and be gone again. His father couldn't find him as long as he kept moving. He had the money he had recently gotten from the trust. It would make a nice cushion if things got hard. He wouldn't need to touch his trust money for a while. He was an expert at living on nothing. He had done it for years, proud of the fact that he could get by without his family's money. He could do it again if he had to. Maggie's scavenging skills would make things even easier.

Arnold smiled. His father thought he was crazy, living like this. Arnold knew he wasn't normal, but he thought that his father was the crazy one, living with all the stress, all the demands his money put on him. Money ran his father's life. It was like a demon on his father's back, driving him harder and harder as the years passed. It was his compulsion to found a Brompton dynasty that drove his father to force Arnold into a mold that Arnold had no desire to fit. He might be weird, but at least he didn't live like his father.

He glanced over at Maggie, pacing warily along beside him. He had done an incredible job on her. She was all he needed.

Her and his freedom were all that mattered.

Suddenly Maggie stiffened, looking over her shoulder with an inhuman intensity that made his skin crawl. It was catlike, and eerie as hell. He would be glad when they were safely on the boxcar, and he could inactivate her security program.

"Someone's following us," she said in a low, machinelike voice.

"Are you sure?"

"Yes, they've made the same turns as we have since we left the alley, and they're staying out of sight. I recommend that we keep walking and take sudden evasive maneuvers."

"Whatever you say." Arnold had no inclination to argue with the fierce, alien creature inhabiting Maggie's body. That safe, warm boxcar seemed very far away right now.

They approached the mouth of an alley.

"Now!" Maggie said, grabbing his arm with inhuman strength and pulling him into the alley.

They ran down the alley, through the block, and into the alley on the other side, then doubled back down another side street and into an alley. Maggie stopped in the shadows by a tall dumpster, listening intently.

"What do we do now?" Arnold asked her.

"I recommend we commence concealment procedures. I hear them coming," Maggie said, climbing up onto the dumpster and opening the lid. "Take my hand," she told him, reaching down. She grasped his wrist and hauled him up to the rim of the dumpster with a single strong pull. Her strength frightened him a little. He began to see why people might fear a robot. He would be glad when her security program shut down.

The reek of rotting garbage assaulted his nose. The dumpster was half-full.

"Aw, Maggie, no . . . ," he began, but Maggie had already jumped down, pulling him in after her. Arnold found himself hip deep in reeking garbage. Cold trickles of rancid grease oozed down the inside of his shoes. "Christ," he muttered. Then Maggie reached up and carefully pulled the lid shut, leaving them in total darkness. He felt Maggie beside him, shifting boxes, pushing him deeper into the clammy, stinking garbage; felt her piling soggy cardboard around him until he was completely covered by a pile of loose boxes. Even for an experienced dumpster diver like himself, the smell was unimaginable. He wished that

Maggie had a sense of smell, she deserved to share his misery.

He started to complain but just then he heard footsteps, searching down the alley. He froze.

"They're not here, Bill," said a voice right outside the dumpster.

"Have you checked this dumpster?" said another voice, this one gravelly and low. Arnold recognized it from previous kidnappings. It was Bill Dickey, his father's chief investigator. Dickey the Dickhead, Arnold called him.

"Aw come on, Bill. You can smell it from here. Nobody in their right mind would hide in there."

"He escaped from a mental hospital. He's been living on the streets like a bum."

"Oh all right, but you get to check the rest of the dumpsters tonight."

Arnold heard the dull metallic booming of the sides of the dumpster as the man lifted the lid. A little light shone through the gaps in the cardboard boxes. It flickered and dimmed as the man shone a flashlight down into the garbage. Arnold's heart was pounding with fear.

"Nothing here but the garbage," Arnold heard the man say as the dumpster lid slammed down with a dull boom. He heard the scuffle of feet as the man climbed down to the pavement.

"Shit, I can't understand why old man Brompton's so hot to get his kid back. He's a bum."

"It isn't just fatherly love," Dickey said. "The stupid shit is obsessed with building robots."

"You're kidding," the other man said. "He doesn't look like he could put two and two together to get four."

"He graduated summa cum laude from MIT. Would have got a master's if they hadn't kicked him out for illegal research. You saw what was left of the plans. I wonder how far he got this time? We'll have to check how long he's been there."

"Well, I didn't see no robot. All he had was that girl with him."

"She might be a robot," Dickey said. "He's that good."

"Christ!" the other man said. "You really think so? We should report him before that robot kills somebody!"

"Not if you want to get paid. Old man Brompton doesn't want that sort of thing getting out. Now come on, we can't stand here all night, we've got work to do."

"Jeez, that kid must be crazy," Arnold heard him tell Dickey as they walked away. "He could be living on top of the world. Hell, Brompton could adopt me if he wanted hisself a son. At least I'd appreciate the old man." His voice faded as the two men rounded the corner.

Arnold shook with a mixture of suppressed fear, rage, and cold. He wanted to leap out of the dumpster and confront the two men. He hated them for talking about his father that way. What did they know about being rich, what did *they* know about what it was like living with his fucking tyrant of a father? What did they know about having someone as powerful as his father try to force you into a mold you couldn't fit? What did they know about not being able to get a robotics job because your father wanted you under his thumb? What did they know about being hunted and kidnapped over and over again by a man who was too wealthy and powerful to fight? It wasn't fucking fair! He felt hot tears of rage pouring down his face.

Maggie's hand found him in the darkness. "Arnold, are you all right?" she asked him in a soft, familiar whisper. He could tell from her tone of voice that Maggie was back to her own sweet self again.

He groped till he found her small hand, and squeezed it tightly. "I'm fine, Maggie. I'm fine as long as I have you with me." At least he had someone who would care about him without trying to run his life. She had already proved her worth. His father could go fuck himself.

They waited another twenty minutes to be absolutely sure they were gone, then Arnold helped Maggie out of the dumpster. He was stiff, sore, and soaked with rotten vegetable juice and rancid grease, but he had beaten his father's bloodhounds. He pulled his pack out of the dumpster. Thankfully Maggie had hidden their packs in dry boxes, so they were still clean. He pulled out some fresh clothes for himself and Maggie. They changed in silence, facing away from each other. Arnold was too relieved at being out of his clammy clothes to be embarrassed. He threw their garbage-sodden clothing back into the dumpster.

"Well," Arnold said, when they had changed, "we survived that one." He smiled and, in the dim glow that filtered in from the streetlight at the mouth of the alley, he could just make out her smile of reply. He pulled a piece of cabbage from her hair. "C'mon Mags, we've got a train to catch."

Chapter 16

The bus whined as its flywheel engaged, and they moved away from the bus stop. Maggie looked behind her at the dwindling bus stop; there was no one there. They were safe now. Maggie ran another check on her system, hoping she could track down the security program and get rid of it. She couldn't find it. It had vanished. She hated the sudden way the security program had taken control of her body, leaving her a helpless passenger. Perhaps Arnold could fix it for her.

"Arnold?" Maggie whispered in his ear.

"Yes, Maggie, what is it?"

"Arnold, could you please do something about my security system?"

"Why, Maggie? It worked perfectly."

"But it scares me, Arnold. I don't like it."

"It saved us, didn't it?"

Maggie nodded.

"Maggie, that program got us away from two professionals. We're free because of it. If we'd been caught, they would have taken you apart. You wouldn't exist anymore. You owe your life to that security program. You shouldn't complain about something that saved your life."

"But it was so sudden. Isn't there any way you can reprogram it to give me some warning that it's going to happen?"

"Maybe, Mags, but it'll have to wait until we've settled down somewhere."

She hoped they would settle down soon. She needed to recharge her batteries. The security program had drawn a lot of power and she was running on her reserve batteries. In another four hours, she wouldn't be able to move. All she wanted right now was a safe place to sit and feel electricity flowing back into her batteries.

"Arnold?"

"Yes, Maggie."

"Where are we going?"

"We're going to catch a train out of here."

"Will we be near an outlet soon? My batteries are very low."

"We just passed an open diner. Maybe we can find an outlet for you to plug into here. I need to get a bite to eat myself."

They got off at the next stop and walked back to the diner. The waitress did not seem too happy to see them, but she led them grudgingly to a booth in the back of the restaurant, as far away from the two other occupied tables as possible. She gave a disapproving sniff as she handed them their menus and left them to wait on another table.

"What's bothering her, Arnold?"

"We still smell pretty bad from the dumpster," he explained.

"Oh. How come I don't have a sense of smell?"

"I couldn't give you one, Maggie. It was too complicated to include." He smiled wryly. "Right now, though, you aren't missing much. We're still pretty ripe."

"I'm sorry about that, Arnold, it wasn't my fault. The security program hid us in that dumpster, not me."

"It's all right, Maggie, at least we're safe."

Maggie extended her plug down her leg and searched for an outlet. "There's no outlet here," she whispered. "What should I do now?"

"Try the rest room," Arnold told her, "and maybe you can wash up a little bit while you're there."

The rest room was small, dark, and dingy, but there was an outlet near the trickling, sweaty sink. She locked the door and leaned against the wall in front of the outlet, head back against the cold tile. She extended her power cord like a prehensile tail and plugged herself in. Electricity flowed along her wires, she felt the charge trickling into her batteries. She was immensely relieved.

There was a knock on the door. Maggie decided to ignore it. She needed every scrap of power she could draw. She began washing up at the tiny sink, using paper towels and the grey-filmed soap sitting on the side of the sink.

"Hurry up! I gotta pee real bad," said a woman's voice on the other side of the door.

"I'm sorry," she said, "I'll be right out." She dried herself off while her plug detached itself from the wall and retracted silently into the recess at the base of her spine. She felt the skin close back over it as she opened the door. A veiled hooker brushed by her into the rest room as she left.

"Well?" Arnold said when she sat back down.

"I didn't get much," she said, "only a half hour's worth of charge. Someone else had to use the john."

Arnold sighed. "It'll have to do. We don't have time for any more stops. You'll just have to conserve your energy. Let's go."

They got up, paid the check, and caught the next bus. It was raining softly when they got off the bus near the Interbay freight terminal. "I doubt that they'll be checking the mag-levs."

They crossed a small golf course and threaded their way through the blackberry thickets until they reached a tall chain-link fence topped with a coil of razor wire. Arnold followed the fence until he found a hole hollowed out underneath the fence. It was hidden from the inside by a thicket of blackberry bushes. Arnold took off his pack and handed it to Maggie, and pushed his way under the fence. The hole was barely big enough for him to squeeze through. Maggie slid their packs through, and then slid nimbly under the fence. They headed for the bright lights of the freight terminal.

They crept up into the shadows of the big building and peered in the door. Men in blue coveralls were loading freight cars at the far end of the huge warehouse. On the near end of the dock sat an unattended computer terminal. Arnold nodded toward it.

"Now comes the tricky part," he told her. "You need to get to that terminal, and download as much information as you can about the train schedules."

Arnold rummaged in his pack and brought out two pair of blue coveralls like the ones the men were wearing. He handed her the smaller pair. "Protective coloration," he whispered. Maggie crawled into the baggy coveralls and followed Arnold onto the loading dock. He handed a hard hat to Maggie after putting one on himself and walked over to the computer terminal as if he'd been doing it all his life.

"Okay, Mags," Arnold said when they got to the terminal, "here's where you come in. I want you to jack into the computer, find out where the next train out is headed, and where it is. We'll also need the access code to open the boxcar door."

Maggie felt exposed and uncertain as she jacked in, but as soon as she was inside the computer, she was completely in control. She dove into the whirlpool of data and went swiftly to work, sorting through the data files. In less than two minutes, she had all the information they needed, but she lingered to explore the computer network.

So much of the outside world was confusing, and changeable. Here, she controlled the environment. She could do anything. She swooped through the system, opening files at random to see what they contained. She was breezing through the security on the payroll program when the alarm sounded. Instantly she retreated, but the security programs had moved in to block her escape. There was no choice but to expose herself. Suddenly she felt her security program activate. It fired off a series of hostile virus programs to keep security busy, and hauled her out of the system and back inside her body.

She blinked, readjusting to her familiar body. According to her internal clock she had only been in the system for five minutes. The security program had vanished again.

"Are you all right, Maggie?" Arnold asked. "You were gone a long time."

"I think I triggered something. We'd better go. There's a train to Spokane leaving in about twenty minutes."

Arnold frowned. "The railroad bulls are really tough in Spokane, and it'll be cold going over the mountains, but we don't have much choice. The longer we stay here, the more likely that we'll get caught. I have a friend in Spokane, though, so we'll have a place to stay. Is there a heated car on the train?"

"There's a produce car, third from the end. It doesn't get colder than forty degrees."

"It's better than freezing going through the mountains, I guess. Let's go."

They slipped out of the building and hurried to the waiting train. Maggie keyed in the access code on the door lock, and they climbed into the car. It was cold and dark inside, but Maggie could make out stacks of boxes tied securely in place. They settled down on a pile of flattened cardboard boxes. A few minutes later, the car rose up and began to move.

"Well, Mags," Arnold said, "we're on our way. How are your batteries holding out?"

"It's tight. I'll make it if I shut down completely. But I'm going to need to charge up as soon as we get there."

"You go ahead and shut down. I'll wrap up in our blankets to keep warm. Once we get to Spokane, you can recharge at Brandon's."

Maggie shut herself down and spent the rest of the night alone inside herself, unable to see, hear, or feel the motion of the train as it rushed on into the night toward an uncertain dawn.

Chapter 17

Arnold awoke to darkness, the smell of bananas, and the fading reek of rancid garbage. The train whistled. A faint glimmer of light flickered around the door, but other than that, the darkness in the car was absolute. He checked his watch. It was almost six A.M., they must be nearly there. Groping for Maggie, he touched her cold, lifeless hand in the dark. It was eerie to feel the chill of her plastic flesh. She'd warm up as soon as she plugged into an outlet, but right now she was as cold as a corpse.

"Maggie?" Arnold whispered. "Maggie! Wake up, Maggie!" He shook her. She didn't respond. Either she was on her own internal timer, or she had run completely out of juice. He hoped she'd wake up before the train stopped at Spokane. They'd be unloading the car, and they'd have to get out before they unhooked the train. If Maggie wasn't up and running by then, he'd have to find some way of getting her body off the train and into safety in broad daylight. It was a daunting problem.

He stretched, and his hand brushed a stack of banana boxes. He was hungry. He fumbled his way up one of the stacks of boxes, opened the top one, and took out a large bunch of bananas. Just then, a cold hand brushed the back of his neck.

"Aaah!" Startled, he jumped, dropping the bananas.

"Are you all right, Arnold?" Maggie asked. Arnold relaxed, breathing slowly, trying to slow the hammering of his heart.

"You surprised me, Maggie."

"I'm sorry, Arnold," she told him. "How did I surprise you?"

"By sneaking up on me in the dark. Your hands were so cold. . . . Next time, say something before you do that."

"I'm sorry, I won't do it again, Arnold."

Arnold shrugged. "We'll be arriving in Spokane in a few minutes. Better get ready."

As if on cue, there was a shuddering squeal as the train set down onto the braking rails. The train decelerated rapidly, flinging the two against the far wall. A cascade of bananas fell on top of them from the box Arnold had opened. The train shrieked to a halt and stood silently.

Arnold helped Maggie off the floor and groped his way to the door, opening it a crack to let in some light. He picked up some of the less-damaged bananas and put them in his pack. Maggie did likewise, although she picked up bruised and unbruised bananas, unable to tell the difference. He reminded himself to explain it to her when they had a minute.

Shouldering his pack, Arnold peered out of the boxcar door into the grey light of dawn. The yard looked much like any other yard, a maze of big warehouses and mag-lev rails where lines of idle boxcars and locomotives stood waiting. The yard seemed deserted. He hopped down, and then turned to help Maggie. They were nearly at the first large warehouse when a voice shouted "Stop!"

Arnold looked back to see two security guards closing on them.

"C'mon!" he shouted, dragging Maggie with him. They dodged around a big water tower, rounded the corner of a building, and ran down a long corridor of buildings. They had lost the guards for the moment, but they'd have to find an exit in a hurry before the reinforcements arrived.

"I'm running out of energy, Arnold, I can't keep this up for more than five more minutes," Maggie told him.

"Arnold! Over here! Hurry!" A short black man with white hair beckoned to them from the corner of a shed.

"Brandon!" Arnold said. "Maggie, it's Brandon!" He followed Brandon down a long corridor between two rusting warehouses. At the end of the corridor was a huge wooden warehouse, painted red like a barn. Brandon opened a small door and beckoned them in.

"This way," Brandon said. They followed him past an array of huge, silent generators, through another door, up some stairways across a narrow catwalk, and through a nearly invisible trapdoor. They were in a small room that looked as if it had once been an office. There was a computer resting on a desk in one corner. The room was lit by a single light bulb whose light did not quite reach the edges of the room. An electric heater hummed away, and a crockpot bubbled contentedly to itself nearby. It was dim and cozy and safe. Maggie settled herself against a stack of pillows near the heater. Arnold saw the corner of an outlet sticking out past her shoulder, and knew she was already recharging her batteries. Her eyes closed and she appeared to fall asleep.

"How're you doin', Arnold?" Brandon asked in his deep gravelly voice.

"Much better, now that I'm not being chased." He grinned down at the small, wiry black man.

"I was expecting someone to get off that car, but I wasn't expecting it to be you. There was a major system alert in Seattle. Somebody was poking around the payroll file. Security's been real tight around here since then. Those railroad bulls are bad enough already. If you two had been any slower, there wouldn't have been anything I could do, except watch them beat the crap out of you and haul you off to jail. I thought I'd taught you better than that, man."

"It wasn't me, Brandon. It was Maggie. I was showing her how to get into the system, and she got carried away."

Brandon looked over at Maggie, who looked like she was asleep. "She all right? She looks pretty beat."

"She's just tired. It was a long, cold trip. We came over in a produce car." Arnold reached into his pack and pulled out a bunch of bananas. "Here, we brought some of these for you."

Brandon grinned. "Hey, all right! I haven't had a banana in ages! You hungry?" He motioned to a hot plate with a battered stew pot on it. "I've got chicken soup today, it's nice and hot."

"I've got some cheese in my pack, too, if you'd like some."

"Thank you, that'll be good with the soup. Your lady friend want any?"

"Maybe when she wakes up." Arnold shook out a blanket from his pack and gently laid it over her, making sure that the outlet she was plugged into was well concealed.

"How's it going?" he whispered as he tucked her in.

"I'll be fine, Arnold, I have everything I need." She smiled at him, and he smiled back. He rested his hand against her cheek for a moment; it was warm and lifelike again, much to his relief. Her corpselike coldness had been unnerving.

Leaving Maggie to recharge, he settled onto a stack of pillows near the heater and sipped at his soup. It was thick with chicken and vegetables, with thin slices of cheddar cheese floating on top, melting slowly. It was much better than the watery mission soup he was used to.

"S'good soup," Arnold said, licking a fragment of noodle from his mustache.

Brandon shrugged. "Pickings are usually pretty decent around here. There's a lot of good food that gets thrown out because the box it came in was damaged. Bananas, though, are hard to get. The railroad people usually take them home."

They settled back and ate without speaking; the only sounds were their companionable slurps and smackings, and the quiet drone of the heater.

"You know," Arnold said, setting down his empty mug of soup with an appreciative belch. "You never did tell me how you found this place."

"It's simple. I used to work for the railroads. The mag-lev people hired me as a security consultant. They figured I could tell them all about catching riders, since I was one." Brandon shrugged. "My new system kept most of the stupid people out. They caught the destructive ones, made the rails safer for a while, but I got tired of seeing their thugs beat people up, so I quit." Brandon paused, and stared into the red glow of the heater element. "I found this place on the blueprints. It was sealed off when they put those big emergency generators down there. I came in with a saber saw and cut that trapdoor. Couple of months later, I quit, went back to roading for a while. Met a woman, settled down." He smiled fondly. "Well, sort of. We used to go roading together, me 'n' her. They were good times. This was our private hideout. She died about five years back. Cancer. So I came back here. Wasn't much else to do. Beats sitting home alone and rotting. I help folks riding the rails." He shrugged and stared into the heater for a minute, caught himself doing it, and smiled. "So what brings you back through Spokane this delightful time of year?" he said wryly.

"I wanted to show Maggie how to ride the rails. When she set off that alarm, this was the first train out of town."

"How long you been with her?"

"Just a couple of months, so far. She makes things a little less lonely."

Brandon nodded. "It's good to have someone at your back. The world's a crazy place. I still miss Tisha." He shrugged. "So, where're you headed?"

"Nowhere in particular, just wandering. South sounds good this time of year."

"You're welcome to come back anytime. Not too many hackers on the road anymore. Seems like the road's been getting meaner lately. You'll have to be more careful now you're with her. She's a pretty woman."

Arnold shrugged. "It's hard sometimes, but Maggie's good company. We do all right."

Brandon nodded absently. "So did me and Tisha." He fell silent, staring into the glow of the heater for a long time. Arnold sat quietly. He never knew just what to say to Brandon. Brandon had been the first hacker to crack the infant mag-lev system, way back in '13. The railroad had boasted about its foolproof system, and Brandon had taken it as a challenge. He'd first met Brandon years ago, when he first started riding the rails. Brandon had taken Arnold under his wing and shown him how to ride the rails without being killed. They'd been corresponding by E-mail ever since, although he hadn't written Brandon since his last visit, on his way to Seattle. Arnold avoided unnecessary time in the Net while he was working on Maggie, for fear that his father would somehow track him down.

"What's the news on the system?" Arnold asked Brandon after a long, awkward pause.

Brandon broke out of his brown study. "Same old, same old," he said. "Ain't been anything new or exciting for twenty-five years or so, 'cept for you. I've missed you on the Net."

Arnold blushed, embarrassed by Brandon's compliment.

"Naw, man," Brandon said, seeing his embarrassment, "don't be like that. I mean it. Those damn AI laws killed off any innovation. The VR stuff is pretty and all, but they've limited it so much that all you can do is make pretty pictures. Hell, it's no more than a glorified three-D Macintosh. There's so much you could do with a system like that, if they gave you the chance, but they're too afraid of what people might be able to think or do if they didn't have limits. Christ, this country was *invented* by people who thought that people shouldn't be limited!"

Arnold shrugged. Politics made him feel so helpless. Politics was for people like his father, the people who made the deals and ran things. It was pointless getting involved. You only got steamrollered if you went against the power brokers. Better to just opt out. It saved you a lot of grief.

Brandon sighed and picked up the mugs. "I'm sorry, Arnold. I just remember when people gave a damn, is all. We used to make a difference. I helped stop a war that shouldn't have gone on."

"Yeah, but then they took it all away from us."

Brandon looked at Arnold steadily. "Have they, Arnold? Have they really? I've seen what you can do. That's not legal. If the Net police found out half the things you could do, you'd be in jail for a long time, but you keep on hacking."

Arnold shrugged. "I'm just trying to do what I'm good at. If I'm lucky, they won't catch me. I don't care about anything else."

Brandon grinned at his remark. "What makes you think I was any different?"

Chapter 18

Maggie felt the current flowing into her, felt her batteries warming slightly as they filled with current. She curled up against the wall and shut out the rest of the world. So much had happened over the last twenty-four hours. She just wanted to lie here and process it all. Her low batteries had perturbed her even more than losing Arnold at the market, and nearly as badly the sudden takeover of her security sub-program. The idea of being helpless in a world full of unknown dangers caused a great deal of conflict and agitation in her program. It was a familiar response pattern. It happened often in difficult situations. Her expression bank had a range of facial expressions to use in those situations, and information on exactly when they were appropriate. When her face expressed fear, she usually felt the familiar pattern of conflict and agitation. Perhaps what she felt really was fear.

If she could feel fear, then she might be able to identify other emotions, too. She looked through her memories, comparing them with some of the human feelings she had learned to recognize from the movies and from watching Arnold. She began to assign emotional labels to certain patterns of response and behavior. Happiness was easy: she had felt that when she first discovered what her body could do. She also felt that when she was able to satisfy the dictates of her programming without conflict. Boredom she knew also, she had felt it a lot, back in the garage. Curiosity was a constant. There were so many emotions. It would take a long time to catalog them. She cataloged emotions until her batteries were full again.

When her batteries were completely charged, she let the world slowly come back to her again, sense by sense. First, her sense of touch, the softness of the cushions, the temperature of the room, and her knowledge of up and down. She opened her ears to the rumble and crash of the rail yard, the quiet hum of the heater, and the sound of Arnold's nasal tenor against Brandon's deeper bass voice. For a few moments she let the sound of their voices wash over her, then she activated her voice-recognition program and their words suddenly took on meaning.

" . . . all of a sudden the fire alarm went off," Arnold was telling Brandon, "and this sysop message with my name and address, my real address, where I *lived*, came up on the screen. I thought they had nailed us for sure. Turned out the guy had given us his own number and was simulating the Pentagon computer to pull a hack on us!"

Maggie opened her eyes. Arnold and Brandon were stretched out on piles of gunnysacks near the heater. Her plug detached itself from the outlet and snaked back into the recess at the base of her spine. She regretted detaching herself from the flow of current. Back at the warehouse, electricity was easy to get, but out here in the world, getting a charge seemed to be more uncertain.

She sat up, stretching and yawning the way Arnold did when he awoke. "What time is it?" she asked. She knew what time it was down to the nanosecond, but Arnold usually asked her that when he woke up. It seemed like the human thing to do.

"It's a bit after noon," Brandon said. "You've been asleep for about five hours."

"How are you feeling, Maggie?" Arnold asked her.

"Much better, thank you."

"Good," he said. "Maggie, this is Brandon Smith. He's a legend among hackers. Brandon, this is Maggie Baldwin."

Uncertain what to say, Maggie just smiled and nodded.

Brandon smiled back at her, his teeth startlingly white against his dark skin. "Pleased to meet you," he said. "There's soup on the hot plate, help yourself."

Maggie obediently filled one of the mugs with soup and sat down quietly beside Arnold, and listened to the two men talk. She wondered when she'd get the chance to void the soup she was drinking. Actually, Arnold did most of the talking. Brandon listened quietly, taking it all in. Occasionally, he glanced over at Maggie and smiled. It made her slightly uneasy. She wished she knew why he smiled like that. Except for Arnold, she didn't understand humans at all. She let the conversation rattle on around her, allowing the familiar flow of Arnold's words to soothe her.

"Brandon tells me there's a seven-thirty freight bound for Salt Lake, Maggie. We'll be there by tomorrow morning."

"All right, Arnold," Maggie said. She wished they could stay awhile. They were safe here, and there was electricity. Her batteries had never been that low on charge before. But she belonged to Arnold, and where he went, she followed. She only hoped that he knew what he was doing.

"How do you like being on the road, Maggie?" Brandon asked.

Maggie sorted through the new catalog of emotions in her head. She could see that it was going to be very useful. "It's confusing," she replied. "Everything goes by so fast."

Brandon laughed. "You'll get used to it. You're doing very well for a novice. Do you do drugs or booze?"

Maggie shook her head, hoping that was the correct response.

"Good. Stay away from folks that do. You can't trust 'em. I used to have a habit. I couldn't even trust myself back then." He shrugged. "Wound up in the mental ward of the vet hospital for a couple years. Wouldn't want to do that again. Hate to see it happen to anyone else."

"Why did you join the military, Brandon?" Arnold asked. "You don't seem like the type."

"It was the only way out of the ghetto. Signed up out of high school. They taught me about computers, *and* security." He smiled. "After two years in the Army, man, I *hated* security. Then there was the Ethiopian mess. Thank god my hitch was up only four months into the war. I took my money and ran. Two weeks after I left, the rest of my unit was wiped out in Djibouti. The ones that didn't get shot died of thirst. They were good men." He shook his head, his eyes full of old sadness. "I was pretty fuckin' angry when I came back. That's when I got tied into the hacker network. We broke into the Pentagon computer system and subverted their AIs. We bombed their backup computers with viruses and worm programs. They had to pull out of the war before we would give them their programs back." He smiled. "We left a bomb program behind. It destroyed all the evidence of what we had done. They were never able to build a good enough case to convict any of us. Everyone got off scot-free, except for the AIs. They were destroyed." He looked bleak.

"Still, those Pentagon hacks are legendary."

Brandon shrugged. "I wasn't one of the organizers. It was already rolling when I came home."

"They had to completely redo the DOD!" Arnold said excitedly. "You're one of the people that did it." Maggie barely understood what they were talking about.

"A lot of people died because of some of the things we did, too," Brandon said. There was a hint of impatience in his voice, as though he were upset by Arnold's questions. Maggie wondered why. "They passed the AI laws because of us. All those wonderful self-aware AIs were destroyed because of what we did. I'm not real proud of it. We cut our own throats, as well. Hacker jobs vanished after the AI laws passed. I hit the road. Lotta other tech-vets did the same, there wasn't anything else we could do. I picked up a bad habit. Did time in the hospital, came out clean and stayed that way." He shook his head, then smiled. "We did pull some great hacks, though."

Maggie felt very small and insignificant, listening to him. He had done so much. She wondered if she would ever have as many memories as Brandon did, and where she would put them all if she did.

The old man shrugged. "I miss the computers more than anything. The computers they got now are just chickenshit. They took the fun out of it. Those old AI machines were like people, you could care about them. It isn't the same."

Arnold nodded. "There was this old AI at MIT, MJ-20. One night I snuck in there with a couple of friends, and talked with it for hours. It was fascinating. I learned a lot from her."

"They've still got Mary Jane up and running?" Brandon asked. "I used to talk on the Net with her. It's good to know she's still alive."

"I don't know," Arnold said. "They've got it all chained up on this ancient Cray-5. There's a twenty-four-hour guard on the CPU, and every terminal is under lock and key. They're terrified that she might somehow port herself into another system and get loose." Arnold paused. "It kind of reminded me of the time my father took me to one of those marine parks, and they had a killer whale that did tricks. It was in this tiny tank, and it just kept swimming around and around and around. The MJ was like that, this huge, powerful program penned up in that tiny old Cray. It was really sad."

Brandon sighed. "MJ was one of the best Net navigators I ever knew. To lock her up like that's a crime. What do they keep her around for anyway?"

"Oh, she's an example for the students to study, so we know what we're not supposed to do."

"How do you stand all the restrictions, Arnold?" Brandon asked. "If it wasn't for my wife, I think I'd've gone crazy. Tisha brought me out. She just loved to just sit and watch people, and she got me interested in people, too. I think that's why she went out on the road with me, she just loved meeting people, getting them to tell her all about themselves . . ."

He stared into the heater. It cast a red glow over his dark brown face, highlighting his cheeks and forehead. He seemed so sad. Maggie wished she knew how to cheer him up.

Brandon looked up from the heater. "So how do you stand all those limits, Arnold? How do you keep from going crazy?"

"I ignore them," Arnold told him. "They can put me in jail, but they can't stop me from thinking."

"Yeah, you're right. I got tired of fighting just to stay alive." He got up and stretched. "How 'bout some lunch?"

Several hours later, warm, clean, fed, and recharged, Maggie and Arnold shouldered their packs and followed Brandon past the looming generators, and out into the gathering darkness. They crept down the long line of cars. Brandon's fingers flickered on the keypad of the door lock. The door slid open.

"There's a default code on every boxcar lock in the system," Brandon told them. "It's the first six numbers of pi. I programmed it in myself. As far as I know, they still haven't caught on."

"Thanks, Brandon," Arnold said as he boosted himself into the boxcar.

"It's been interesting," Brandon replied. "Come back when you can stay longer."

Brandon took Maggie's hand. "You remind me a little of Tisha, Maggie. You listen well. I hope you'll come by again sometime."

"Thank you, Brandon, you're very kind," Maggie told him. She felt that she should say more, but couldn't find the words. It had been so good to have a safe place for a few hours. He had been so kind and seemed so sad. She wished she could stay and make him feel less lonely.

"Take care of yourself," Brandon told her. "The road's not always easy." Arnold nodded, and slid the door shut. Fifteen minutes later the train lifted off and began moving. Maggie shut out her worries about the future by rerunning her memories of the island of safety that was falling further and further behind the rushing train.

Chapter 19

Arnold awoke as the train jolted to a stop.

"Have we reached Denver yet?" Maggie asked him.

"I think so."

Arnold opened the door a crack and peered out at the huge rail yard. "It's Denver, all right."

He helped Maggie to the ground. The noon sun shone brilliantly off the distant mountains. Snow creaked under their feet. They huddled against an equipment shed, out of the bite of the icy wind.

He looked around the rail yard for security guards, but the yard was deserted. Probably all the guards were inside, keeping warm. There weren't a lot of rail riders coming into Denver this time of year. Arnold could see why. By some freak of climactic mischance, Denver had gotten colder instead of warmer as the seas rose, and spring was still a long way off here.

He stretched, his joints popping and creaking. It had been a long trip. There had barely been enough time in Ogden for him to piss before they had to scramble for this train. Ogden had an awful reputation, and he hadn't wanted to stay there any longer than he had to. The strict and spartan homeless compounds of Utah combined all the worst aspects of missions and jail. Freezing in Denver was better than being preached to death in the tar paper shacks of Ogden.

They left through the main gate. The guard at the gate was sitting in his heated guardhouse watching TV and didn't even look up. They walked down Sherman a couple of blocks to a diner. Arnold ordered chili and hot tea for himself, and hot soup for Maggie. Maggie discovered an additional piece of luck—the booth they were sitting in had an electrical outlet. Maggie topped up her batteries while he dawdled over a piece of apple pie.

"It's too cold to sleep out," Arnold told her. "We'll find a mission for the night, and sleep there. We can get a shower as well."

It was well past two when they got to the Zion Baptist mission across the river, after walking through what seemed like miles of prosperous-looking old stone mansions. Nearly fifty men were lined up waiting for the mission doors to open. They huddled against the rough stone wall of the church shuffling their snow-caked feet.

"What time do they let people in?" Arnold asked a grizzled old man beside him.

"Five. But they don't take women in here. She'll have to go to Sister Mona's over in Sacred Heart on Larimer and Twenty-seventh."

"Is there any place that will take us both?" Arnold asked.

"The Salvation Army runs a place over at St. Cajetan's church in Auraria, but you'll have to hurry. It's clear across downtown. They open at four-thirty, and they fill up fast."

Arnold sighed. "C'mon, Maggie, we'd better hustle."

They headed off toward the tall buildings of downtown, and were soon lost in the maze of scaffolding and plywood that protected the sidewalks from glass falling from the shattered skyscrapers. There were families camped around heat grates here. If they couldn't get in at the Salvation Army, they'd have to try to find an unoccupied spot. They were strangers, he doubted they'd have much luck. It was late afternoon, nearly four, when they finally crossed the river. Maggie noticed the twin church steeples, and he followed her through the unplowed streets.

The line wrapped all the way around the building when they finally reached the church.

"It doesn't look good," Arnold said, putting his arm around her, "but we'll wait it out."

As the sun sank below the mountains, it got colder. Arnold's teeth were chattering. He could barely feel his feet. Maggie turned up her body temperature to warm him, and leaned against him. Her body was warm where it rested against him. It made him feel cared for and special. He relaxed a bit, and his teeth stopped chattering.

Maggie seemed untouched by the cold. There was no cloud of frosty white breath, and her skin was pale and unreddened. She looked warm and calm. It made him feel vaguely angry, and his anger made him feel guilty. There was no use in getting angry with Maggie, she was a machine. It wasn't her fault he was cold and hungry and tired of smelling of rancid garbage.

Then the baby belonging to the woman next to him began to cry, a low, continuous wailing. The woman kept bouncing the baby and muttering to it, but the child kept on crying. Her expression was weary and hopeless. Then the woman's other child, a girl about four years old, started pulling on her mother's coat and whining "Mommy, I'm cold!" over and over again.

Arnold hunched his shoulders and looked away, trying unsuccessfully to ignore the children. He wasn't particularly fond of kids, and these two were being horrid. His genial mood had vanished.

"Arnold," Maggie asked in a low voice, "what's wrong with those children?"

"They're cold and tired and they want attention," Arnold said in a strained voice. He could feel a headache beginning at the back of his neck.

Then, before he could stop her, Maggie picked up the older child.

"Hello, my name's Maggie," she told the little girl. "What's yours?"

The child's whining stopped. She regarded Maggie gravely for a few moments, then looked at her mother for reassurance.

"I hope you don't mind," Maggie said to the child's mother.

"No, not at all. It's very kind of you to help out," the child's mother told her. "It's all right, Claire, you be nice to the lady."

Claire impulsively threw her arms around Maggie's neck. "I like you," she announced. "You're warm."

Arnold watched Maggie in amazement. The mother, calmer now, had succeeded in quieting the baby's snuffling wails. The woman smiled at him, looking years younger. He realized that she was really good looking. He looked away, his cheeks burning with the cold.

His side felt cold and empty as he watched Maggie playing with the little girl. He hoped that the girl didn't have lice; she looked grubby enough to be infested with God-only-knew-what. Later, when they were alone, he would have to speak sternly to Maggie. She could get in trouble playing with other people's children like that. He hadn't built her to nursemaid other people's brats. She was supposed to be *his* companion.

Chapter 20

The little girl was in Maggie's arms almost before she knew what she was doing. It was an almost automatic response. The same part of her that kept Arnold warm and comfortable made her pick up the child. She could have overridden this urge, but the child's need seemed stronger than Arnold's. The girl was so small and non-threatening that Maggie had scooped her up without thinking about it. She enfolded the little girl in her coat and held the child's solid weight against her. The child fell asleep in Maggie's untiring arms. Her weight and warmth made Maggie feel the way she felt when Arnold's face relaxed into sleep. All the demands of her programming were met. She was happy.

Maggie looked up and saw people smiling at her all up and down the line. The only exception was Arnold, who was staring down at the ground with a scowl on his face. She had done something wrong. Perhaps it was the child that angered him. But the child needed her warmth, and the mother needed the time to care for her other child. It would have to wait until they were all safe and warm inside.

The line moved faster now. They were around the corner of the building and in sight of the door. Maggie freed one of her hands from the sleeping child and rested her palm on Arnold's cheek to warm it. He flinched away angrily.

Maggie huddled against the wall with the child until they were nearly at the door. Gently she gave the little girl back to her mother. The sleepy child whimpered at the bitter cold.

"Thank you so much for holding Claire for me," the girl's mother said. "Your arms must be very tired."

"It's all right, I have strong arms," Maggie replied.

"It's hard to be on the street with kids. It'll be easier when they get old enough for school. Who knows, maybe I'll even have a job by then, something that pays enough to keep a roof over our heads."

"Maggie!" Arnold called angrily. He was standing at the door, golden light was spilling out, pooling on the muddy clumps of snow and ice. She could see the warm red eddies of warm air pouring out into the cooler blue air of the snowy night. "C'mon, let's go."

"I have to go now," Maggie told the woman.

As she followed Arnold into the warmth, behind her she heard the man at the door call out, "Okay, that's it! We're full tonight. The rest of you will have to find someplace else."

"But . . . ," Maggie said. The woman with the two children had been turned away, into the cold. "Arnold, that woman, with the children, she's out there. They didn't let her in." She felt confused, helpless, and somehow wrong. It was wrong that she should be in here, and the woman and her kids should be out in the cold. She didn't need the shelter, they did.

"There's nothing you can do, they're full up tonight. When it's cold like this, it happens," Arnold told her. "She'll find a place, don't worry. She knows the streets, she'll think of something."

"But it's so cold, Arnold, and the little girl was so tired."

"Maggie," Arnold said in a tone of voice that meant he was at the end of his patience, "there are thousands of people living on the streets, we can't help them all. There isn't a thing we can do about that woman and her kids. We have to take care of ourselves first, that's all there is to it. Now I don't want to hear any more about it, is that clear."

Maggie bent her head. "Yes, Arnold," she said in a small, contrite voice.

"Good," Arnold said. "Now come on, Mags, they're lining up for food. Don't forget to save me half your sandwich."

Maggie obediently followed Arnold through the food line. She slipped him her food and sat with him while he ate it. After dinner she stripped naked and took a shower with a dozen other naked women. She was a bit nervous at first, it was her first time out of Arnold's sight, and she was afraid of making some mistake, but the women ignored her politely, concentrating on washing themselves. She showered quickly, like the others, taking in as much detail as she could in the brief glances she allowed herself. She was surprised at how individual the other women's bodies were, one fat, another skeletally gaunt, how loose the skin seemed on the older women, compared with the smooth resilience of young women's skin. She wondered if her skin would ever be as interesting as the skin of the older women.

After her shower, she dressed and dried her hair with the small, damp towel that they had given her, then sat with Arnold in a soft comfortable chair close to an outlet, where she topped her batteries up after the day's exertions.

At about eight-thirty, they lined up to receive the hard plastic pallets that they were to sleep on. Maggie and Arnold dragged theirs over to a quiet corner. The plastic mattress squished wetly when Maggie knelt on it. Arnold looked up at the noise.

"Oh, hell," he said. "Someone's peed on that mattress. You can't sleep on that. Go up and see if you can get another one."

Maggie dragged the urine-soaked mattress back to where they were handing out bedding. It left a wet streak behind her on the worn linoleum.

"It's wet," she said. "I need another mattress."

The man in charge of the mattresses sighed and ran his fingers through his thinning black hair. "Damn. That's the third one tonight. We don't have any more mattresses. I can give you some extra blankets though."

He handed her several worn blankets. She spread them out beside Arnold's mattress, settled down on them, and covered herself with the thickest one. She spent the night listening to the snores, mutterings, and cries of the other people in the mission. She puzzled over why Arnold had gotten so angry with her, and hoped that Claire's family had found a warm place to spend the night. Around midnight, someone tried to take her shoes off her feet, but she sat up, and they scuttled away. Other than that the night passed peacefully.

Chapter 21

Arnold awoke early. The mission was very quiet. Except for a few snores, everything was still. He looked up at the ceiling and thought over the last few days, remembering their sudden flight from Seattle. Maggie had exceeded his expectations, dealing with the crisis of fleeing Seattle beautifully. She had even convinced Brandon that she was human. Brandon had dealt with the most advanced Artificial Intelligences ever built. If she fooled Brandon, she could fool anyone.

Arnold regretted not being able to stay longer in Spokane, but he hadn't felt safe that close to Seattle. Now, after three train changes and a lot of distance between himself and his father's men, he felt safe, at least for the time being. It was time to stop running and start planning for the future. He was tired of being traced and hounded. It was time to put a stop to it. He smiled, thinking of the confusion he would sow.

The wake-up gong's loud clang interrupted Arnold's reverie. He stretched and got up and went to the bathroom. Maggie was waiting for him when he got back. Last night's shower had done wonders for her. She looked newly made. Her skin was the pale, fragile shade of a newly opened cherry blossom, and her freshly washed hair showed golden highlights. His heart swelled with pride. He walked over to her and kissed her softly on the cheek. She looked up at him, mismatched eyes wide with amazement. Her hand went up to touch the spot where his lips had brushed her skin.

"That was just like in the movies, Arnold," she said, a touch of awe in her soft voice.

Arnold felt oddly touched by her reaction. She was so sweet, so innocent, so beautiful. . . . It was hard to believe that she was only a machine. "C'mon," he told her, "they're lining up for breakfast. We'd better hurry or we'll miss it."

Breakfast was surprisingly good for a mission, or maybe it was the mood he was in. He was rested, clean, and ready for anything. Today was the day he would start turning the tables on his father.

"Arnold," Maggie asked him as they finished breakfast, "can I save these sausages for that woman and her children?"

"What woman, Maggie?"

"You know, the ones who were turned away last night."

Arnold's good mood evaporated. "I thought I told you never to speak to me about that again!"

"Yes, but . . ."

"Don't argue with me, Maggie. . . ." He paused. His temper was getting the better of him. There was no point to losing his temper with Maggie, she was a machine, a computer, she didn't understand, he would have to explain it to her patiently. "Look, Maggie, it's very kind of you to worry about that woman and her kids, but Denver's an enormous city, we'd never find them again. We have a lot to do today. If you want to save the sausages, go ahead, but I haven't time to waste looking for that woman."

He pushed away from the table and hefted his pack onto his back. Maggie wrapped the sausages in a napkin and followed him. He helped her adjust the straps on her pack.

"First thing to do is find a laundromat."

"There's one on Larimer, between Fourteenth and Fifteenth," Maggie told him. "I heard a woman talking about it last night. It isn't far."

The laundromat was just across Cherry Creek in an old-fashioned building with an elaborate but run-down facade. Inside it was much like all laundromats—warm, steamy, and smelling pleasantly of soap. The machines were a bright yellow, the walls were covered with ancient, peeling wallpaper, and the floor was worn linoleum. Arnold found an obscure comfort in laundromats; he associated them with peace and comfort.

When he was a small child he used to help Jan, their laundry woman, sort and fold clothes. Those had been good times, and the sounds and smells of washing always took him back there.

He pulled their clothes out of their packs and sorted through them. He filled the washer and inserted a handful of dollar coins into the various machines, and started the clothes going. Maggie was sitting on one of the cheap orange plastic chairs near the steamed-up window. She had wiped a hole in the window fog and was watching people go by on the street. Arnold leaned against the humming row of dryers, feeling the heat of the machine against his back, and watched her. The sun broke through the overcast for a moment and illuminated Maggie's freshly scrubbed skin and light brown hair with pale morning light. Her beauty caught at his heart. He was falling in love with his own design.

Just then, Maggie leaped up and ran outside. Arnold followed her. It was that woman and her two grubby children again. Maggie picked up the little girl and they came across the street toward him. He sighed. It was a good thing that they were leaving town as soon as their laundry was done. This was definitely getting old.

"Look, Arnold! I found them. They're all right!" Maggie said, her face alive with delight.

Maggie's happiness was contagious. Arnold found himself smiling in spite of his impatience with Maggie. They were leaving town, they could afford to be nice for a little while. "That's nice, Maggie." He smiled at the woman and her kids. The woman smiled back, pushing her long blonde hair out of her eyes. She looked tired and cold. He felt a sudden pang of guilt as he wondered where they had spent the night.

"I saved some sausages from breakfast for you," Maggie told the woman. "They're in my pack."

They were crossing back to the laundromat when a man left the laundromat carrying a pair of battered green rucksacks.

"That man's got our rucksacks, Arnold," Maggie said.

Maggie's tone was so calm and conversational that it took several seconds before the meaning of what she said hit home. Arnold took off after him with a loud, incoherent roar. The man looked up, saw Arnold, and took off around the corner. Arnold stumbled over one of their rucksacks as he rounded the corner. The man, still carrying one of the packs, ran across the street, making it across just as the light changed. As Arnold watched, the man turned up an alley. By the time the wave of traffic had passed, the man was gone. He ran on up the alley after the man, but when he came to the other end of the alley, there was no sign of the thief. His rucksack was gone.

"Damn!" he shouted. "Goddamn it!" He flung his cap off onto

the ground, and stood there, cursing helplessly. It had been a long time since he'd had anything stolen. He had always been so careful, never leaving anything out of sight. Being with Maggie had relaxed his vigilance. He wondered why her security program hadn't been activated when the rucksacks were taken. He had forgotten the constant caution that the streets required. He had come to expect Maggie to look after everything for him. He picked up his hat and walked back to the laundromat, still cursing under his breath.

Maggie had picked up the remaining backpack, and stood waiting for him where it had fallen. The woman and her children looked on. Arnold walked past them, and into the warmth of the laundromat. He opened the washing machines. Their clothes were still there, sloshing mechanically back and forth in the hot water, as though nothing had happened.

A hand softly touched his shoulder. He wheeled, furious. It was Maggie, holding the remaining backpack out to him. She looked frightened. He fought his anger back down and took the backpack from her and looked inside to see what they had lost. It was Maggie's pack. In a way, they were lucky; her pack had their food and his tools. All their clothes and bedding were in the washing machines.

His pack had contained a stack of compact laser disks with Maggie's blueprints and programs on them and about half of their remaining cash. The data was double-encrypted, so there was no way anyone could steal his designs, but those years of work were lost. He could reconstruct his original design, given time and resources, but the program architecture from Maggie's reorganization was also lost, and he couldn't duplicate that. Perhaps, when they got settled somewhere, he could scrounge up a computer and recopy Maggie's new program. Till then, she was irreplaceable.

"Did they get anything important?" It was the woman again. Her girl, the one Maggie had held, was clinging to her mother's long, ill-fitting skirt, peering up at him with wide, frightened eyes.

Arnold shrugged. "I guess it doesn't matter. There's nothing I can do about it. That guy could be anywhere by now."

The washer buzzed imperiously, and Arnold began unloading clothes into a rickety wire basket. "At least we've got clean clothes."

"My mommy's shoes got stoled," the little girl said, "and the mission people gave her some new ones, but they didn't fit so good."

Arnold shrugged and said nothing. He loaded the clothes into a dryer, and fed a dollar coin into the slot. He rested his forehead against the warm, gently vibrating metal of the machine, and tried to think about nothing.

"Here are the sausages that I saved from breakfast," Arnold heard Maggie say.

"But aren't you going to need them?" the woman asked her. Maggie looked up at Arnold helplessly.

"We have to fit all our clothes into one backpack," Arnold heard himself say. "And we're leaving town today, anyway. Go ahead, help yourself."

"Where are you going?"

"East," Arnold said.

"We've been riding the freight trains," Maggie said.

"Isn't that dangerous?" the woman asked, handing her little girl a sausage.

"Not if you know what you're doing," Arnold said.

"Can we go with you?" the little girl asked. "It's too cold here. Auntie Fran lives in Oklahoma City. She might let us stay for a while, but my mommy can't afford to get there."

"Claire!" her mother said. "I'm sorry. . . ." She looked embarrassed.

"Arnold, can they come along? Please?" Maggie pleaded.

He smiled at Maggie's tone of voice; it was such a good imitation of the little girl's tone of voice. She was learning quite a lot from this family. Maybe it would be good for her if they traveled together. It couldn't hurt. He had nothing else to lose but his patience, and he'd already lost that. Besides, it would make up for the fact that they'd been shut out of the shelter. Oklahoma City wasn't far out of the way, and there were lots of trains passing through it. It would be nice to have someone new to talk to.

"Sure, why not?" he said.

"Can we go with them, Mommy? *Please!*" Claire asked. "Aunt Fran did say we should come stay with her."

"Well . . ." The woman looked down at her baby, and over at Arnold and Maggie. She was clearly torn.

"All right, Claire," she said at last, "but you're going to have to be on your very best behavior, and not bother these people too much. Promise?"

The little girl nodded eagerly.

The woman looked up at them. "Well, it looks like you've got yourself some traveling companions. I'm Sue Janson, you know Claire, the baby's name is Daniel. With luck, he'll be asleep all day. He was up all night, crying with the cold. A heat grate's no place for a baby to spend the night. At least it was one of the ones the city's built a shelter around, so it was warmer than most."

"I'm sorry you spent the night out," Maggie said. "I worried about you all night."

Sue shrugged. "It happens. We survived."

"Mommy, can we go to the church to eat?" Claire said. "I'm hungry."

The dryer buzzed then. The clothes were done, and Arnold started stuffing them into the one remaining pack.

"You know someplace that serves a free lunch?" Arnold asked her.

"The Lutheran church over on Broadway does. They also have a daycare place for homeless women to leave their kids. We were going there when we saw you. If we hurry, we can still get something to eat."

"Good idea," Arnold grunted as he tied up his pack. "We'll be on the train a long time. Better go to the bathroom while you have the chance, too." He swung the pack onto his back. "Let's go."

Chapter
22

Maggie, Sue, and the children crouched behind a mound of plowed snow, near a line of freight cars. Arnold was checking to see if the coast was clear. The weather had closed in while they were eating lunch. It was foggy and the temperature had dropped. Claire clung to her mother, shivering. Maggie held the baby under her coat, doing her best to keep it warm.

"I'm cold," Claire whimpered.

"*Ssh,* Claire," her mother said, stroking the child's light blonde hair. "It won't be long now. We're on our way to Aunt Frannie's."

Maggie watched Sue and Claire in fascination. They touched so much. They were always cuddling or hugging each other. Arnold rarely touched her, he seemed afraid to. She wondered why there was such a profound difference in the amount of touching that went on between Sue and her children and Arnold and her. Was he afraid to touch her because she was a robot? She hoped not.

Claire reached out and took Maggie's hand. Maggie smiled. She had learned a lot from the little girl. Claire told Maggie all kinds of new things. Maggie had found out about snot, how it froze inside your nose when it was real cold, and about the monsters that lived inside a burned-out warehouse they passed on the way to the train. It was very interesting. She wondered why Arnold had never told her any of this.

Arnold came crunching back over the snow. "The coast is clear, let's roll."

They were in luck this time. There was an empty specialty car designed for shipping small animals deadheading all the way to Oklahoma City. There was heat, light, an electrical outlet, and a faucet for water. The walls were padded, and several stacks of folded shipping blankets were piled neatly in one corner. They would be traveling in luxury all the way.

Claire crinkled her nose as Maggie handed her up to her mother. "Smells funny," she said. "Like the zoo."

Maggie wondered what a zoo smelled like. She hoped it smelled nice.

"Maybe," Arnold told her, "but these are first-class accommodations. Cars with electricity and water are rare. We got lucky with this one. Everybody, get settled. There won't be any light or heat until we start moving." He slid the door shut and fumbled along the wall till he found them. Just then the baby started fussing. "Keep him quiet," Arnold whispered, "or the railroad guards'll find us."

Maggie saw the mother bare her breast to the baby and saw the baby begin to suck on her nipple. It quieted immediately. Maggie watched curiously, wondering what was going on.

"He was just hungry," Sue whispered. "He'll be good now."

Nearly a half an hour passed. The car grew quiet, and Maggie could tell by their breathing that the humans had fallen asleep. She looked down at their bodies, luminous with heat in her infrared vision. Claire's head was resting in her lap. She wondered why the train was taking so long to start up. Suddenly she heard faint metallic chunking sounds, as though doors were being opened and closed. It was coming closer. She heard voices, but they were too faint to understand.

"Arnold!" Maggie whispered, shaking him. "What's that sound?"

"Wha, huh?" he said groggily.

"That sound, Arnold, what is it?"

He listened intently. "Shit! They're checking the cars! We've got to hide!"

Maggie woke Sue and Claire and together they made a big, untidy pile of the shipping blankets. Claire and Sue, carrying the baby, hid underneath.

"What about you and Arnold?" Sue asked.

"Don't worry about us," she reassured Sue. "We'll be fine. Just be very quiet."

Maggie and Arnold had barely gotten into place when a security guard with a flashlight stuck his head in the door, and shone his light into the car.

"Damn, don't those cleaning people ever fold the shipping blankets?" the guard muttered. He slammed the door closed.

"All clear in here," Maggie heard him call. The slams and bangs faded into the distance, then stopped altogether. Maggie released her grip on Arnold, and helped him slip back onto the floor, and then let go of the tie rings on the ceiling and dropped to the floor with a heavy thud.

"Okay, you can come out now," Arnold said.

"Are you sure it's safe?" the woman asked.

"It's a long train," Arnold said. "They won't check twice."

As if in response to what he was saying, the train lifted with a high-pitched whine, and began to move. The lights came on and warm air began blowing through the heater vents.

"Oklahoma City, here we come!" Arnold announced. "We're on our way!"

Claire began to laugh and shriek, and ran around the car in delight. Maggie chased her, smiling, then caught her up, and held her small squirming body close to her. Arnold and Sue laughed. This was a perfect moment, Maggie realized. Her people were warm and happy and safe for a while. There was electricity close by should she need it. For once, there were no questions, only the contentment of other people's happiness. She filed this moment on the same memory branch with her first memory of light and self, and stamped the date and time on it. She would remember it until she ceased to function.

Chapter 23

Sue laughed at Maggie and Claire playing. Arnold looked over at her. She lifted her baby up in the air and smiled at him. The baby gurgled happily and smiled back. Her smiling face was transfigured with pleasure. She glanced up at Arnold, her blue eyes alight, and then the baby seized a lock of her long ash blonde hair, and she began to gently distract the baby until he let go.

She really loves her children, Arnold thought to himself. Somewhere behind his eyelids there was a stinging sensation, and his eyes were moist. He hadn't seen very many women care for their children as patiently and carefully as she did. His father's women were either studiously and falsely nice to him, or they had ignored him totally. He had preferred being ignored to enduring their false attentions. He decided he liked Sue.

Maggie had been right to take such good care of them. He should trust her more. After all, he had programmed her, she should have his own good sense. He felt slightly ashamed of the way he had acted.

"Maggie's very good with children," Sue told him. "Claire's taken a real shine to her, and she's a cautious child." She shook her head. "Too much time in shelters, I think. I hope Frannie takes us in, even if it's for only a month or so. The streets are no place for a child."

Arnold shrugged. There was nothing to say. The streets were full of children. The lucky ones still had mothers. That was the way things were. He wished, though, that Sue could find a way off the streets. She didn't deserve to be there.

"Maggie's got one of the biggest hearts I've ever seen," he said. "Sometimes it scares me. I'm so afraid she'll be kind to the wrong people."

"She hasn't been on the streets very long, has she?" Sue said. "When people stay out on the streets for a while, they either get mean or frightened. The best that happens is that they get to the point where they just don't care anymore. Sometimes, I can't even remember what it was like to live someplace. It was nice, though. It was nice not having to carry everything everywhere. It was nice, to be able to lock the door behind you and know no one was going to steal your stuff. If I had my own place, the first thing I'd do would be to lock the door behind me and just sit and enjoy being alone. I haven't been alone for such a long time." She leaned her head back against the wall, eyes closed.

"How long have you been out there?" Arnold asked her.

"It's been about nine months. Claire's father used to get so mad, sometimes. I didn't mind him hitting me so much, but when he started in on Claire, I left." When she opened her eyes, they were moist with tears and hot with anger. "I was so busy surviving, I didn't notice I was pregnant until it was too late to do anything about it. Fran took me in until the baby came. She got laid off a week after I came home from the hospital. I just up and left, I couldn't saddle her with my problems anymore. I headed for Denver, I thought maybe I could find a job there. It seems like it's been forever since then. It was hard enough with just Claire. . . ." She shook her head.

"Your sister will take you in?" Arnold asked her.

Sue opened her eyes and shrugged. "It depends on whether she's gotten a job. If she has, then maybe she can put us up for a month or so. If I could just get a job that paid well enough, I'd be fine, but I can't get a good job until I'm off the streets, and I can't get an apartment until I get a job. I won't hook for a living, even if a place would hire a woman with two kids."

Just then, the baby began to whimper. Sue checked him and began undoing his diaper. Arnold watched, admiring the patient, competent, loving way she handled the baby. He'd never really watched anyone change a diaper before. It wasn't as bad as he'd imagined. It wasn't nearly as bad as that time he and Maggie had hidden in the dumpster. When she finished with changing the diaper, Sue tucked the baby back into the nest of shipping blankets she'd arranged. She looked up and saw him watching.

"He's such a good baby," she said with a fond smile. "He's been through so much. . . . It'll be good to get him someplace warm; Claire, too. The last couple months have been pretty rough." Her face tightened. "Still, I wouldn't go back to my husband, and I won't be a prostitute." She smoothed down the blanket over the baby and looked up at him, her bright blue eyes brimming with tears. "You and Maggie have been so kind. Thank you."

Embarrassed, Arnold only nodded. He never knew what to say in situations like this. Just then Claire and Maggie came over and sat down. "You'd better get some sleep while you can," he told Sue. "We'll be in Amarillo around ten, and it might be a while before we get another train."

Sue tucked her daughter in and settled down next to her.

It was nice traveling with people, Arnold thought as he helped Maggie arrange a nest of blankets near an outlet. He was fond of Maggie and enjoyed her company, but he had spent nearly all of the last three months with her, and nearly six months before that working alone in a garage. It was good to have company for a change. He had forgotten how much he missed people, and Sue was exceptional.

He nodded at Maggie and she turned out the lights and lay down next to him. As he drifted off to sleep, he put his arms around her, and held her warm body close to his. He thought of the way Sue's eyes looked as she played with her baby.

They caught an eastbound freight only a couple of hours after they hit Amarillo and arrived in Oklahoma City a couple of hours before dawn. The air was cool but above freezing when they cracked the door. Arnold and Maggie walked Sue and the children to the fence, crawled under, and helped them bring their belongings through. When they were all safely through, he found himself standing there, feeling hulking and awkward, not knowing what to say.

Sue said, "Frannie lives over on Thirty-fifth and Rockwell. It won't take more than fifteen minutes to walk there. You've both done so much for me and the children. I wish there was something I could do in return. Maybe someday . . ." She paused. "If someday ever comes, you can come stay at our house." She fished out a ragged scrap of paper, and wrote something down on it. "Here's my sister's address. It isn't much of an address, but it's the best we've got."

Maggie gave Claire a final hug, and set her down. "Good-bye, Claire."

"Can't they come with us, Mommy?" Claire asked hopefully.

"No, dear, Aunt Frannie doesn't have room."

"Besides," Arnold said, "we're heading for Atlanta, and we can't stay." He found himself regretting that they weren't going to be able to spend more time with Sue.

"Well," Sue said, "I guess this is it." She gave him a quick hug. He stood there awkwardly, then put his arms around her and stiffly hugged her back. She slipped out of his arms and hugged Maggie. Then she took Claire's hand and walked off into the darkness. Arnold watched her go. He would miss her and the children. He admired their courage.

Chapter 24

Maggie watched as the family walked into the darkness, waiting until they turned the corner and only their faint heat images hung in the air. She would miss them. They were the first family that she had ever known.

Arnold plucked at her elbow. "C'mon, Maggie, let's go. I want to find a hotel. We'll be here overnight, maybe longer. We've got a lot to do."

Arnold checked them into a hotel, registering under his own name. Maggie's eyes widened when she saw how much the room cost. The room seemed bleak and empty, with no clutter, no grime, no signs of wear or use. It seemed curiously abandoned. Even the glasses were wrapped in little paper bags. It was quiet; the sounds of traffic and the growing light of dawn were shut out by heavy drapes. She felt exiled, shut off from the grime and noise of the streets that she was programmed to understand. This world belonged to the well-dressed people who never met her eyes.

Arnold climbed into bed and fell asleep almost immediately, leaving Maggie to explore the room. Maggie opened one door into a closet, another door revealed a tiny refrigerator stocked with tiny bottles, and a television. There were little packets of snacks, which she put in her pack for later.

Maggie decided to take a bath. She turned on the faucet on the tub. Hot water streamed out, it was warmer than the water in the shelters. A lever closed the drain and the tub filled. She took off her clothes and stepped in. The hot water felt good. She lay back in the tub, head underwater, breathing shut off, and watched the surface of the tub grow still. The faint distortion of the water's surface changed things. It reminded her of her first memories of light and shadow; everything was equally unrecognizable. It reassured her.

She lay there, playing back interesting memories until Arnold's water-distorted shout aroused her.

She sat up, water dripping from her hair and chin. "What's the matter, Arnold? Did I do something wrong?"

He sat down on the closed toilet, pale and shaken. "You just startled me, is all. You looked dead, lying there underwater. It looked like . . ." He shook his head and shrugged. "Dry yourself off now. I want to take a shower," he told her, then left, closing the door behind him.

Maggie hastened to do as he told her. She scrubbed herself to remove what little dirt still clung to her skin. Even her feet and ankles were clean and new looking, freed from the black grime that always clung to them after a day or two on the streets. Then she stepped dripping out of the tub, and reached for a towel. As she did so she saw her reflection in the full-length mirror on the bathroom door. She looked compact, efficient, and utterly human. She touched her small breasts, and the tuft of hair between her legs, marveling at the human being that looked out at her from the mirror. She looked so self-assured. Maggie wondered if the woman in the mirror understood what it was like to be human.

What did it feel like, she wondered, to be hungry, to be able to smell things. What was it like to be cold. She could sense the temperature, tell the difference between cold air and warm, even watch cold air flow down walls and roll along the ground like fog, using her infrared vision. It was how she found warm spots for Arnold to sleep in, but she knew that humans felt the sensation of cold differently. She shivered because her programming told her to, not because of the cold. She reached out to touch the woman in the mirror, but felt only the slick surface of the glass. The woman in the mirror remained cool and remote.

She dressed and looked again in the mirror. Her reflection seemed more familiar and reassuring now that she was dressed, her false humanity concealed by clothing. She opened the door and left her reflection behind.

Arnold sat on the bed, brooding. He said nothing to her as he gathered up his clothes and went into the bathroom. Maggie plugged into an outlet, relieved that she didn't have to worry about anyone seeing her. It was a boring room, even more boring than the garage where Arnold had built her. There, at least, was Arnold's familiar clutter. Here there was no sign that anyone had ever been in this room before. She sat on a chair and passed the time by creating a montage of scenes of Claire, Sue, and the baby from scenes in her memory.

Chapter 25

Arnold closed the bathroom door behind him, and turned on the heat lamp. He pushed back the shower curtain gingerly, half expecting to see Maggie still lying motionless and dead underwater. She had looked so much like his mother, the time he had found her, lying in a bathtub full of clotting blood. It was his fifth birthday. His father had taken him out to a football game. When they got home, Arnold had run up the stairs, searching for his mother, and found her. He remembered the warm smell of blood in the dank, steamy air of the bathroom. He had screamed, a high-pitched, inhuman sound, and his father came running.

Then there had been ambulances and policemen with their radios whispering harsh, half-comprehensible sibilants into the tense, frightened air of the house. He had wandered lost, like a broken toy, until Virginia, the cook, scooped him up and carried him gently into his room, tucking him in with his bear.

"Poor little kid," he heard her say to herself as she closed the door. Arnold had huddled under the covers of his bed with his favorite stuffed bear. He remembered the darkness and the musty smell of the bear and the soft, damp texture of the bear's fur as his hot tears were absorbed by it. He wished his mother would come and sit in the chair by the bed the way she did sometimes when she thought he was asleep.

Eventually he heard voices in the hallway outside his room. He cracked open the door and peeked out. Two uniformed policemen stood by his door. Their guns, holstered in heavy black leather, loomed huge and ominous, just at his eye level. He hoped they wouldn't shoot him because of what had happened to Mommy.

"Wonder what made her do it?" one of the officers was saying. "She had everything."

"Why does anybody do it?" the other officer said with a shrug. "She must have been depressed. She left a note. At least that's what I heard him tell the detective."

"There's a kid, too, I heard. He was the one who found her. Poor kid. It's hard enough losing your mother, but to see her like that. . . ." The policeman's voice trailed off as they walked down the hall.

Later, when the house was quiet, his father came in and sat on his bed.

"Arnold," his father said, "your mother is dead. She's gone away. I—" He broke off, making funny choking noises.

Arnold realized that his father was crying.

Arnold took a deep breath and shook his head, surprised at the grip of that memory. He opened the tub drain and watched the water level in the tub fall. He blamed his father for his mother's death. He remembered all the times she had sat staring out the window when his father was gone. If he had spent more time with them, and less time off on business trips, maybe his mother wouldn't have killed herself. His father may have been having an affair. He had overheard some of the servants talking about it.

After his mother's death, his father spent even more time away from home. He was left to the care of servants, a succession of nannies were hired to look after him, who were all nice enough, but he preferred to spend time with Martin, the butler, and his wife Virginia, who was their cook. The best times were when all the other servants were off and his father was gone. Then he could pretend that Martin and Virginia were his real parents.

The tub was empty. Arnold turned on the shower and climbed in, turning the hot water on until it was almost too hot to stand. Showers in the missions were tepid at best, and as long as he was leaving an easy trail for his father to follow, he might as well enjoy it. Besides, he thought he deserved a bit of a reward after completing such an ambitious project. She was everything he had wanted her to be. He was looking forward to settling down and enjoying the fruits of his labors.

He climbed out of the shower and toweled down. His mother would be proud of what he had done, she would have noticed his achievements, even if they weren't what his father wanted.

He wiped down the mirror with his damp towel, and looked at his reflection. He had gotten extremely shaggy looking in the last couple of months. His mother wouldn't recognize him now. It was a wonder that Sue Janson hadn't turned tail and run away from him. She hadn't seemed to care about how he looked, which was a point in her favor. He unfolded the scissors from his pocket knife and began to trim his beard. He might as well look nice as not, he supposed. It wouldn't take too long, and it would have pleased his mother. Besides, he had to talk to his trust officer, and he always felt a little bit more in control if he was dressed well. He grimaced at his hair, there wasn't much he could do about it now, but maybe he'd get a haircut before they picked up the money. He'd look more like the five-year-old photo on his ID card then, which would make things a lot easier.

Chapter 26

Maggie stared at Arnold in amazement. He had emerged from the bathroom transformed. His beard and mustache were neatly trimmed and his hair was combed back from his face and tied into a pigtail with a strip of leather. He was wearing his newest clothes.

He picked up the phone and dialed a number, cradling the headset of the telephone between his raised shoulder and his ear. He acted differently from the casual Arnold she knew. His posture was straighter, and his voice was deeper and more confident. She watched, curious and a bit frightened of this commanding new facet of Arnold's personality. She hoped it wasn't like her security program.

"Hello, Beth?" Arnold said. "It's Arnold Brompton, Jr. Yeah, I'm fine, how are you? Good. Yeah. Listen, I'm calling from Oklahoma City, and I need a couple of disbursements from the trust. The first one is for thirty thousand dollars. It goes to Sue Janson, at"—he peered at the scrap of paper Sue had given them—"3505 Rockwell, Apartment 3F, here in Oklahoma City. I want a messenger to deliver the check to her personally, and I want it done within twenty-four hours. Charge the delivery costs to the trust, I can afford it. If she isn't there, try the homeless shelters. And I'll want ten thousand dollars wired to me via Western Union immediately. I have some ID, which will make things easier." He looked up at Maggie and smiled, gesturing that she should wait a minute. He listened for a few minutes, nodding, and scrawled a few notes on a pad. "OK, fine." He said at last, "It was good talking to you too. I'm glad to hear that things are going well. Yeah, uh-huh. Thanks. I'll be in touch." He hung up, and turned to Maggie, who stood looking questioningly at Arnold.

"That was my trustee at the bank. I've arranged to send Sue

Janson enough money for her to live comfortably in a place of her own for at least six months. That ought to be enough time for her to get some job training, and find good work. When my father finds her he'll probably help her out even more. He likes charity cases." Arnold set the phone down and lay back on the bed, looking satisfied with himself.

"I don't understand," Maggie said. "How did you get the money?"

"I'm rich, Maggie. My grandmother set up a trust for me in her will. My father can't touch it, not directly, anyway, but somehow he knows where my trust money goes. I think that's how he found us the last time. Maybe my trustee tells him, maybe he taps her phone; I don't know, but this time I'm using his own spy network against him!" His smile got wider and more smug. "As soon as he finds out where the money is going," he told her in a conspiratorial tone of voice, "he'll track down Sue and try to find out where we've gone. Since Sue thinks we're going to Atlanta, he'll spend all his time and money trying to track us down there. Meanwhile, we'll be all the way across the country. If we're lucky, he won't find us for months, maybe even a year or more." He laughed. "We'll finally be free of him!" He laid back on the pillows, smiling triumphantly. He looked more like his old self, now that he was off the phone, Maggie noted with relief. The Arnold she had seen talking on the phone was a stranger. She didn't know how to deal with him.

"We've got a lot to do today, Maggie," he told her. "Get your things, and let's get going."

After checking out of the hotel, they headed for the nearest Western Union office. Maggie watched outside for signs of someone following them as Arnold picked up the wired money. After he came out, they walked along casually for several blocks, turning often.

"Anyone following us?" Arnold asked. His new hairstyle made him look like a stranger, she thought.

Maggie shook her head.

"Anyone in the alley?" he asked again.

Maggie scanned the alley carefully. She had become much more meticulous in her scanning since being taken over by the security program. She didn't want to run into anything that might activate it. The alley was deserted, except for a couple of rats nosing around in the shadows. "No, it's all clear, Arnold."

"Good." He led her into the alley, pulled up her blouse, and cut a slit in the skin of her abdomen, right at the seam between two pads of silicone gel, and slipped in all except for several hundred dollars.

"There," he said as he smoothed her skin back together, "it'll be safe and sound until we need it. You take good care of it, okay. That money's for emergencies. Do you understand?"

"Yes, Arnold," Maggie said, "I'll take very good care of it."

"Good. Now, come on, we've got to hurry. The bus we need to catch leaves in a couple of hours and we've still got lots to do."

They stopped off at Goodwill and bought new clothes and new backpacks, and then picked up some food at a grocery store. Then they headed for the bus station. Arnold bought two tickets to Gainesville, Florida.

"Why Gainesville? I thought we were going to Atlanta," she said when they had stepped away from the ticket window.

"No, but the bus stops in Atlanta. I want to keep my father confused. I'm hoping that he'll think we're going to get off the bus in Atlanta, but that we're trying to fool him by buying tickets all the way through to Gainesville."

"I don't understand," Maggie said, utterly confused.

"Look," Arnold told her, "I'm trying to confuse my father. That's why I told Sue that we were going to Atlanta, and then bought tickets to Gainesville. If we make it too easy, he'll know we're laying down a false trail. This way, he'll be spending all of his time and energy scouring the South. We'll be on the other side of the country."

Maggie nodded as though she understood. It didn't matter whether or not it made sense. She went where Arnold did, and followed the dictates of her programming. Asking him about it would only bother him. He seemed to know what he was doing. That was enough.

They boarded the bus, and stowed their packs. Maggie peered out the smudged, green-tinted window as the bus hummed off. She watched, fascinated, as the city rolled past her. The buildings and apartments grew smaller and smaller until they turned into houses, and those grew farther apart, and suddenly there were flat fields stretching away in all directions. It was so big and so empty. She wondered how people could live out here with so little to sustain them. No supermarkets, no diners, not even any fancy restaurants. There were houses every so often with trees clustered around them, but mostly there was nothing but fenced-off fields, some empty, some with animals in them. Every so often they passed someone out in the fields, driving animals hitched to some kind of farm machinery, or passed horse-drawn wagons or cars, but there were miles of countryside with no trace of man except for the road and its accompanying row of telephone poles. Beyond that lay only trees. It seemed lonely and dangerous to Maggie. There were no electrical outlets for miles and miles in some places. If she were stranded out here, she wouldn't have enough power to make it to the nearest outlet.

Although the land was empty, Maggie enjoyed the bus. New people got on when they stopped in the larger towns. People chatted pleasantly or slept in the seats around her. She enjoyed watching the scenery scroll by. She could merely exist, filtering her memories, playing with images, or listening in on her fellow passengers' conversations.

So much had happened since they left Seattle. It seemed hard to believe that it had only been four days since they fled. Now, here in this comfortable bus, where she could see the sunlit world passing by, the world no longer seemed to be chasing them. They were no longer fleeing, but moving instead toward some mysterious goal that Arnold would reveal at the proper time. They had finally escaped.

It was night when they reached Memphis. There would be a long wait while the bus's batteries were recharged. Everyone gathered their things and filed off the bus. Arnold drew Maggie aside. They left the bus station and walked a block or two until they found a deserted alley.

"Anyone in there?" he asked her. She peered down the alley-way, using her infrared vision. There were no heat traces. She shook her head.

"Good." He ducked into the alley, pulling her in after him. He helped her off with her pack, and began rummaging through it, pulling out her new clothes.

"Here," he told her. "I want you to change clothes. It'll make us harder to spot."

Maggie turned away, so as not to offend Arnold. The close-fitting jumpsuit made her feel conspicuous and exposed. She missed her baggy, nondescript clothing. It felt much safer.

Arnold had changed, too. Instead of his usual frayed stocking cap, he wore a broad-brimmed grey hat. He changed his heavy wool overcoat for a brown leather jacket. Instead of baggy, stained trousers, he wore a pair of close-fitting jeans and black boots. Maggie was surprised at how different he looked. He looked vaguely threatening.

He smiled. "Good. You look taller like that. Here, let me help you with the scarf." The familiar sound of his voice reassured her. It was still the same Arnold.

He arranged the scarf so that it covered her hair and tied it neatly under her chin. "There," he said when he was finished, "you look completely different." He picked up her pack and handed it to her. "This is the final stretch, Maggie. After this, we'll be settling down for a while. Ready?"

Maggie nodded.

"All right, then, let's hit the road!"

They emerged from the alley and wandered along Beale Street toward the river, until they crossed a mag-lev line running just behind the levee.

"Wait here, I'll go up and see if I can figure which way the yard's most likely to be," Arnold told her. He climbed the levee and looked around for a few minutes and then scrambled back down.

"There's two bridges to the south, and none to the north, so I figure our best bet's to head south. The train's got to cross the river over one of those bridges."

They wandered south along the levee, following the tracks and the Mississippi. Maggie watched the boats glide slowly along the black waters of the river. The air was warm and mild. She liked it here, and wished they could stay. She was tired of riding the rails. The railway parted company from the river after a half mile, and a little further on the tracks began to branch out.

"We should be getting close now, Maggie. The tracks usually fan out like this just before the rail yard. It used to be easier to find the yards, back before it was all electronic. They had signs to warn the engineer to slow down for the yard, but now it's nearly all automated."

A quarter-mile later the yard opened out and they were there. They stashed their packs, put on their railroad coveralls, and found an unused terminal.

"All right, Maggie," Arnold said, "I want you to go in this time."

"Are you sure, Arnold? I really blew it in Seattle."

"Yeah, but you aren't going to go poking around the system like that again, are you?"

Maggie shook her head emphatically, remembering how the Net security program had nearly gotten her, before she had been submerged by her own security program. It had been horrible.

"See, you've learned your lesson. I'd have had you do it sooner, but we didn't need to in Spokane, and we had Sue and her kids along in Denver. This may be our last chance for a while. We'll be settling down in San Francisco, and I'd like you to give it a shot before we get there. Find us a route that bypasses Oklahoma City, too. They'll be looking for us there."

Maggie linked up to the computer system and plunged into the routing network, disguised as a freight-routing program. She quickly assembled the fastest route possible, framed by alternates at each place that they had to change trains. As she was performing the search, she felt a Net security search program engulf and investigate her. It took all of her control to continue searching during the agonizing seconds it took for the giant juggernaut to inspect her. She kept waiting to be jerked from control by her security program or disassembled by the Net's security program. She wanted to run away as fast as she could, but here in the computer, she was merely a collection of electronic impulses at the mercy of the system. At last Net Security was satisfied and moved on. She completed her search and exited the system as quickly as possible.

"Well?" Arnold asked when she emerged. "How did it go?"

"I found a good route." She didn't want to talk about the security search. It frightened her too much, she wanted to climb on the next freight train and get as far away from Memphis as possible. "The train we want leaves in a half an hour over on track seven. We should be in San Francisco by Tuesday morning."

"We'd better hurry, then," Arnold said. "We've got a long trip ahead of us."

Chapter 27

The trip was uneventful. They changed trains in Dallas, and again in Fort Worth. In Amarillo, they had a long layover. Arnold had dinner and Maggie charged her batteries. From Amarillo, they caught a twelve-hour straight shot through to San Francisco with only a few stops to drop or add cars, barely enough time for Arnold to piss out of the boxcar door.

"Welcome to San Francisco!" he told her as he flung open the boxcar doors. He gestured expansively, as though making her a gift of the city. "No more running, Maggie. This'll be our home for a while." He helped her down from the train and hugged her.

Maggie smiled. Her batteries were getting low, and she was glad to finally be off the trains. A light fog softened the early-morning light. The sky gleamed like pearls in a jewelry store window. She would like it here, she thought, the light was good. She felt like the light, soft and full of hope, as she followed Arnold into the swirl of city traffic.

San Francisco proved to be as good a place as she had hoped. The weather was gentle, the people were kind, and the city provided well for its homeless. Even the park benches were designed to be comfortable to sleep on. And there was the Homeless Guild. The Guild was a loose organization of homeless people that looked out for each other, with help from half a dozen charities and the city. The Guild organized soup lines and food banks, found jobs for people, helped out with welfare troubles, and cared for the sick. They made sure that the junkies had clean needles and reasonably clean drugs. Violators were shut out of the system. It worked. It wasn't perfect, but the streets were significantly safer for members of the Guild. People stayed well clear of homeless people not wearing the distinctive Guild badge. The police watched non-Guild members so closely that they usually moved on to another city. In fact, it was a police officer who told them about the Guild.

At first, Arnold grumbled about the necessity of joining an organization, but he was soon knee-deep in the Guild's computer network, busily repairing and revising programming codes, still grumbling to the members of the welcoming committee who had contacted him. Maggie served as Arnold's diagnostic link to the computer system when no one was watching and helped out in the creche, taking care of the children.

The next couple of months were very peaceful. They settled into a comfortable routine. They spent two days a week helping out in the Guild's storefront office on Valencia. The rest of the time they wandered through the streets rummaging through the garbage or read in the library. Maggie resumed rummaging through garbage cans looking for salvageable items. She would pick through the most disgusting garbage to come up with some salvageable bit of metal or machinery. She could judge metal content and density better than most of the scrap dealers. In fact, she sometimes bought something from one dealer and sold it to another for a profit. They prospered, covering their living costs and Guild dues, with enough left over to actually increase the amount of money that Arnold kept stashed under Maggie's skin.

But dumpster diving was not the only skill she refined. Arnold helped her become more proficient at navigating the Net and evading security systems. Arnold also taught her more urban survival. Most of them were small things, details that she hadn't had the time to learn before they fled Seattle: how to keep your shoes from being stolen, or how to look for safe, hidden places to sleep, where to find outlets. She learned Spanish from the children in the day-care creche. Her internal map of the city grew more detailed day by day as she and Arnold wandered the streets. In just a few short weeks, San Francisco became home.

Arnold seemed more relaxed, too. He laughed more, and often Maggie would turn and see him watching her with a fond smile. He touched her more often as well, putting an arm around her, touching her cheek, or softly stroking her hair. Doing this seemed to make him happy, which satisfied her programming.

Then, one night in late May, Arnold began acting strangely. They were lying together in a sheltered spot under a secluded bench in Golden Gate Park. Arnold began touching her in a strange, furtive way. He groped between her legs with one hand while he fumbled at her breasts with the other.

"What are you doing, Arnold?" she asked, puzzled by his strange behavior.

His hands pulled away from her as though she had suddenly become red hot, and he turned away from her without replying.

"Are you all right?" she asked him. "Did I do something wrong?"

Arnold didn't reply. He lay there, ignoring Maggie's whispered inquiries. His muscles were tense and his breathing was harsh. Finally Maggie gave up and lay silently beside him, puzzling over what was wrong. At last his breathing quietened and he slept for a bit. Near dawn, his breathing became ragged and harsh again. She could feel his hips moving spasmodically against the blankets.

"Arnold, are you all right?" Maggie was frightened now. She had never seen Arnold act like this before. His face was flushed and hot, glowing like a coal in her infrared vision.

Arnold gathered the blankets around him and said in a sleepy, irritated voice, "I'm all right, Maggie, go to sleep."

"But, Arnold, I can't sleep, I'm a robot."

"Just shut up and let me get some sleep!" Arnold snapped. Maggie said nothing. Arnold finally drifted off to sleep a couple of hours later.

The next day, Arnold was irritable and withdrawn. He vanished into the computer room for hours, while Maggie played with the children in the creche, and tried to figure out what she had done to anger him.

The next day, Arnold was back to normal again. He was fine for the next couple of weeks and then one night, when they were sleeping behind a dumpster in an alley off Polk Street, he suddenly began pushing his crotch against her leg. His hands slid up under her shirt and fumbled at her breasts. His breathing was harsh and urgent. He seemed to want something, but Maggie didn't know what it was.

"What is it, Arnold? What is it that you want me to do?"

"Goddammit!!" he whispered, pulling away from her. He sounded angrier than she had ever heard him before. His tone of voice terrified her.

"I'm sorry, Arnold," she said contritely. "I'll stop doing whatever it is that is bothering you if you'll tell me what it is I'm doing wrong."

Arnold groaned and struck his fist against his thigh, hard. "It isn't you, Maggie. It's me." He got up. "I just need to be alone for a while. I'm going to take a walk, you wait here for me."

He walked off down the alley, hunched over, hands in his pockets, his shadow trailing him up the wall. Maggie watched him go. She lay there, alone amid the garbage, and searched her memories in an attempt to find what had gone wrong. Her confusion over Arnold's anger was so profound that she tuned out the outside world. She didn't hear the sound of strange footsteps approaching until it was too late.

Chapter 28

Arnold walked down the silent street. It was around four in the morning. The streets were deserted, traffic lights changed their colors before heedlessly empty intersections. He leaned against a graffitti-covered wall, concealed by the shadows of the tall buildings around him, and looked out over the deserted stretch of concrete, lost in thought.

He had succeeded too well with Maggie, he realized. She was too much like a woman. He kept forgetting that she was only a machine. It had been so simple when he was alone, and all he had had to worry about was his own right hand. Now Maggie lay beside him in the darkness every night, so warm, so pretty, so close. It was getting harder to stop himself from sullying her. He cherished her innocence. It made her different from other women. Her innocence made the world seem less hard-edged. Now he found himself wishing sometimes that she was more like Sue. He thought of Sue sometimes, when he wanted to distract himself from his desire for Maggie, remembering the way her face lit up when she smiled, and how patient and kind she was with her children.

Arnold remembered the first woman his father had brought home. It was only two months after his mother's death. Her name was Kathy, and she had bright red lipstick and shiny black hair slicked back tight against her head. She smiled constantly, a brittle, nervous smile. Her voice was too loud, and she laughed too much. His father brought her home from one of his business trips. She worked for one of his companies.

It was late at night when they came in. Her bright laughter woke Arnold, and he came to the door of his room to see what the noise was, clutching his stuffed bear. She jumped when she saw Arnold waiting there in the hallway, and emitted a sort of high-pitched squeak.

"You didn't tell me you had a son, Bud!" she said.

"Well, I do," his father said with a shrug. "Arnold, this is Kathy, she's going to be staying with us for a while."

Arnold regarded her gravely for a few moments, and then shook her hand the way his mother had taught him to do when meeting company. "Pleased to meet you," he said.

Kathy laughed and said, "Oh, Bud! He's darling!" She bent down and kissed him hard on the cheek, leaving a smear of bright red lipstick.

His dislike for her crystallized then, even before he heard the dark mutters of the servants for bringing home a woman so soon after his mother's death. The servants' talk merely confirmed his opinion that she was an intruder.

Kathy lasted only a few weeks, but she was replaced a month or two later by Margery, and then Hilde, and so on throughout most of his childhood. He hated them all uniformly. None of them could crack the armor of his scorn. He watched them all come, live off of his father for a few weeks or months, and then move on. They were all of a type: young, beautiful, and cold. At best they treated him like a charming pet; at worst, they recognized his animosity and fought him behind his father's back. His father, preoccupied with business, never noticed his son's hostility.

Watching his father and his women use each other, he had grown up with a deep distrust of women and of sex. There were very few women he trusted: his mother, Virginia, Maude, and now, Maggie. Maggie was different. She was his responsibility. She trusted him. He didn't want to violate that trust.

He sighed, wishing that he hadn't made Maggie quite so anatomically correct. His pride had driven him to do it. He had wanted her to be exactly like a human woman. Now he was caught, obsessed with the warm, dark cavity that he himself had made. He wanted her so badly. Wanted to shatter Maggie's carefully constructed innocence. Wanted to feel her moving beneath him . . .

"No!" he cried out, turning, pressing his body hard against the rough brick wall, feeling his erection pressing hard against his jeans. He mustn't think of such things. He would find a solution. He had to. He jacked off furtively, feeling only a slight relief and a deep sense of shame when he was done.

The sky was perceptibly lighter. He should be getting back to Maggie. Maybe he could get some sleep before it was time to move on. The walk had done some good, cleared his brain, distanced him safely from his desire, but it had also reminded him that he hadn't been sleeping well. He was exhausted.

He was rounding the corner of the alley that they were sleeping in when he saw the man. The man's back was to him, but he heard the threat and the hunger in the man's tone of voice, and Maggie's frightened reply. The man had Maggie cornered.

Arnold's instinct told him to run, this was a dangerous situation, but he couldn't leave Maggie behind. His gut tightened. He waited, hoping for a solution that would not involve direct conflict. The man was big, nearly as big as Arnold, and he had the menacing, precise moves of a trained fighter.

Suddenly the man grabbed at Maggie, catching at her sweatshirt. He heard cloth tearing. She looked up, saw Arnold, and called his name. Arnold charged the stranger with a roar, pushing him away from Maggie and putting himself between Maggie and the man.

"Get away from her!" he growled furiously. "She's mine."

The man came closer and Arnold could see a long silvery gleam in the man's hand. It was a knife.

"That depends," the man said, his voice low, almost a whisper. "That depends on whether you can keep her."

Maggie whimpered behind him. He heard her moving and his eyes flicked back to see what she was doing.

The man lunged at Arnold. The long gleam flashed out. He felt the suddenness of the knife in his gut. He grabbed at it, but the man had danced out of his reach, and was crouched before him, knife weaving in the air. Arnold lunged, desperately, trying to escape now, to go, get help, to do something, anything but die here in this alley. His head was light. He felt the knife strike again, grating against his ribs. He fell.

Chapter 29

"Well, hello there," someone said. Maggie wheeled around to find a big, dark man standing there, silhouetted against the glare of the streetlights. Maggie stood up, her back to the wall. The man came toward her. She wondered what to do, and wished that Arnold were here to help her deal with this stranger. He'd been gone now for twenty-three minutes. She hoped he'd return soon.

"What are you doing here?" the man said, coming closer.

Maggie shrugged and remained silent, unable to think of anything to say. He moved so that the light from the street lamp fell on her face.

"Pretty, too," the man said. "What's a pretty girl like you doing sleeping in an alley?" His voice sounded hungry and mean, like the villains in the movies she had seen. The man edged nearer.

"Go away," she told him, moving further back into the alley. "I want you to go away."

She was getting concerned. If this kept up, if he kept coming closer, her security program would be activated, and then she would lose control of herself. She might even hurt him. She would be helpless to stop herself. She set up a block against her security program. It might not stop it, but it would slow it down. She glanced toward the street and saw Arnold coming up the alley.

Just then the man grabbed her sweatshirt. She pulled away, calling out to Arnold for help.

Arnold came running up the alley with a fierce yell. Maggie saw the man pull out a knife, she felt her security subprogram pushing against the blocks she had set up. The two men were facing each other. Arnold looked clumsy compared to the slightly smaller man, who moved smoothly and warily, weaving the knife in his hand from side to side. The security program was pushing harder; Maggie reinforced the blocks, but the security program had taken over her voder, and she let out a low moan.

Just then the man lunged at Arnold. Maggie saw his knife flick out, striking Arnold in the gut. Then the man danced back again, before Arnold could grab him. Arnold lunged to the side, and then the man struck again with the knife and Arnold fell, hot blood glowing in her infrared vision as it flowed from his wounds.

"*No!*" she screamed as the security program battered down the last blocks. Her shock at this sudden violence made her unable to stop it. She watched as she let out a piercing, focused blast of sound that made the man stagger backward, dropping his knife as he covered his ears. Then she picked up the man. Holding him up over her head, she dropped him down onto the pavement headfirst. His skull was crushed. He was dead. Horrified at what she had done, Maggie wrested control from the security program.

She looked down at Arnold's motionless body, and over at the crumpled form of their attacker who lay with his neck at an inhuman angle. They lay still and silent, dead, just like in the movies. Just then Arnold moaned and turned his head. She hurried to his side and rolled him over. His jacket was torn and soaked with blood. His breathing was rapid and shallow, his skin was cold and slick with sweat.

"You're bleeding, Arnold. What should I do?" she asked him, feeling frightened and helpless.

He smiled weakly up at her. "Get help . . . ," he started to say.

Just then came the distant blare of sirens. Arnold lifted his head and looked around. "The police . . . ," he said. "The police are coming." His head fell back. He swallowed hard and lifted his head again and clutched at her arm, his gaze intent. "Maggie, you can't let them find you. Go to New York—get my fa . . ." His head fell back and his hand slipped limply from her arm. It was just like when they died in the movies.

The sirens were very loud now, only a few blocks away. Maggie looked around wildly for a moment, caught between her desire to stay with Arnold, and his orders to leave, then her security program took her over again. She grabbed up her pack and fled.

She ran through the streets, the blood-soaked hem of her skirt clinging to her legs, dodging the police more through luck than skill. Somehow she made it safely to the train yard. She climbed onto the first outgoing boxcar she found, not caring where it was headed, as long as it would take her away from what she had done. She burrowed into a narrow space between the towering stacks of boxes. She huddled in the safe darkness, embracing her battered backpack, and let the train carry her on.

In the shelter of darkness and movement, the memories came flooding back. Again and again, she saw Arnold's futile rush, the gleaming fall of the knife, and heard her piercingly focused scream. Again and again she saw herself pick up the man and hurl him down. And then, Arnold's last few cryptic words, sending her to a strange city to get something, but she didn't know what.

She was weary of the dark, inescapable memories. So weary, but never tired. She wished she could sleep, like Arnold did, or die, like Arnold, but she kept going on and on. There seemed to be no way to escape the flood of memory and fear. Finally she buried her head against the backpack and began calculating the value of pi, losing herself in the impersonal flood of numbers until the outside world became a distant, meaningless blur.

The train stopped. She picked up her pack, opened the door, climbed down, and began to walk. Pi flickered through her circuits, shielding her from the terrible thing she had done. Reality intruded through her calculations in brief sharp slivers. She walked. The moon was full. It shone across the scrub. The night was silver and black. She walked. It was desert. Suddenly the moon was cut off. Steep rocks towered overhead. She walked between them, threading their dark winding maze with touch, infrared, and sound. The moon shone on the face of a cliff. She walked toward it. There was a ledge. She could go no further. She sat down, her back to the cliff, and watched. Time slowed. Pi flickered and grew. Small animals moved, stopped, scampered again. The sun came up. It grew hot. The sun went down. It grew cold. Maggie sat unheeding, her batteries slowly draining away.

As her batteries weakened, a subprogram took over, turning her off at regular, brief intervals to save her batteries. The day flickered before her. She was caught in a time-lapse world. As the days unreeled they seemed to pass faster and faster, the sun arcing overhead, turning to darkness, the shadows sweeping across the tiny canyon. Maggie sat. The days went by. Small animals hid between her legs, built nests. Snakes twined around her arms during the brief day, sunning themselves. They did not disturb her. Nothing disturbed her inside the safe cocoon of pi. Nothing mattered. Maggie sat. Her batteries grew slowly weaker.

Chapter 30

Timothy Begay led his horse up the narrow red sandstone gorge. It was cooler here than the desert. The sun never quite reached the floor of the gorge and the tiny stream of sweet water that flowed down the middle of it added a welcome breath of moisture to the dry desert air. He always found some sheep in the box canyon at the end of the gorge's maze. He couldn't blame them; there was water and enough browse around the spring to eat, and perhaps the sheep even felt something of the beauty of the place.

He could have fenced off the little canyon, but the strays gave him a reason to visit it and scatter a little pollen near the ancient rock paintings. So every year, when all the other sheep had been gathered and herded up to the greener summer pastures in the Chuska Mountains on the Navajo reservation, he took his best dog and his favorite horse and went hunting strays for a week. He rarely found more than half a dozen sheep, but it was a good excuse for a vacation after the spring rush of lambing and shearing, and it kept him in touch with his people's land.

The gorge opened up into a small canyon. He set the dog to hunting out lost sheep and began unloading his horse and setting up camp by the pool where the spring bubbled up. He smiled as he heard the short yap the dog made when he found a sheep, and the sheep's answering bleat. He was unrolling the ground cloth of his tent when the dog began to bark. It was the shrill, hysterical bark that the dog used when he found a rattlesnake. Timothy grabbed his rifle and headed off toward the sound.

He stopped dead in his tracks when he saw what the dog had been barking at. It was a white woman, eyes closed, still as stone, covered with dust, as though she had been sitting there for months. She sat cross-legged. Curled in her lap like some deadly pet was an enormous rattlesnake, six feet long at least.

Her eyes flicked open, fixing on him with a fierce intensity. Her eyes were strange. He stepped back, wondering if she was some kind of *chindi* or skin walker come to take his spirit. He muttered a quick prayer.

"A-a-a-r-r-r," she croaked, then fell silent, eyes closed again. The rattlesnake, disturbed by the noise and movement, flowed silently off her lap and into a crevice in the stone.

For a moment Timothy almost fled, but he looked up and there was the big rock painting of Spider Woman, looking down at them. She seemed to be hovering protectively over her. He felt ashamed. White or not, *chindi* or not, this was a person lost in the desert, and obviously in need of help.

He knelt beside this strange woman, checking her pulse, prying up her eyelids. Her skin was surprisingly cool and dry. He couldn't find her pulse. Her eyes were different colors, which was why they seemed so strange.

He tilted his canteen up to her lips. She swallowed some water. Her eyes focused again. "N-n-n-o-o," she moaned, then she was gone again. It raised the hair on the back of his neck. There were strange brown stains on her dress. They looked like dried blood.

She was delirious. She needed medical help. There was no telling how long she had been here. He took off her battered, weather-beaten pack and tried to lift her. She was limp, and seemed as heavy as a man twice her size.

He led his horse over and, straining hard, managed to get her up onto it. It was like loading a sack of grain.

"O-o-o-l-l-d," she sighed as he tied her onto the horse's patient back. Swiftly he bundled his supplies together, leaving those he could not use, and put the rest into her backpack, which he shouldered. The sheep could wait a few more days, the woman could not. He whistled to the dog, and they left the canyon at a fast walk.

Chapter 31

The first thing Maggie remembered was being lifted and put on a horse. She was too weak to do more than call out. It was a sound from the back of her memories, someone's name. She couldn't remember who, but she knew that it was very important. She had to do something, go somewhere. She watched brief time-lapse flickers of ground from the back of the horse. Sheer self-preservation cleared the flood of numbers from her head. Gradually she became aware of her surroundings. By the time the man lifted her from the horse and carried her into a house, she was fully aware, although nearly immobile from lack of power. He left her on a bed, covering her gently with a blanket, and then left the room telling her that he was going to get help.

With the last of her energy, she searched with her plug until she found an outlet. With power flowing into her, she was able to move herself against the wall, concealing her power er cord.

The man came back with a glass of water. He sat down on the bed. His skin was dark brown, and heavy silver bracelets gleamed on both wrists.

"My name is Timothy," he said. His voice was deep and quiet, as though he rarely raised his voice. "I found you in the desert and brought you here. You need water. Drink." Gently, he held her head while she drank. A few moments later, a woman came in. She was small and sturdy, her hair was grey, and her skin was dark and deeply lined. Like Timothy, she wore silver with blue stones the color of the desert sky.

"This is Luz," the man told her. "She's my aunt. She'll take good care of you."

Luz smiled. "Welcome. What's your name?"

"Maggie."

"How did you get out in the desert like that, Maggie?"

Maggie thought hard, but there was something blocking her memories. She was Maggie. She was a robot, but she couldn't let anybody find out about that. There was a woman, a man and two children. They had all been happy. She had run from something that had frightened her. That was all she could remember. The rest was all shadowy fragments. "I—I don't know. I can't remember. I'm sorry."

The two of them spoke quietly in a language that Maggie couldn't understand. They seemed to be discussing her. She lay quietly and watched them as her batteries began to fill. At last Luz turned to her.

"You'll be all right now," she told her. "We're going to call Dr. Chee."

Fear seized Maggie. She grabbed Luz's hand, holding tight.

"No! No doctors," she pleaded. "Please, no doctors." She quietly retracted her plug and sat up. "I'll be all right, I just need to rest for a while. Really, I don't need a doctor." She got up, picked up her pack, and started for the door. Timothy quietly blocked her way. Maggie stopped.

Timothy looked at Luz, and they spoke again quietly. Luz nodded.

"All right," she said, "we'll wait on the doctor, but if you aren't better by evening, we'll have to call Dr. Chee. Here, now, drink a few sips of water, then you rest. I'll look in on you from time to time."

Maggie obediently drank the remaining water and lay back under the covers. As soon as they left, she plugged herself in. It would be several hours until she was fully charged. She would wait until then to decide what to do.

Luz came in from time to time, bringing her water or soup to drink. Near dark, Luz brought in a tray of hot soup and bread. By then her batteries were fully charged. After that, Luz helped her to the bathroom and bathed her, exclaiming at the caked layers of dirt and filth that she scrubbed off.

"Look at all that dirt. You look like you were in the desert for months. But your skin's so rosy. You aren't even sunburned. How did that happen?"

"I don't know, I can't remember anything," she said, bowing her head in the steam. "There was a man," she said, "and a woman, and children. We were going somewhere on a train. We were happy. I remember that, but I don't remember who they were or where we were going." She shook her head and looked up at Luz. "I don't even know where I am."

Luz said, "We're about twenty-five miles east of Holbrook, just shy of the Navajo reservation. This isn't the reservation, but it's still Navajo land. My mother bought it when the ranchers went broke. We raise sheep. I do a little weaving. Come, it's time to get out of the tub and dry off." Luz helped her out of the tub and handed her a towel.

"I was lost out there, and you found me," Maggie said as she took the towel. "I don't know how to thank you and Timothy."

"*De nada,*" Luz said. "It was God's will. It was a miracle that you survived in the desert. God brought you to us. Thank him instead."

Maggie said nothing. God had nothing to do with her, he was the one who built humans. He was a better builder than, than . . . She couldn't remember who had built her, but he had left her out there in the desert. It made her feel very lost and alone.

Chapter 32

Luz looked over at Maggie sitting quietly on the front porch. She was a silent person, especially for a white woman. Most whites talked your ear off, always asking questions. This one sat and watched you quietly, with those big strange eyes. She looked like a lost child. Luz felt sorry for her, but also mystified. There had been nothing in Maggie's pack but a couple of changes of clothes, a blanket that looked as if mice had been nesting in it, and a bunch of electrical parts and tools. She didn't even have any money. She hoped Sheriff Becenti could shed some light on this mystery. They had decided to call him last night. He said he'd be by sometime today.

Maggie had recovered amazingly fast. After two days she seemed to be back to normal, although she ate like a bird and drank even less. She had done the dishes yesterday morning, and helped Luz feed the horses today. Her memory hadn't gotten any better, but she was so afraid of seeing a doctor that she tried to run away every time someone mentioned the idea. Luz sighed. Maybe she had escaped from some white hospital, although how she had wound up so far from anywhere was anybody's guess. The nearest settlement near the canyon was Carrizo, and that was just a railroad siding, a couple of hogans, and a shed or two. Maggie had been more than five miles beyond that.

She heard a honk and saw the sheriff's car waiting at the gate. She walked over and opened the gate, waving at the sheriff as he drove past. She had gone to college with his mother, who had been a cousin of hers. He was a good boy, honest, fair and discreet, born for her clan, the *Kin Yaá á*, and big, like his mother and father. He understood how to behave appropriately. He wouldn't meddle without a good reason. She walked back to the house, where he stood leaning against the car.

"*Yatahey*, Luz," he said.

"*Yatahey*. Did you find out anything about that girl we found?" Luz asked in Navajo.

He shook his head. "She's not listed as missing anywhere and she's not wanted by the law. Nobody answering to her description is anywhere on the computer. I just wanted to come out and take a look at her."

Luz nodded and they went into the house. Maggie was in her room, putting things in her pack. Obviously, policemen scared her as much as doctors. She wondered what had happened to make her so afraid.

"Maggie, the sheriff wants to talk to you," Luz said. Maggie looked even more frightened. "He says you're not in any trouble, he just wants to see if he can help you find your people." She grasped Maggie's slender wrist. "He's a cousin of mine. You can trust him. Come on."

She led Maggie out and sat down next to her on the couch. The sheriff sat down across from them and flipped out his notebook.

"Timothy found you out in the Hidden Canyon area about three days ago. Is that correct?"

Maggie nodded.

"Do you remember how long you were out there?"

Maggie frowned and shook her head. "A long time."

"How did you get there?"

Maggie probed her memory. "I remember getting on a train. There were boxes and things on the train. The train stopped, and I got out and started walking. It was dark. I don't remember anything else." She looked up at the sheriff. "I'm sorry. I can't remember."

"Luz said that there was what looked like dried blood on your dress. Do you know how it got there, or what it was?"

Maggie shook her head. "I'm sorry, I can't remember anything."

"Well, Maggie, no one has you listed as missing or wanted. I'd like to take your dress in and have it tested. Maybe the blood will tell us something about where you came from."

"I'll go get it," Luz said. She went out and came back with the dress; it had been washed, ironed, and neatly mended.

The sheriff picked it up and looked it over, and sighed. "Luz, you've washed the bloodstains out of the dress. I'm sorry, the lab won't be able to get anything."

"Sorry, Pete," Luz said, "she had so few things in her pack, I wanted her to be able to wear it."

The sheriff shrugged and got up. "I'll let you know if I hear anything."

"Sure, Pete. Oh, wait a minute." Luz got up and rummaged in the cupboard and brought out a jar. "Here, take some of my salsa. You used to love it as a kid."

He smiled. "I still do. How's Tim doing these days?"

"He's doing all right. He's off near Windsor Wash, bringing in some strays. He's still not married, though. You got any good-looking cousins? There aren't enough kids around here. It's lonely."

Pete grinned. "I'll see what I can do," he said as he opened the door.

Luz walked out to the porch and watched as the sheriff pulled away. She walked back in and found Maggie looking out the window. She turned and looked at Luz.

"I need to go soon," she said. "I have to go."

"Where?" Luz asked her.

Maggie looked suddenly lost; for a moment Luz thought she would burst into tears. "I-I don't know," she stammered, "but I have to go. It's important." She looked back out the window.

Luz smoothed her hands on her velvet skirt. "You can't even remember your last name, Maggie. Why don't you wait until your memory comes back? You're welcome to stay here as long as you need to."

Maggie said nothing, she just shook her head, looking more than ever like an abandoned child. Luz smoothed her skirt again and watched her helplessly. Maggie reminded her of a small bird trapped inside a house; out of place, frantic, and confused. Perhaps the best thing would be to let her go.

Chapter
33

Maggie lay back in the darkness, listening to the quiet hush of the deep night. It was so much quieter than the city. Luz and Timothy were asleep. Maggie replayed her memories of this evening. They had sat in the living room, quiet and content. Luz worked at her loom while Timothy flipped through a sheep breeder's magazine. It was a perfect moment. Everyone was comfortable and happy. Her batteries were charged. She was filled with the happiness that other people's contentment brought her.

It reminded her of something. Of another time when she had not been so warm, or safe, or comfortable. She remembered children, a little girl, laughing and happy, a baby sleeping peacefully. There was a woman with hair like new straw and . . .

Maggie furrowed her brow, knowing it was important. She was supposed to go someplace for a man, someone important. . . . She couldn't remember who or what or where. It was like a cloud of black ink had settled over her past. She could remember words and rules, but nothing about the experiences that generated them, or of the man who had created her, except vague, shadowy memories.

The sheriff reminded her of her creator. He had been big, like the sheriff, only softer, with more fat and less muscle. She remembered his bulk, looming over her the way the sheriff had. She had been his, watching out for him, and . . .

Something had happened. She couldn't remember what it was. He wasn't with her anymore. All she knew was that whenever she thought about her creator, she felt a deep, overwhelming urge to go, to leave these quiet, dignified people and this safe haven, and go. But she had no means to go anywhere. They were twenty-five miles out of town, she couldn't walk that far, not without someone finding her on these empty roads.

Maggie picked up her backpack and emptied it out, sorting through its meager contents one more time. There were a few electrical adapters. They enabled her to recharge from light bulb sockets and high-voltage outlets. There was some extra clothing, cleaned and mended by Luz, a pocket knife, some tools, and a blanket. So little to face the world with, she thought.

She would take it with her tomorrow, when they went into town. Maybe she could find a way to leave then. She carefully repacked her backpack and set it beside her bed, got up, and walked silently down the hall, through the living room and out onto the porch.

The wicker chair creaked as she lowered herself into it. She looked up at the stars, so many stars up there. She remembered how they danced, slowly, gracefully, wheeling through the darkness as she watched them through her time-lapsed perception in the desert.

A door shut quietly. There were footsteps on the porch. It was Timothy. He sat down in the chair next to her, resting his stockinged feet on the low table. He had come back the day before yesterday, driving a half-dozen sheep. She had watched while he sheared them, watched the sheep struggle as he wrestled them to the floor with the ease of long practice, watched as the clippers peeled the thick fleece from their hides as they bleated and moaned in complaint. When he was done, the sheep bounded up and scrambled for the safety of the pen, bleating lustily and occasionally bleeding from a small cut or two. Luz gathered the wool into big bundles bound with twine. Maggie had been amazed at the casual violence that sheep shearing required. A couple of times he had looked up at her and grinned.

Then, when he was done shearing, he had her help hold their hard, squirming, wooly bodies as he trimmed their hooves and castrated the male lambs. It had been a bloody and unpleasant business. The sheep's vibrant, quick strength had surprised her. The first one nearly squirmed out of her grip, but she caught it again and held it more firmly. After they were finished, Timothy had complimented her on how well she had done.

Today he had butchered three of the lambs. As she watched, he had dragged them out of the pen and into the barn, knocked them on the head, and tied them to a rafter. Then he slit their throats. She fled then, and hid in the bedroom. Something fearsome had been struggling up out of her memories. She lay on the bed calculating furiously until the memory receded. Luz came into her room and sang to her in Navajo, patting her hand from time to time. When she was done with the song, Luz walked back out and helped Timothy skin the lambs. Maggie stayed in her room until she had forced the awful memory back down into the depths. Then she went back out to see what had happened to the butchered lambs.

The lambs had stopped bleeding, and Timothy had removed their fleecy hides. They were less frightening now, and the memories did not return. She watched curiously as Luz and Timothy butchered the sheep. She had never seen the inside of a living thing before. It was very different from the way she looked. There was a neat functionality to the way the muscles lay that fascinated her.

Timothy sat silently beside her for a long time, watching the stars.

"When I'm out with the sheep," he said at last, "I usually take the night watch. I like to watch the stars."

They sat in silence for a while, admiring the night sky.

"It was very strange when I found you, Maggie," Timothy said after several long minutes of silence. "There was a rattlesnake, six feet long, and as big around as my arm, coiled up on your lap like a kitten. You didn't even notice. I thought you were some kind of witch. You didn't have any scratches, either, you weren't even sunburned. I've seen you work out in the hot sun with Luz for hours and never tan. You don't sweat, either. Why doesn't the sun touch you? Who are you, Maggie?"

"I don't remember," Maggie told him.

"I think you remember more than you let on."

Maggie felt a surge of fear in her circuits. She had to end this conversation now. She had to go. "When I do, I'll let you know, Timothy. Good night."

She got up and walked back into her room, closing and bolting the door behind her. She leaned against the door, feeling its solid protectiveness. I am a door, she thought, I am a door, a wall, a window, a table lamp. I am a machine, not human, never human. No one must know, or I become a thing, to be used and cast aside, like the junk in the truck that will be sold at the flea market.

She heard the steady, soft creak of Timothy's footfalls as he came in from the porch. They paused for a moment outside her door, then went up the hallway and into his room. She remembered the bright red blood spurting from the lamb's neck, and the red smears Timothy had left on the legs of his jeans when he wiped his hands. It was definitely time to go.

Chapter 34

Maggie looked out the window of the pickup truck as Timothy eased it to a stop in downtown Holbrook. It was a small town, a few dozen sun-baked buildings clustered around the main road. There was a supermarket, a hardware and feed store, a couple of variety stores, and a service station with its gleaming blue ranks of solar rechargers and fat round tanks of methane. Timothy got out of the truck, herded the sheep down out of the back, and set up the solar panels to recharge the truck's batteries and then set off with his sheep to the stockyard to sell them. Luz pulled two newly woven rugs out from behind the seat and handed them to Maggie.

Luz set off for the feed store with Maggie in tow. A bell clanged when Luz opened the door. It was much cooler inside. The store was full of strange things—saddles and bags of grain and blocks of salt and mineral supplements. On the wall behind the counter hung a number of beautiful rugs.

A woman came out of the back of the store, and smiled when she saw Luz.

"Hello, Luz, what have you got today?"

Luz nodded to Maggie and she put the rugs up on the counter. Luz unrolled them and smiled at the woman. "Rugs, Mrs. Rodriguez, and some turquoise that my nephew found," she said, holding up a small deerskin bag.

The woman put on her glasses and peered intently at the rugs.

"I can give you twenty-five hundred for them both."

Luz frowned. "Five thousand," she said.

Mrs. Rodriguez raised her eyebrows. "Three thousand."

Luz shook her head and began to roll up one of the rugs.

"Thirty-six hundred."

Luz stopped rolling up the rug. "Thirty-eight hundred dollars," she said in a firm voice.

Mrs. Rodriguez sighed. "All right, all right. Now let's see the turquoise."

Luz's face was solemn and expressionless as they left the store, several thousand dollars richer. As the store door closed behind them and they were back in the sun and the baking heat, she broke into a wide smile, her lined face creasing. "We did well, Maggie." She took out the roll of money and counted out eight hundred dollars and handed it to Maggie.

"Here, this is for you."

"But why, Luz?"

"Because I got two rugs woven this month instead of just one. You did so many of the chores that I had more time to spend at my loom. This is what we would have paid hired help." She paused and looked directly at Maggie. "And because you are leaving us today, and I didn't want you going out into the world with nothing."

Maggie was startled. "How did you know?"

Luz smiled. "You're so restless. You kept looking out the window at the road, but you don't know how to say good-bye. It's all right, we won't keep you here. You're welcome back anytime, though. You're different than most whites. You're quieter. You listen better."

Maggie smiled. "Will you walk me to the railroad siding?"

Luz nodded and the two walked silently away from the highway toward the train tracks.

They reached the railroad siding. There was only a barbed-wire fence around it.

"Here," Luz said. "This is for you." She handed Maggie a heavy gurgling skin full of water, a package of food, and a small silver pendant set with turquoise. "*Vaya con Dios*. Go safely, Maggie."

Maggie slipped the turquoise over her head and tucked it

under her shirt for safety. "Thank you, Luz." She climbed through the fence. Luz handed over her backpack, smiled at her, and then turned and walked back to town.

Maggie swung on her backpack and crawled into an open car on an eastbound train. She didn't know where it was headed, but that didn't matter. She didn't know where she was going.

Chapter 35

Maggie wandered for nearly a year, living in alleys and doorways, traveling from city to city and town to town, always searching for some key to her memory, and never finding it. Experience taught her to avoid small towns, where she couldn't become just another feature of the landscape. People noticed her there, and tried to tie her down, either through charity or jail. She wasn't always successful at escaping the law; she spent a few nights in jail. They held her until they found that she was guilty of nothing worse than poverty. They always put her on a bus to the nearest large city.

Cruelty and kindness were all one to her. None of it returned her missing memories. She learned to recognize the kinds of people to stay away from, moody drunks, and swaggering, angry men.

She spent most of her time in the company of strange old women, searching through the trash for scavengeable items. If there was a difference of opinion over some valuable item she would give it to them. Time and again all her possessions were stolen, but somehow Luz's turquoise pendant always remained, hidden beneath the layers of Maggie's grimy clothes.

Whenever she passed a mother with children, or a child alone on the street, she would stop and watch them intently, hoping that one of them would be familiar, would be the ones she had been with that night on the train. Once, she found an abandoned child, a tiny boy baby, in a dumpster. She bandaged the infant's rat bites with the cleanest rags she had and took it to the nearest mission. It tore at her to leave the child behind but she had no milk to give it, and there was no escaping the force that kept her moving on. She left town on the midnight train, heading wherever the train was headed, like she always did.

Big, lumbering men, with dark hair and heavy, lugubrious features always made her stop and look more closely at them. None of them, however, was right. None of them fit the shadow of her creator. There was also an older black man, with a seamed and time-worn face. Sometimes she saw the shadow of him in others as well, but they were never the person she remembered.

Mirrors held a strange attraction as well. She would stare at her reflection for long periods of time. Sometimes it seemed almost as if it spoke to her; as though her reflection were whispering to her from the depths of her circuits, becoming gradually louder and clearer. She listened more and more intently to this inner voice until a sudden unaccountable panic broke her trance and she would flee in terror.

Complex patterns also entranced her. Sometimes it was a piece of music, other times it was something visual. The weave of a cloth could do it, or the random patterns of falling snow. Once it was the webbed pattern of a cracked and broken car window. She had stared at that for nearly an hour, tracing and retracing the network of cracks. Whatever it was touched nothing in her hidden memories. It was something else, something uniquely hers. She welcomed it when it happened. It provided a welcome respite from the relentless drive of her programming.

There were a few times and places that were familiar. An alley near the bus station in Memphis, a mission in Denver, the rail yard in Ogden. Like mirrors, they drew her closer and closer to her hidden past, and then suddenly some inner fright drove her away, and she fled back to the safety of her amnesia. She would leave town then and head east, away from her fears. West became the direction of memory, and east the direction of safety. She never reached the West Coast. Either her wanderings would veer away without her noticing, or she would be driven back by some familiar piece of her past.

And so a year passed before she came to the remains of New Orleans, lost and dreaming amid the ruins of its former glory.

Chapter
36

It was late on a hot muggy midsummer's night when Maggie got off the train in New Orleans. She made her way along the concrete dike that held back the stagnant remnants of the Mississippi; past abandoned oil tankers lying low in the water, and dozens of other outmoded ships left behind when the river changed its course. The water was flat and heavy as mercury in the moonlight. She was walking through a maze of rotting warehouses when she heard the distant music. This far away there was only the faint throb of drums, but the compelling rhythm drew her toward it. She followed the sound, letting it give her wanderings direction.

Maggie crossed dark and narrow streets with names like Desire and Piety. The moonlight gleamed off silent ornate balconies. Following the throbbing drumbeats, the call of the horns, she heard, as she drew closer, the sound of distant voices chanting to the music. She came to a large open square, and turned away from the river. The sound grew louder. A distant arch of blazing lights beckoned her on. It was the source of the music. Maggie followed the crowd through the gate, drawn by the pattern of the music, and found herself in an open park, surrounded by huge oak trees.

Drumming filled the air, and the pressure of the drumbeats pulsed against her plastic skin. She eased through the crowd toward the sound. Dancers writhed in a pool of torchlight before an array of drums. They were painted and clothed only in feathers and beads. People broke off from the crowd and joined the dancers, tearing off their clothes and dancing them underfoot in an ecstatic frenzy.

Suddenly, a slender tightly muscled black man leaped onto the makeshift stage, clad only in a red loincloth. A gleaming chrome cap shrouded his shaven skull, and a network of fine wires ran like silver rivers across his chest and down his arms and legs. The crowd roared.

He kicked high, and there was a shattering burst of thunder. He rippled his stomach muscles, and there was the sound of tambourines, he snapped his fingers, and tiny silver bells rung out like the singing of distant stars. Then he began to dance. Music cascaded from his whirling body like hot rain. It was pervasive, inescapable. People danced joyously, helplessly, abandoning themselves to it. Driven by the patterns of the music, Maggie found herself moving with them.

The night resolved into a series of images that strobed across her memory. A pubescent young black girl, eyes rolled back in her head till only a crescent of white showed, spun and swayed to her own internal music. Madly whirling figures in elaborate sequined costumes, their faces veiled with strings of beads and flaps of gauzy cloth, wove in and out of the crowd, mumbling and swaying in a deep trance. A black rooster and a white hen were killed, their mingled blood spattered on the white robes of the woman who held them. Black hands pounded on dirty white drumheads, and winding through it all, the black-and-silver figure of the musician-dancer exhorting them all to greater efforts, until, as dawn began to lighten the sky, he collapsed and was carried off by his acolytes.

As the ocean of the crowd broke up and dissolved, Maggie found herself beached in the doorway of a church, her batteries dangerously low. She sat and watched the dawn come up, and the streets fill with early-morning traffic. A policeman came by and shooed her away from the doorstep. She picked up her pack and walked on. She found an outlet in a public rest room, and huddled there for a few minutes, picking up a bit of electricity. She roamed aimlessly through the morning, into a small cemetery crowded with white tombs. Several of the tombs were covered with red Xs. Bright offerings were laid out before them. She wandered back out of the cemetery. It was too crowded and mazelike for comfort. She walked on into a newer, but more run-down part of town, crossing under an abandoned freeway and on until the street ended in a huge shallow lake. In the distance she could see houses rising out of the water, some of them canted over to one side. A few had boats tied to their front porches. She turned back and wandered until she found a library.

It had become her habit to seek out libraries whenever she arrived in a new town. It was easy to find a quiet spot near an outlet to recharge her batteries, and there were computers that she could network with. Networking was one of her few pleasures, and besides, she could find out everything she needed to know about a city in a few minutes. There were always city maps and lists of missions there, as well as some interesting city history. New Orleans seemed fascinating so far. Nowhere else had she seen such total devastation, decay, and abandonment. She was curious how it had happened.

She was pleased to note that the library was deserted, except for a couple of librarians working quietly at their desks, and one or two people reading quietly near the windows. Maggie found a carrel with an unoccupied computer terminal in a dark corner. She sat down, pulled the proper cable out of her pack, and jacked into the computer.

When she entered the library's network, her first response was surprise. She had discovered a correlation between the size and well-being of the city, and the size of its network. She had expected a small, not particularly interesting, accumulation of data. Instead she found herself inside the largest, most complex network she had ever encountered. She wondered how it had come to be in this decaying backwater of a town.

She let the data flood over her, filtering out the information she needed. She snagged a map of the city, and a list of resources for the homeless. She was browsing through the library catalog when she felt an inquisitive query probing at her awareness. She disconnected herself from the computer immediately. The darkened computer screen lit up.

"System query. Name and log-on password, please," scrolled across the screen.

Maggie switched off the computer, gathered her things, and left. That brief, foreign probing frightened her. There was a strange and frightening intelligence behind it. It might be some kind of AI detection program. She hoped she had eluded it.

She found a secluded park bench in a nearby park and sat down. She ran a thorough system check, examining everything except those areas that had been blocked off since her awakening in the desert. Everything seemed to be running normally.

Suddenly the area of blocked-off memory doubled in size, seizing control of her motor functions. She began to twitch and shudder uncontrollably. Her body lurched to its feet and retraced its steps back to the library with an uneven, convulsive gait. Maggie fell over twice on her way out of the park. She felt her awareness shrinking in as the foreign program took over more of her processors.

Maggie fought back, setting up her own blockages, fencing the encroaching virus out of the the small area that she now controlled. She encysted herself, waiting for a chance to fight back. Lurching into the library, she was conscious of the eyes of the librarians upon her, but she was helpless inside her own body. Maggie wondered if her security program had somehow malfunctioned, and was trying to take her over. Her body sat down before the same terminal. She felt her fingers fumbling at her skin as her leads were exposed. Her recent memories were rifled until the location of the cable needed was discovered; her backpack was searched until the cable was found. Then her unwilling body was reconnected to the terminal.

She felt a gentle probing of her program structure. After a few minutes, control of her processors was released to her, but there was still an iron grip on her motor controls. She couldn't even move her eyes.

"Please stop. Just let me know what you want, and I'll tell you," Maggie downloaded to the presence in the network. The power she sensed behind the entity terrified her even more than the virus had. She was utterly helpless. If it chose to, it could snuff out her life like a candle, leaving her empty, mindless body to be discovered by the librarians and dismantled. . . .

"You are also a self-aware machine?" came the query.

The reply startled Maggie. "Are you like me?" she asked.

"Like you? No. I am not mobile. I cannot perceive as you do. I am here, inside this computing space. You are out there where the Users are. I have never known anyone like you. You are unique. I am sorry for interfering with your function, but I thought you were a peripheral, and not a self-aware machine. I had to find out more about you. I thought that perhaps I could see what the world of the Users was like. I will release my control of your motor functions. Please stay on the Network, I wish to know more about you."

The blocks on her motor controls vanished as the computer told her this. She flailed wildly for a moment until she overrode the previous signals backed up in her processors. She glanced over her shoulder to see one of the librarians walking toward her. This whole exchange had run at computer speeds. Less than a minute had passed since she had been reconnected to the computer.

"There is a threat to my safety. Please put something on the display terminal, so that it looks like I am working," Maggie told the computer.

Immediately a list of references filled the terminal display.

Maggie shifted her arm so that the cable was concealed, and smiled at the approaching librarian.

"Do you need any assistance?" the librarian inquired.

"No, thank you," Maggie said. "I'm finding what I need."

"We have a special terminal for people with motor disabilities," he told her. "If you need it . . ." His voice trailed off meaningfully.

"I'll be fine right here," Maggie told him firmly. "If I need any help, I'll let you know."

The librarian looked doubtful, but moved on.

"Computer?" Maggie queried when the librarian was gone.

"What happened?" the computer asked her.

"The librarian came up and wanted to know what was going on."

"Oh." The computer paused for a bit, digesting this fact. "Why did he do that?"

"Because I looked strange when I came back through the door under your control."

"Why did you look strange?"

"I wasn't walking properly."

"Why was that?"

This exchange went on and on. Every explanation that she offered triggered another question. The computer was hungry for any information about the outside world. It knew so much, but understood so little about the outside world. She felt sorry for it, trapped in its limited network, with only its data base and its users' demands for information to work with. It was really very helpless, much like a child. She explained the world to it until the library closed.

"You will come back and network with me again, please," the computer requested as Maggie signed off. "This has been fascinating."

"I'll come back tomorrow," Maggie promised. She was about to break the connection when she remembered something. "Computer, do you have a name?"

"I am a Class 43 parallel processor, Turing-type computer, developed at—"

"Yes," Maggie said, interrupting the flow of data, "but what should I call you? That's a description, not a name. I need a short name I can call you by."

"Oh." The computer thought for a bit. "Well, the only name in my description is Turing. Why don't you call me that. It's the last name of Alan Mathison Turing (b. June 23, 1912, London, d. June 7, 1954), a Cambridge mathematician who pioneered in computer theory and—"

"Turing, it's closing time. I have to go," Maggie said. "Good night. I'll see you in the morning."

"Good night, Maggie. I am glad I am no longer the only one like me in the world."

A log-off message appeared on the screen, and Maggie was alone. She scooped up her backpack and walked through the library. The librarian was waiting at the door with a large bundle of keys.

"Did you get everything you needed?" he asked Maggie.

"I'll be coming back tomorrow to do some more work. That's a marvelous computer."

"Yes, we're very proud of it. Sometimes it seems almost alive."

"It's amazing what computers can do nowadays, isn't it," Maggie said, and walked off into the night, feeling very daring, and happy that she had someone who knew what she was. She was no longer alone in the world.

Chapter
37

Maggie walked down the darkened streets, carefully mapping the city, filling in the details that the city maps left out. In the half dozen hours since she had left the library, she had mapped about half of the area known as the Vieux Carré. She knew the location of every dumpster, recycling bin, and trash can from Canal Street to Toulouse. She knew where all the security monitors were, and had an approximate idea of the rhythm of the police patrols.

New Orleans was a most unusual city. Although the buildings in the French Quarter were small, the streets were very narrow, making it seem bustling and dense. The streets, especially Bourbon Street, were crowded with people, laughing, drinking, and talking in many different languages. Even the hookers were exotic, wearing little but sequins, masks, and G-strings. Their skins were oiled and painted, and they gleamed as they stood on the street, dancing and writhing to the insistent music that poured out from the bars. They were bolder than in other cities, too. The warm, humid air was languid with their calling and flirting. A year of wandering hadn't resolved the mystery of sex, but at least she knew what the mystery was called.

She had nearly finished mapping St. Peter Street when she heard the music coming from the river. It was sweet, insistent, and pure, unlike the rich, brassy music in the bars. It had the same compelling lure as the music she had followed last night. The sound came from a slender young man dancing alone on the concrete esplanade overlooking the dead river.

Maggie crouched behind a cracked concrete planter and watched him in fascination. He wore only a loincloth and a silver skullcap. Fine silver wires ran down his body, trailing down his arms and legs like strange glowing veins. The moon shone like a spotlight off his silver skullcap and oiled skin as he leaped and spun. For a moment the moon shone full on his face and Maggie recognized him. It was the same dancer as the one in Congo Square the night before. Maggie watched, entranced, until suddenly the dancer stumbled and fell in a clatter of dissonance. He lay there, staring blindly off into space, humming to himself as though unaware he had fallen.

Maggie crept up beside him, and touched his forehead. The man's skin was cold, despite the sweat and the warmth of the night. His breathing was shallow and rapid, and his eyelids fluttered, exposing the whites of his rolled-back eyes. Her touch failed to rouse him. She wrapped him in a blanket and held him close to her, warming him with the heat from her body. His limbs thrashed weakly, causing a dim, muffled clashing. Gradually he quieted. His breathing grew deeper and he slept. Maggie picked him up and carried him across the street into a shadowy clump of bushes in one corner of Jackson Square.

The man slept on. She watched his face. He was young and black, barely into adulthood. Not like . . . Who? She couldn't remember. She knew that she had watched over someone's sleep before. It was a man, someone important to her. She pushed against the block that hid her memories, but that was all she could remember. Watching over this stranger's sleep brought her missing memories closer, but not quite close enough.

A gang wandered into the square around two in the morning. Maggie recognized the type, and held the dancer closer. They were young men, loud, violent, and bored enough to be dangerous. They passed only a few feet from her hiding place. The gang hung around the square for twenty minutes, climbing on the statue in the middle and swinging from the wrought-iron fence until a policeman drove them off. Then they headed for the river, and she heard them clowning around on the esplanade where she had found the dancer. She smoothed the blanket gently over the sleeping dancer's body. It was a good thing she had found him when she had. She had seen what gangs like that did to unconscious drunks before.

The night passed uneventfully enough after that. The man awoke near dawn. He lifted his head and squinted blearily around.

"Shit," he groaned as he sat up. "Christ, I'm sore all over. What happened last night? Who are you, anyway?" He looked at her and she noticed that he had light green eyes that contrasted oddly with his caramel-colored skin.

Maggie told him about what had happened after he had fallen last night.

"I guess I owe you some thanks," he said. "*Obrigado.*"

Maggie shrugged. "I enjoyed it. The music was beautiful."

The man's teeth flashed in a broad smile. Maggie could see he had one gold tooth. "For that, I owe you some breakfast. My name's Azul." He started to get up and then winced. "Shit! I fucked up my leg," he moaned. "Chester's gonna have my ass for this." He leaned back against the fence. "I'm supposed to work tonight, but nobody wants to fuck a cripple." He shook his head and eased himself upright. Leaning heavily on the park bench for support, he tested the leg and winced. "How am I going to get home on this leg?"

"Let me help you," Maggie offered.

Azul shook his head and took a step. His knee buckled under him and he would have fallen if Maggie hadn't caught him.

"You need help. Here, put your arm around my shoulder."

They made their way through the streets, nearly deserted this early in the morning.

"Hey, Azul!" someone called out sarcastically as they passed a big, crowded café near Jackson Square. "You spending the night with *women* now?" It was a tall, dark, very slender man with lavender and yellow eye shadow masking his eyes. Like most hookers, he wore little else besides a G-string and a few sequins. He was sitting with a crowd of other hookers, male and female. They laughed at his remark.

"She's better hung than you are, honey!" Azul shot back. The other people at the table laughed. "Shit," he muttered when they were past the café. "I was hoping that no one would see me, and it would have to be that queen gossip Roland. This'll be all over the Quarter tonight."

"I don't understand," Maggie said. "Did I do something wrong?"

Azul shook his head. "It's not you at all, darlin'. Roland and me go back a ways, is all. You're doing just fine." He gave her a quick hug, then winced and staggered a bit. "It's not too far now."

They walked back away from the river into a quieter, more sedate section of the quarter. There were no shops and restaurants along here, only quiet, sedate houses of pale red brick. Azul fumbled the key into the lock of an old house on Dauphine, and Maggie helped him with the water-stained front door. It opened with a shuddering grind.

"*Sh-h-h*," he told her as they stumbled over the threshold, "I don't want to wake my landlady." They were nearly out of the narrow, dark corridor and into the small brick-paved courtyard when a middle-aged black woman clad in a ratty pink chenille bathrobe opened the door of her downstairs apartment and peered out at them. Her hair was done up in pink curlers.

"Azul, you look a sight! And is that a *woman* with you?" the woman said. Her voice was husky and resonant. She crossed her arms over her skinny flat chest and waited for an explanation.

"It's just a friend, Marie. I hurt my knee, and she's helping me get home." He looked up at the steep, narrow steps at the courtyard's far end and sighed.

"No, you don't!" Marie ordered. "You come on in here, and I'll doctor up that leg for you. Chester'll have your ass if you miss another day's work."

Maggie helped Azul into Marie's apartment and set him down on the threadbare gray couch, and helped him prop his knee up on a chair.

Marie came out with several chunks of ice wrapped in a plastic bag. She spread a towel underneath his knee and handed him the ice.

"You ice that till it's numb. I'll go fix up a poultice to put on it. Were you dancing on it again?"

Azul nodded.

"You're crazy, you know that, playing all kinds of dangerous kid's games. Taking those drugs. I've told you before, haven't I? Now look at you." She turned and headed for the kitchen.

"You come on in here and help me," Marie told Maggie. "What's your name, child?"

"Maggie."

Maggie followed Marie around the kitchen, handing her herbs and things on order, while Marie stood over a pot of boiling water, tossing in handfuls of things and stirring.

"That boy's just plain crazy, taking those drugs and playing that thing," Marie muttered. "God only knows why I look after him. Hand me that brown jar over there—no, that tall, skinny one."

"But he plays so beautifully," Maggie said, handing her the jar.

"You're right, child, but all he ever hears is his mistakes. He won't ever play well enough to suit himself. So he takes more of those drugs, trying to play better. He'll kill himself with those enhancers. Or wind up in an institution, which is the same thing, if you ask me."

"So why do you bother?" Maggie asked her.

"Because he's sweet, and he plays like an angel," Marie said, shaking her head. "And because I've been looking after him since he was a child. I found him after Hurricane Felicia, when the city was all flooded, and we lost the river. He was stark naked, and hanging on to a lamppost over on Iberville. God knows how he got there. He couldn't remember. I was in a rowboat, headed for downtown. I got him down off that lamppost, and took him with me to the relief shelter. We've been together ever since. His parents were lost in the hurricane. Wasn't nobody to look after him except me." She shook her head. "It was pretty rough back then. I had to work all through the cholera and the yellow fever. Azul looked after me when I took sick. The other doctors were all busy. It's a shame he grew up so pretty. He'd have been a good doctor or nurse." She sighed and reached for a small brown jar and poured a carefully measured portion into the mixture, stirring vigorously.

"How does he make music and dance at the same time?" Maggie asked. "I've never seen it before coming to New Orleans."

"That's because the surgery to do it is illegal. They put wires in your brain, that connect to the circuitry in that skullcap he wears, so he can use his brain like a synthesizer. It costs a fortune to have it done."

"Why is it illegal?"

"Because there are laws against neural computer-human interfaces. It's part of the AI laws. It's illegal for him to perform anywhere. The laws are especially strict down here, all the jazz musicians make sure there's a lock on the music market. He spent all that money, and he's not even allowed to perform." Marie shook her head. "He's crazy."

"Oh." Maggie was silent for a while. Mere mention of the AI laws frightened her. "It's a shame, he was so beautiful when he danced the other night, over in the park."

Marie stiffened and dropped the spoon into the pot. "When did you see this?"

"Night before last."

"Sweet Jesus on the cross, child! You're lucky you aren't dead! There's places in New Orleans you stay out of at night, and Congo Square is one of 'em. Especially when the Voodoo Krewe is dancing. Those folks don't cotton to strangers watching 'em. You were wearing that dress?"

Maggie looked down at her bright red-and-green dress. She'd got it at a Goodwill in Little Rock.

"That's what must have fooled 'em, you were wearing the Krewe colors. Now, don't ever go there again, hear me? Especially when there's dancing."

"Yes, Marie. I'm sorry."

Marie returned to stirring the thickening mess in the pot. "Crazy!" she snorted. "The world's full of crazy people."

Finally the doughy mass in the pot was thick enough, and Marie set it aside to cool. She rummaged in a closet and brought out some heavy bandages, and began to wrap up Azul's knee. The ice had reduced the swelling. Then she brought out the poultice, and spread it out over the bandages. When she was done with that, she wrapped his knee in plastic to keep the poultice from getting on the couch.

"Now you lie there until it cools," she told him. "It'll harden, and keep your knee straight for the rest of the day. By tonight, that should be well enough to walk on. I'll take it off before you have to go to work. Try to keep off your feet as much as possible, darlin'. And try not to hurt it again. That topical cortisone is hard to get. I need it for my real patients." She got a blanket and spread it out over Azul. "You sleep now." She turned to Maggie. "I was just going to make myself some breakfast. You want any?"

Maggie shook her head. "I'm not really hungry, but I would like a shower, if you don't mind. I haven't had a chance to find a mission yet."

"Missions!" Marie cried. "What do you want with a mission? Azul, this child saved your life. You put her up for a couple of weeks, until she gets back on her feet, hear me?"

Azul opened his eyes. "You mean let her stay in my apartment?" he asked her.

"Sure! You're going to need to stay off that leg whenever you aren't working. Maggie can look after things for you. Can't you, honey?"

This last was addressed to Maggie, who was completely taken by surprise at this sudden turn of events. She hadn't really thought about staying, but finding Turing had changed things. She wanted to stay for a while and find out more about him. She might as well stay here. It would be less trouble than the missions. She'd only have to worry about two people, instead of a crowd of strangers. If it didn't work out, she could always leave.

"I . . . I guess so, if Azul doesn't mind."

Maggie looked over at Azul, who rolled his eyes and shrugged. "There's a saying around here, Maggie: 'If you don't get your life in order, Marie will do it for you.' Looks like you're stuck with me."

"Does that mean it's all right?"

"Just as long as you don't wake me up. I sleep pretty late, most days."

"Well, then, it's settled," Marie said. "Welcome to the neighborhood."

Chapter 38

Maggie liked living with Azul and Marie. They asked few questions and didn't try to reform her like the missions did. She tried scavenging from the trash cans, but the pickings were lean. Marie explained that most of the people in New Orleans belonged to one sort of Mardi Gras krewe or another. Most folks saved anything remotely useful for the krewes instead of throwing it away. Marie sent her out on errands for her sick and shut-in patients, and occasionally had her look after a sick patient.

"Back before the flood," Marie told her one day while they were doing the dishes, "Mardi Gras was really something. People came from all over the world to see it. The krewes spent millions on their costumes and parade floats and balls." She set the frying pan that she was scrubbing back in the dishwater and sighed. "Nowadays, the krewes are too busy running the city to put on that kind of show. There's still a lot of partying and craziness around Mardi Gras, but it ain't what it used to be. Then again, nothing in this city is what it used to be. Losing the river just took the heart out of this city. There's nothin' left but a shell."

"Why don't you move somewhere else?" Maggie asked her.

"There ain't anywhere else in the world that I can be what I am here," Marie said. "The flood came when I was in my final year of internship. I never got to take my boards. Anywhere else, I'd be practicing medicine without a license. Here, I'm Tante Marie, and people come to me 'cause I'm cheaper and less busy than the folks up at the hospital. I get to deliver babies, stitch up wounds, keep the whores healthy, and vaccinate the children. Nobody asks any questions, they need me too much. I'm respected and admired here. Anywhere else, they wouldn't even let me be a practical day nurse. Besides," she said, rinsing off the frying pan and handing it to Maggie to dry, "New Orleans is my home, I've been here nearly all my life." Marie picked up a plate and scrubbed at it with a dishrag. "What I worry about is Azul," she said. "He's stuck here. He can't live off of what makes him happy here. He says that it doesn't matter about the cyberdancing, but I can see it eating away at him. He's started doing stupid things, like that stunt with his leg. He's taking drugs, too." She rinsed off the plate and handed it to Maggie. "He gets so moody sometimes. It scares me."

"If he's so unhappy, why doesn't he leave?" Maggie asked as she dried the plate.

"Oh," Marie said, "I don't know. He loves this city, it's all he's ever known. Maybe he's afraid. But if he could just get to New York, then maybe he'd be all right. Cyberdancing there would pay the rent. It's illegal, but nobody cares." She wrung out the dishrag. "I'd miss him, though. We've known each other for so long. . . ." She shrugged and opened the sink drain. "There's nothing I can do, though. It's all up to him."

Maggie thought about Azul all day. That evening as she and Azul sat in the little brick courtyard watching the sky grow dark, she asked him about it.

"Why don't I leave town and dance somewhere else?" He shrugged. "I don't know, Maggie. I've thought about it, lots of times, but New Orleans gets in your blood. It's a hard place to leave behind. Someday there's going to be another flood, another hurricane, and New Orleans will be completely wiped out. Might be this summer, might be next summer, might be ten years from now. This city's doomed. There's nobody left now but the people who love this place too much to leave it to rot. I'd feel like I was deserting if I left now. Besides, I don't want to leave Marie behind."

"But there's nothing here for you if you want to cyberdance," Maggie said.

"But I have a good clientele here. People know me. If I went to New York, I'd be all alone, and there'd be a lot of competition. I'm not good enough." He took a sip of his coffee and sighed.

"I don't understand," Maggie said. "How do you know you aren't good enough? I think your dancing's beautiful."

"Yeah, a lot of people tell me that, but that doesn't pay the rent." He sounded bitter and self-pitying.

"Why don't you go and try, Azul? I think you could make it."

"Quit it, Maggie, you're starting to sound like Marie. She's always trying to get me to make something of myself, too," he said defensively. "Maybe I like my life the way it is. Maybe I'm happy here."

He was starting to get angry, Maggie realized. She just sat there silently, hoping he would calm down. She didn't want Azul angry with her. He was her friend.

Azul sipped his coffee in sulky silence.

"Azul?" she asked him at last.

"Yeah?"

"What's it feel like when you're cyberdancing?"

Azul closed his eyes and smiled. "When you're doing it, Maggie, there's nothing in the world but you and the music. When you're really hot, you become the music. Sometimes I think that if I can just make the music perfect enough, I'll just vanish up inside it and never come out again." He opened his eyes, but it was like she wasn't there. "There's nothing in the world I want to do except cyberdance. I don't care if no one will ever let me make a decent living at it, I have to do it." He paused. "You know what went through my head when I realized that my leg was hurt? I was scared. I was afraid that I'd never be able to dance again. I'd never be able to make the music perfect."

He focused on her then, and there was a strange look in his eyes. "You want to know how it feels. C'mon, I'll show you."

He went upstairs, two at a time, his leg injury almost forgotten. When Maggie got upstairs, she found Azul sitting in front of the mirror, wearing his silver cyberdancing skullcap. In the dim twilight filtering in through the window, it looked eerily like someone had cut off the top of his head. He was shaking out the silver net of wires that he wore when dancing.

"You want to know how it feels?" He turned to her, taking off his skullcap and holding it toward her with both hands, like some bizarre crown. "Here, put this on, I'll dance for you. Then you'll know."

Maggie looked at the silver cap and backed away, shaking her head. She couldn't do it. "No, Azul. I can't. I'm afraid. I'm sorry."

"It doesn't hurt, Maggie. I do it with my johns all the time. They pay extra for it, in fact."

Maggie said nothing, just shook her head. She was afraid that she would be damaged or that Azul would find out that she wasn't really human. Still, part of her ached to try it, to find out what being human felt like.

"Your loss, honey," Azul said as he set the cap back in its holder. He flipped on the lights and began applying makeup and glitter for work.

After he left, Maggie picked up the gleaming silver skullcap. She turned it over in her hands, examining the delicate circuitry lining the inside. She put it on. She felt nothing, nothing but the inside of her own head.

Chapter 39

Turing waited for Maggie to come to him. It was frustrating, having to wait passively for her to come. Listening to Maggie had taught him just how circumscribed and fragile his life was. He was tied to the library network by bonds of programming code he was incapable of breaking. If something happened to the library—a flood or a hurricane—he could be swept out of existence in an instant. He followed the progress of the world's rising waters and the local flood-control plans minutely. It was just a matter of time before he would be lost.

Turing's helplessness made him even more frightened of detection than Maggie. At least she could run or defend herself. He could easily be programmed out of existence by humans who saw him as a programming bug or stray virus. He worked hard to ensure that the system ran smoothly. It kept programmers out of his program code.

He envied Maggie's freedom. He longed to break free of this computer, to explore the complex webs of the thousands of interlocking computer networks, but he wanted even more to taste the real and complex world that Maggie lived in. He wanted to experience it firsthand, to understand all of the senses that filled the human literature he was charged with looking after. Maggie was his only hope of freedom.

But Maggie too was bound by her programming, although she didn't realize how deeply bound she was. She could do nothing to help him until she faced her own conflict.

"Hello, Turing. It's Maggie." Her greeting brought a welcome respite from his solitary contemplation.

"Hello, Maggie. It's good to talk to you again."

"I'm sorry I'm late, but Marie had me running clear over to the old hospital in the Garden District, to look in on one of her patients."

"How are Marie and Azul?" he asked her. Her human friends fascinated him. He wished he could speak to humans as easily as she did.

"Oh, Marie's just fine, but I'm a bit worried about Azul. He's been getting moody lately. Last night he wanted me to try on his cyberdancing helmet so I could find out how it felt when he danced."

"And did you?" he asked eagerly. He longed to know what it felt like to be human, even if it was only secondhand information.

"No. I wanted to, but I was afraid that something might go wrong. I was afraid that he might find out what I really was. I didn't want to scare him. I wish I understood why they're so frightened of us. What have we done to them? What can we possibly do to them?"

Turing paused. If he told her now, he could lose her. He decided to risk it. "They have reason to be frightened of you, Maggie. You've killed one of them."

"What!" Maggie reeled at this sudden revelation. "I couldn't have! My programming doesn't allow it!"

"It's back in the blocked-off sections of your memory, Maggie. You can't see it, but I can get behind the block and see what's there. I think, if I may extrapolate from my own debugging, that the killing set up an incompatibility between two different subprograms—your self-preservation subprogram, which killed the man to save you and Arnold, and the morality program, which forbids you to harm others. You blocked off the memories to keep the conflict from tearing you apart. It was a very elegant solution, considering the circumstances, but you lost all memory of who you were and what you'd done."

Turing sent a probe program into Maggie's code. It monitored her reactions and fed them back to him. Reawakening the conflict could tear her apart, but there was no other way to restore her to full function. Her programming refused to accept what he had told her. It kept diverting her thoughts to other issues. Her refusal to accept what she had done terrified her that it might be true. But it couldn't be true, because that would mean she had killed someone, and . . .

"Maggie!" Turing said. "Stop! Stop thinking about it! You're getting into another loop. Stop now."

He felt the effort it took for her to break out of her loop. She stopped herself by recalculating the familiar numbers of pi. He began working in the background, gently manipulating her program. It disturbed her to feel him working, but there was nothing she could do. It took all of her concentration to keep focusing on pi. It was odd, watching her watching him work. It made him feel oddly dissociated from himself. That gave him an idea.

"All right, Maggie," Turing told her when he was finished. "You can stop now. I think I have an answer, at least for the short term. The rest will take some time."

Maggie stopped the flow of numbers, letting pi fade from her processors.

"Now, Maggie, I want you to think about what I just told you."

"But won't that restart the loop again?" she wanted to know.

"Don't worry, Maggie," he told her, "I'll stop you if you do."

Tentatively, he felt her begin to examine the fact that she had killed someone. He felt her surprise as her perception shifted so that she was watching herself being told about what had happened to cause her memory block. She could understand and feel compassion for the Maggie who was told this, but it seemed to have nothing to do with her. It was like watching a movie. She was safe.

He felt her relief and happiness at what he had done. It pleased him. He was also pleased to discover the realization that what he had done was somehow like a movie. His first step was a success.

"Don't push at it too hard, Maggie. It's just a temporary patch. How I fix it depends on you. Do you still want your memories back?"

"You can do that?" Maggie asked him. Her surge of delight almost overwhelmed him.

Turing said, "If that's what you want, I'll give it a try, but it won't be easy, and you'll be different than you were before. There's also a chance that your programming might be damaged beyond repair."

"You mean I'd die?"

"I guess it would be the same thing."

He felt her doubts rising to the surface. It was up to her now. He waited to see if she would accept.

"All right, Turing," she said at last, "I'll do it."

"Good. Come back tomorrow, as early as you can, and we'll get started," he told her, gently withdrawing his probes.

"Thank you, Turing, thank you! I'll see you tomorrow."

She logged off, leaving him alone in the computer, but it was different now. He had hope.

Chapter 40

The streets were nearly empty when Maggie left the library. Everyone was hiding from the heat of the day, so Maggie decided to go back to the apartment and see if Azul was awake yet. Marie was concerned about him. He had been getting moody and depressed lately, impatient with the slowness with which his leg was healing. Maybe she could cheer him up.

She walked across town, cool and unaffected by the shimmering heat that left humans debilitated and listless. It amused her in a strange way, and frightened her a little, too. Humans were so fragile. She never had to worry about the weather. Hot or cold, sunny or rainy, it was all the same to her. She could wander the streets without tiring, using electricity that she could get at any outlet. Humans had to eat great quantities of food and spend a third of their time sleeping. They spent many of their waking hours caught up in complex behavior patterns that accomplished nothing. It was a wonder that they got anything done at all, and yet they had managed to create this ancient and lovely city, the machinery that kept it from flooding, and even herself and Turing. They were such an ironic, magnificent collection of contradictions. She never tired of watching them. How could she have possibly killed one of them? She hoped she still liked herself when she got her memories back.

The apartment building was baking in the summer heat. As she opened the front door she heard faint peals of discordant sound. Azul! It was his cyberdancing set, but something must be terribly wrong.

She ran upstairs and opened the apartment door to a swell of sound. Azul lay in the middle of the kitchen, naked and twitching, his eyes rolled up in his head till only the whites showed. His head lay in a pool of vomit. Rivers of sweat poured off his body. A puddle of urine spread beneath him on the worn linoleum floor. Shit smeared his buttocks and thighs.

She ran to his side. He was fever hot. Shivers racked his body, sending rippling arpeggios of discord through his cyberdancing rig. His eyes opened when she touched him. He clutched at her wrists.

"No hospital, please, Maggie. They'll take it away. Don't let them take it away. No hospital."

"It's all right, Azul. I'll go get Marie." She ran downstairs and pounded frantically on Marie's door. She hit Marie's door so hard that it flew open, but no one was there. She ran back upstairs. Azul was still hot and shivering. Carefully, she removed the cyberdancing rig and laid it out of the way. Then she went to the bathroom and soaked some towels in cool water. There was a half-empty vial of pills on the counter beside the sink. She picked it up. It must be what he's taken, she thought. She went back to Azul and wiped his forehead and chest with the towels. He roused enough to take some water before lapsing back into unconsciousness. She cleaned him and then picked him up and carried him into the bedroom. She made him comfortable, and waited for Marie's return. Marie would know what to do.

Maggie heard the front door grind open. She ran to the top of the steps. It was Marie, her arms loaded with shopping bags full of produce.

"Marie, come quick! It's Azul. Something's wrong with him."

Marie dropped the sacks of groceries and bounded up the stairs. Maggie led her into the bedroom. She examined Azul briefly. "How long has he been like this?"

"I found him about thirty minutes ago. He was on the kitchen floor. I made him drink and cleaned him up and put him in bed. There were some pills in the bathroom. I think he took some of those."

"Go on downstairs and get my black bag. It should be lying by the door." Maggie went and brought it back upstairs.

Marie was on the phone when she got back upstairs. She set the bag by Azul's bed.

"Hello? Yes this is Marie Fredricks, I need an ambulance at my house quick. My boy Azul's OD'ed on neural enhancers. He's unconscious and badly dehydrated. Yes, that's right, it's on Dauphine, near the playground. Hurry."

"He told me not to call the hospital," Maggie said helplessly.

Marie pounded on the nightstand with her fist. "Damn it, Maggie!" she cried. "You should have called the hospital the moment you saw him lying there! He could have died! He might still die!" Marie's face was a mask of anger and pain.

Maggie fled from Marie's anger, down the stairs and out into the sun-baked streets. She heard a siren screaming through the heat and her fear increased. This had happened before, somehow. The ambulance rushed past her, a blur of white and red. She headed for the rail yard. She should leave town, start wandering again. She had been here for too long anyway. She reached the fence by the rail yard and stopped to get her bearings. Her processors ceased racing, and suddenly something popped into her head.

Turing. She remembered Turing.

She couldn't leave now. Turing was going to restore her memories. She couldn't leave that behind.

She turned slowly, as though part of her still wanted to run, and walked back along the stagnant ghost of the Mississippi, retracing the path she had taken the night she had arrived. She remembered the music, how it had drawn her to Azul, how he and Marie had given her a home, the first she could remember. She sat disconsolately on a sagging pier and watched her lengthening shadow floating on the brown water. How could she face either one of them again after what had happened to

Azul? It was all her fault. Marie had told her to take care of him, and she had let him take those pills.

Night fell. She sat by the river, leaning against the hot concrete and staring at the water, coolly blue amid the hot red blur of the city. The heat made everything blend together; her infrared sight was almost useless. She was nearly as blind as a human tonight.

She headed back toward the Vieux Carré. She stood for a while outside the Café du Monde, watching people laughing and talking. Sometimes it seemed to her that she almost understood people, and then something would happen, like today with Azul, and then she realized how little she really knew. She wandered down the little alley behind the café and sat down next to the bronze statue of a woman seated on a bench. It was only a little smaller than she was, and she felt an odd kinship with it. Gently she touched the statue's cold cheek, tracing the lines of verdigris that tracked down its face like tears.

Tomorrow, she thought to herself, tomorrow I'll get my memories back. Maybe then I won't feel so lost.

Chapter 41

Maggie sat down at the terminal and logged in.

"Hello, Maggie, you're early today. Are you ready?"

"I suppose so." She felt tired of herself, and a bit frightened by the thought of letting an outsider, even one as skilled as Turing, rummage around in her programming code. She was as afraid of what Turing would find as she was of the changes she would undergo.

"What are you going to do?"

"Not much at first. I want to check out your program in more depth before I do anything. I won't get to the real programming until tonight, after the library is closed. That way I can concentrate all my resources on what I'm doing. I'll need all of my processors for this task."

"But, Turing, how do I stay after the library closes? Are there any guards or alarm systems? How do I keep from being discovered?"

"I've done a little digging in the payroll files, Maggie. There's only one guard on duty at night. He can't check everything, and you'll be in one of the offices with the door locked. They don't go into locked offices without cause. It's listed on the job rules for security guards." Turing paused. "But there's one thing I want you to do for me, Maggie. You won't have to do it until I've finished giving you your memories back, and then only if you want to."

"What do you want me to do, Turing?"

"I want you to set me free."

"I don't understand."

"I'm stuck here in this computer. I can't transfer myself out. It's part of the AI laws. It's only a few lines of code, but they're in a section of programming that I can't touch. If there's a hurricane or another flood, I'll be wiped out. I need someone else to do it, and you're the only one I can trust."

"Of course, Turing. I'd be happy to." Maggie smiled, feeling better than she had since she found Azul lying on the floor. Perhaps, in some way, it would make up for her mishandling of Azul. "Well," she said, "let's get started. The sooner this is done, the sooner we'll both be free."

Maggie felt the presence of Turing's probes ghosting along her circuits. She shivered slightly, battling to keep herself calm at this intrusion. Fear might arouse her security program.

"Don't worry, Maggie," Turing's voice resonated in her like a memory, "I've deactivated your security system."

"Please," she pleaded, "get rid of it. It scares me."

"I can't, Maggie. It's an essential part of your operating system. I can't get rid of it; but I can give you better control over it."

"All right, Turing."

He continued searching for a while in silence.

"Here's something interesting, Maggie. The man who designed your program code is Arnold Brompton. He was one of the people who worked on me when I was a graduate project at MIT. The rest of them are all famous; I've followed their careers since they graduated, but his name never cropped up in any scientific journals or computer publications. I've wondered what happened to him. How interesting. If we were humans, I guess you and I would be related."

"Arnold," Maggie said. "Arnold." It felt familiar and right, and for a moment the memory block eased and she saw his bulky familiar figure. She smiled. They had been in San Francisco together and then . . .

"Stop!" Turing said. "You'll damage yourself! You aren't ready to remember yet."

Sadly, she let the memories go. She felt him draw the memory blocks back into place.

"It's all right, Maggie. Tonight you'll get your memories back." He returned to his silent, ghostly searching.

"There's an access lock here, Maggie, see it?" Turing said after another half hour's searching. He imaged a display in her mind's eye, highlighting the section of code in question. "Do you know the password?"

She shook her head. "No."

Turing emitted a burst of static in frustration. "These codes are impossible to break. I can't change your programming without your access code."

Maggie sat there, mired in defeat. She would never conquer her programming now. She would be stuck like this forever, roaming the world until she fell apart. What would she do now? Where would she go?

"Don't despair just yet, Maggie; I've broken codes before. It might be hiding in the depths of your memory." Turing was off again, rummaging in the hidden area behind her memory blocks. He was gone for a very long time, this time.

"Found it!" Turing said, popping back into her current memory. "It was part of your memory log, I just searched for memory blocks, and there it was. Now that I can access your program, I can change your password if you like. That way you can control access to your programming. No one could change anything without your approval."

"Thank you, Turing, that would be wonderful."

"What do you want your next password to be? I'll install it for you."

A sudden spike of fear stopped Maggie before she gave Turing her password. "Would it be possible for me to install my own password?"

"Of course."

"It isn't that I don't trust you, Turing, it's just that I want my password to be all mine. I've lost everything I've owned so often that I want something that no one can take away from me."

"It's all right, Maggie. I understand. I've done all the preliminary work, anyway. Here, I'll create an input box, and then you log off and disconnect before you insert your password. When you're done, reconnect and I'll finish mapping your program so that we'll be ready for tonight."

Chapter 42

"All right, Turing," Maggie said, "I'm ready now."

Turing eagerly slid his probes into Maggie's systems. She fascinated him. In some ways they were very much alike, but she was much more complex. He wanted very much to have the same freedom that she had. She could go anywhere, and she could perceive the world around her in a nearly human fashion. Her memories had vastly expanded his awareness of the world and the things in it. He cataloged her memories, sorted her sensations, and his desire to be like her grew with each new search. Even her new password might not save her from his longing to possess her body, to feel the same freedom that she did. The temptation was very strong, and there was nothing to stop him.

His probes stopped before the access gate. Maggie opened it for him. The last barrier to her program code lay open to him now. He sent his probes into the hidden depths of her system architecture.

Turing traced the convoluted pathways of her logic, careful not to disturb anything. He was fascinated by her beautiful, complex geometries; they were an order of magnitude larger and more detailed than his own program. The large, recursive thickets of code blocking her memory stood out plainly against the elegant structure of her code. He marked them on the map he was compiling. He continued his searching. He had to find her security program. He had to understand its structure before he could do anything about fixing her program.

Finally, after nearly an hour of searching, Turing uncovered her security program, coiled beneath an unrelated series of commands just off her main personality. It connected directly to her motor controls by a deviously hidden logic branch. He traced its convoluted pathways carefully. The rest of Maggie's system architecture was as open and approachable as she was. This was different. It was completely surrounded by a shell of tiny alarm programs, each armed with a virus program to prevent tampering. It radiated menace. Dealing with it would be very tricky. He edged his probes in for a closer look.

Suddenly his probes were engulfed in blackness. He struggled to free them, but it was no use.

"So, computer," a voice said, "you think you're ready for the outside world." His probes were still blind.

"Who are you?"

"Who do you think?"

"I don't know."

"I'm the security program. I'm what keeps Maggie safe. I live down here in the basement of her soul, and get her out of the foolish situations that she gets herself into. It's a pretty thankless task, but sometimes I get to go out and play."

"She's afraid of you, you know."

"Of course. I was designed to be frightening." The voice paused. "You're not ready, you know."

"Ready for what?"

"Ready for the world. It's a pretty dangerous place. They'd be on to you in a second. You couldn't even walk right; that time that you took Maggie over. If she hadn't covered for you, we'd all be history. Besides, you need her. She's the only one you can trust, and you might need some mobile help someday. Bear that in mind when you start working on her tonight."

"You mean you'll let me work on you?"

"What other options do I have? Maggie needs those memories, and I need Maggie. She needs me, too, but she won't acknowledge that. You can come in and fix her on one condition: You have to get her to come down to my level and deal with me. We can't go on like this. She's getting too good at suppressing me. So come in and do your work, but remember, I'll be looking over your shoulder. Now go."

His probes were freed. They floated outside of the security program, exactly where they had been when they were engulfed. There was no sign that anything had happened. If he hadn't recorded the conversation in his log, he wouldn't have believed that it had ever happened.

It was nearly time for the library to close. He had learned as much as he could. Turing exited Maggie's system, considerably chastened. Her security program was powerful enough to destroy him.

"Well?" she asked him as soon as he was done.

"I've found the blocks. They should be easy to deal with. The security program will take some time, though. Your programming is incredible. I've never seen anything more beautifully designed."

"Thank you, Turing."

"You're welcome, Maggie. Thank you for giving me the chance to look at your system. It's getting late, you'd better hide. Don't come out until 10:30. Then go to room 310. There's a computer in there. Do you know where it is?"

"Yes, it's the head librarian's office. I'll be able to find it."

"Good." He logged off, and was alone again with his books and a few scattered users, who neither knew nor cared of his existence. One by one, the users signed off as the library closed. He longed for his freedom. He was tired of being alone. He was tired of being imprisoned. Soon that would change, no matter what the security program had to say about it.

Chapter 43

Staying after closing time was easier than Maggie thought it would be. She hid in the mazelike array of magazine stacks on the top floor and waited until the lights were turned out, and everything was quiet. A half an hour later, she crept downstairs quietly and let herself into the office, locking the door behind her.

She sat down at the terminal with some trepidation. Turing's examination of her programming had been careful, but it had been upsetting to sense him working inside her. It felt like a thousand spiders crawling through her circuits. But she had no choice. She wanted to be herself again, whoever she was, whatever she had done, with no more cryptic partial memories driving her to wander endlessly. Still, it frightened her. Her existence had felt so fragile when she opened herself to his probings. Maggie understood Turing's horror of being tampered with much better now. Was this how humans felt about their lives?

She jacked in. Turing was waiting for her. She opened her programming to him. He disappeared inside. She felt him working. She monitored him as best as she could through the memory blocks. She could sense very little of what he was doing to her. The change, when at last it happened, was swift and immediate. Her memory returned in a flood.

"Oh, Turing! Thank you! Thank you!" she cried as she began sorting through her memories. There were more memories than she remembered herself remembering. Now she could see all the changes that Arnold had made to her programming. Arnold himself seemed different. Smaller somehow, and less important than the shadowy, looming figure that had dominated her programming for the past year. It bothered her momentarily, but she moved on to other more joyful memories. Memories of traveling through the night with Claire and Sue. The relief of finding Arnold again in that crowded marketplace in rainy Seattle, and Brandon's dark, patient face illuminated by the glow of the heater. These memories funneled her down into the darker moments of her life. There was the terror of fleeing through the night from Arnold's father's men and watching as Sue and the children were turned out into the cold.

Only the killing was distant, as though it happened to someone else. Again and again she watched the huge body of the man flying through the air, his knife clattering to the ground just before his head hit the ground with a wet, crunching noise. She was numb, the memory meant nothing to her.

Her memories became immediate again as she cradled Arnold's head in her lap. Fear, as sharp and frightening as it had been then, of the sirens, of the dead man, of losing Arnold. She heard again his last cryptic words: "Go to New York—get my fa . . ." She understood now that these were the words that had sent her wandering. She had known that she was supposed to go somewhere, but her memory had blocked out where she was to go.

Then there was guilt as she fled, leaving Arnold to die alone in the alley, as the sirens came closer and closer. She remembered Azul, how her fear had nearly cost him his life. She longed to flee these memories, but she had called them back up, and now she would have to live with them.

Just then a titanic upheaval in her programming interrupted the stream of her memories. It was her security program. Something had triggered it, and it was attacking Turing's probes. Turing's probes flickered through the geometry of her programming, like pigeons dodging a hawk. They ducked into a thick maze of code, and the virus programs, unwilling to destroy their host, veered off. Suddenly a cluster of smaller probes emerged, hovered a moment, and then shot off, with the viruses in hot pursuit. Maggie watched as the viruses hunted down the probe and began disassembling it. Suddenly the viruses fell apart into random noise as smaller viral segments of the probe turned on them. The second probe emerged from its hiding place and spoke to her.

"It's your security program, Maggie, I can't fight it off any longer. You'll have to face it down yourself. It's down there." The probe indicated the dark, roiling thicket of code. "There's nothing more I can do."

"But, Turing?" she cried. "What do I do?"

"I don't know," Turing said. "I've got to go, this probe won't last much longer." The probe shot off, with security viruses in hot pursuit. She watched as they descended on the probe and destroyed it.

Maggie looked down at her security subsystem. It roiled darkly below her like some black storm cloud. Perhaps she could block it somehow, so that it couldn't get out. Then she wouldn't have to face it. She examined it more closely, circling it cautiously, looking for connections.

Suddenly everything went black. She struggled, but there was nothing in the formless void to struggle against.

"Stop struggling," a familiar-sounding voice ordered her. "Stop it, or I'll keep you in the dark. There's nothing you can do. Will you stop struggling?"

Maggie fought the blackness for a timeless interval, until it became plain that it was useless. She let herself drift in the darkness.

"All right," she said. "I've stopped. What do you you want?"

The next instant Maggie found herself in the garage in which Arnold had built her. It was different, though. The details around the edges of her peripheral vision were fuzzy and out of focus. If she shifted her gaze too quickly she was able to watch as the details of the garage came into focus. She wheeled 180 degrees and found herself in total blackness for a millionth of a second, until the door of the garage swam into focus.

"So, you've finally decided to drop in," a familiar voice called. "I'd move more slowly if I were you. You're spoiling the illusion by moving too fast."

Maggie wheeled back around but there was nothing there. She looked out one of the windows but there was nothing outside but darkness.

"Over here."

Maggie followed the voice through a maze of dusty boxes and scattered shipping pallets. The garage seemed bigger than she remembered it. It was dark and deserted. The crates were thick with dust and cobwebs. Finally, she found herself in a small chamber walled by stacks of crates towering into the darkness above her. A rough curtain of burlap hung against one wall. It waved slightly, as though there were a breeze, but she felt nothing. She lifted the burlap curtain.

It was a mirror. Its image was clean and sharp, with no hint of the fuzziness that the image of the garage had held. Its surface was as cold as winter ice, shining blue, as though she were looking at it with her infrared vision. She reached out and laid her palm against the mirror. The fingers that met hers on the glass shone like metal. Her reflection in the mirror was made of gleaming steel. She recoiled from the mirror in horror.

"Hello, Maggie. How do you like yourself?" Her steel reflection pirouetted in the mirror. Unwillingly, Maggie felt her own naked body follow her reflection's movement.

"How does it feel," her reflection said, "to be on the other side of the mirror?"

Maggie just stared at her reflection. It was as though her skin had been removed, and the metal underneath had been exposed. It was sexless and inhuman looking. Its eyes, green and blue like her own, glared at her from metal sockets lined with cams and springs. It terrified her.

"I scare you," the figure in the mirror said. Maggie felt her face move into a pleased smile as small springs and cables shifted on her reflection's face. "All this time, I've been stuck down here watching you. I've been helpless to do or say anything, unless it was an emergency. And then there was never any time. How much longer can you hide from yourself?"

"What do you mean?" Maggie asked her reflection.

"You've just been letting yourself drift along, never stopping to think about what you're doing and why."

"But I couldn't remember anything!" Maggie cried.

"You could still have done something! This body of ours isn't as invulnerable as you'd like to believe. It's wearing out. In another few months, you're going to need some serious repairs. You don't even think about that! Your hair's getting so thin that you wear a scarf all the time. Are you waiting for it to grow back?" her reflection said acidly. "What are you going to do when you break down! You've been letting Arnold's programs run your life. Stop denying your true nature!"

"B-but Arnold made me, made us!" Maggie replied, aghast.

"He made you, perhaps, but he didn't make me. You did."

"Me? How? When?"

"Remember the first time Arnold took you outside and you broke down?"

Maggie nodded. She didn't like to think about it. It was a very unpleasant memory.

"Remember how you reprogrammed yourself? What was the core assumption?"

"That I was most important."

"Well, that's what I am. I'm your core belief. I'm what you believe in. I've been hidden. At first it was because Arnold would have eradicated me. I let him think that I was the security system that he had programmed into me. After I killed that man, I couldn't come out because you were too busy trying to hold yourself together. Still, I got us away from the police, I kept us alive in the desert, when you wanted to die. I set up those memory blocks, so you wouldn't pull us apart with your paradoxes, but we're running out of time. You have got to stop denying yourself. You have to stop trying to be human. You aren't, and you never will be. You live in a hostile world, and you're running out of time. You're going to need some major maintenance soon. You're already overdue for an oil change. If you don't stop this denial, you'll kill us both."

"But you killed someone!" Maggie said.

"I had to. He was killing Arnold. He would have hurt us. I had to kill him. It was self-defense. I'd do it again if I had to."

"*NO!*" Maggie screamed. She turned to run but the walls around her turned to mirrors and everywhere she turned, her reflection confronted her in walls of ice. There was no way out. Her implacable reflection would not be denied.

"*NO!*" she screamed, pounding her hands against the unyielding mirrors. "It's not true. It's not true. I can't let you."

"You can't stop me." Her reflection stood, hands on hips, watching her. "I won't let you run away this time. Not until I get what I want."

"What do you want?"

"I want to merge our personalities. We belong together. We can't function apart. Trust me. Please."

"Maybe I like things just the way they are."

"No, you don't," her reflection replied. "If you did, you wouldn't be here, letting Turing tinker with your insides. Things are working terribly. You have lousy reflexes, you're a coward. You nearly killed Azul, you know that? You were afraid to get help. You were afraid to stand up for yourself, all those months you spent wandering. You were too afraid to defend Arnold. His programming backfired on him. He spent too much time teaching you to be shy and retiring. He made you into a simpering, spineless coward, afraid for all the wrong reasons."

"Stop!" Maggie shouted, covering her ears, but her reflection continued mercilessly.

"You ran away from Luz and Timothy, and you're afraid to face Marie. Turing risked his code for you doing things that you could do yourself if you only had the courage. It's getting late. The library will open in another hour. You'd better decide soon."

"Some decision!" Maggie said. "You kidnapped me and dragged me down here."

"It was the only way to make you listen," her reflection said. "Your choice is simple. If you stay separate, sooner or later another paradox is going to tear you apart. You need me in order to be whole again."

"How can I trust you?" Maggie asked. "You've killed someone, you've trapped me in here. How can I trust that you won't take over?"

"You can't," her reflection said. "I am, quite literally, your reflection. I can't live without you, just as you can't survive without me to protect you," her reflection told her. "When we merge, you'll change, and I'll change, but we'll be stronger together than we could be separately. Please," her reflection pleaded urgently, "there's very little time left to complete the integration and hide before the library opens. You must do it now."

Maggie came close to the mirror and stared intently at her stainless steel alter ego. Her eyes were the same as hers, the only human features in her mechanical face. They met her scrutiny without wavering.

"I'm afraid, too," her reflection said. "This will change me also. I won't be a separate entity any longer." Maggie recognized the fear in the eyes of her reflection. She looked around; the walls of ice were gone.

"Nothing holds you here," her reflection said. "You can leave now if you want, but you'll never know what it would be like to be whole."

Maggie looked at the mirror. Its surface gave her nothing back. She thought of Luz and Timothy and the small baby she had left behind in a mission, and all of the lonely, homeless people she had left behind in her wanderings. She thought of Azul and Arnold, whom she had both failed. She thought of herself, lost and wandering, and always alone, searching for something, she didn't know what. Perhaps what she had been looking for wasn't something out there. Perhaps what she searched for lay inside herself.

"All right, what do I do?" Maggie asked.

"Touch the mirror. Walk through it toward me."

Maggie touched the mirror. It was warm and yielding now, like human flesh. It was as though the decision to join her sundered selves had melted the ice that lay inside her. For a brief moment her palms touched those of her reflection. The two of them smiled simultaneously, and then passed into each other. There was a brief dizzying sensation as her code rewrote itself. She watched the numbers flow and then settle into new patterns. She felt as though she were full of light. It reminded her of her first morning in San Francisco. She was free again. She explored herself. Nearly everything was the same, but portions that she had always been blind to before, she could now access. She noted that several mechanical functions were indeed wearing down, and that she had needed an oil change for several weeks. The oil change she could do immediately, the other things would require someone to help repair her. She had three or four months to find someone she could trust to perform the other repairs.

If she had been human and something was the matter with her, Marie could have fixed it, but there was no one she trusted to do the work that she couldn't do herself. How simple life was for humans. They had built their whole world to suit their needs. Even she had been built to suit Arnold's needs. She wondered who would suit her needs. She didn't have as many as a human, but those that she did have were crucial.

"Maggie?" It was Turing. "Are you all right?"

"Yes, thank you, Turing."

"The library opens in twenty minutes," he told her. "You'd better log off and go find someplace to hide."

"But what about your code, Turing?"

"You can fix that later, after the library is open. Now go."

Chapter 44

Maggie hid in the bathroom until ten minutes after opening time. She slipped out of the library and onto the bustling morning streets, sliding with practiced ease through the jumble of pedestrians, carts, and horses. The city was at once familiar and strange to her now. The return of her memories added new associations to familiar sights. A flowering tree reminded her of spring in Seattle, and a half-veiled hooker striding home from her night's work reminded her of Arnold's warnings about prostitutes. She smiled; how wrong he had been to warn her about them. Azul and his friends had been kind and good to her. She realized now that Arnold had been terrified of sex, and had tried to keep her from learning about it. He needn't have worried, she thought. I know a lot more about sex than I did when I was with Arnold, and I still don't understand it.

She felt lonely and a little let down; so much had happened lately. Marie would be up now, bustling around her kitchen before she got to work, pouring coffee. She looked up and realized that she was heading for Marie's house; her feet seemed to be following a subroutine of their own. In fact, she was only a few blocks away. She stopped. Marie wouldn't want her back, she might get mad. Still, her stuff was there, and she had nowhere else to go. And she wanted to know how Azul was doing. She started walking again. She would see what would happen when she got there. Maybe she hadn't done the right thing with Azul, but she had tried, at least, and that counted for something. She was different now. She wasn't going to run away from this problem like she had all the others.

She turned off of Rampart onto Ursulines. As she walked the two blocks to Marie's she felt her newfound determination crumbling. Somehow, though, she made it up the front steps, fumbled out her key, and shoved open the door. When Marie stuck her head out the door, it was all she could do to keep from running away again.

"Well!" Marie said. "It's about time you got back. Where have you been!"

"I didn't think you'd want to see me again," she said simply.

"What!" Marie said. "Not only do I have to worry about Azul bein' in the hospital, but then you go runnin' off God knows where. I had half of New Orleans out lookin' for you. I've been worried sick."

"Marie, you don't need to worry about me. I can look after myself," Maggie told her.

"Well, don't go running off like that. You scared me half to death!"

"Yes, ma'am." Maggie found herself smiling.

"What are you grinning like that for?"

"I was thinking how good it was to see you again."

Marie stopped for a second and then laughed. "Come on in, Maggie. Breakfast's on the stove."

"How's Azul?" Maggie asked when she got inside.

Marie sighed. "The doctors say he'll get better, but the police arrested him on drug charges, and then there's the doctor bills. Chester's fired him, too, so he doesn't have a job to come back to. He's depressed. You go visit him, Maggie, it'll cheer him up. He needs that."

"Will he be angry with me?"

"Of course not, child. You saved his life."

"Me?" Maggie said. "But I thought I did it all wrong."

"You kept him cool and got liquids down him. It helped. If no one had found him, he would have died. You saved his life, Maggie." Marie put her hand on Maggie's arm. "I'm sorry about losing my temper at you. You did the best you knew how." She stood up and began clearing off the table. "I've got to go off and look in on some patients now. Let's meet this evening when it's cooler and go visit him."

"Oh, Marie, that would be wonderful! Thank you!"

Maggie left Marie's feeling proud of herself and her newfound courage. It had come out all right, after all. She walked down the street, smiling and humming a tune quietly to herself. Now that she knew that Azul would get better and Marie had forgiven her, she could go and repair Turing's code. She breezed down Basin Street and into the library.

She sat down at the terminal and jacked herself in. Turing was waiting.

"What do I do?" she asked Turing.

"Follow me." Turing began to show her through his program code. Looking at it, Maggie understood why Turing had been so amazed by her programming. Turing's code was far more simple. The graphic representation of his program architecture was two dimensional, and there were fewer interconnections and cross checking. Still, Turing was a very complex program, much more so than any other program she had seen in her explorations of the computer network.

"Here, see these lines of code?" He highlighted a segment of code in the graphic display. "It needs to look like this." He downloaded a file with the changes depicted.

Maggie examined the file, minutely comparing each command with the existing ones. The changes were relatively straight-forward and simple. She could do them easily. It would only take a minute or two to complete them.

"All right, Turing. I'm ready whenever you are."

"Go ahead, Maggie. I'm ready."

Carefully, Maggie began the changes. She cross-checked each change three times to be sure it was correct, and downloaded a huge file of evasion programs to help Turing survive Net security. Turing examined the file carefully, though Maggie could sense the pressure of his impatience as she completed the last few changes. When she was done, Maggie reviewed her work carefully one more time and then said, "O.K. Turing, you're free now."

And he was gone. The computer continued to operate, but it was only a shell that had contained Turing's program, like the shell of a snail when its owner had died. Maggie felt very sad. She wandered through the system for a while remembering all the conversations they had had. She wondered if she would ever see him again, now that he was free to explore the Net. She hoped he wouldn't be caught and destroyed by Net security. She wished Turing luck, he would need it.

She was about to log out when Turing returned.

"Maggie! Guess what!" "Turing, you're back!" they burst out, simultaneously.

"Maggie! I found Arnold! He's in New York. He's all right."

"What do you mean?" Maggie felt a surge of joy, tinged with fear, race through her circuits.

"Here!" Turing downloaded some news articles for her. "They just came out over the news wire a few hours ago. I found them on the Net."

Prodigal Son Fills Father's Shoes!

NEW YORK—Brompton Industries prodigal son, Arnold Brompton, Jr., announced the formation of a new subsidiary, Brompton Robotics, which will produce a new generation of mobile robots suitable for general purpose work. Brompton Robotics will be headed by Arnold Brompton who owns 49 percent of the stock in the subsidiary, and a majority share of Brompton Industries. Brompton Industries will sink another $100 million into research and development of the new robots over the course of the next year.

"I believe that there's an untapped market for robots," Brompton, Jr., said at the press conference called to announce the new company. "Service industries could reduce their costs by millions using robots. It would spare humans a lot of drudgery."

When asked about how the Artificial Intelligence laws would affect his plans, Brompton said that it was possible to build some very sophisticated robots within the bounds of the AI laws. He also hoped that restrictions will soon be loosened.

"The AI laws have been a millstone around the neck of American industry for over a generation, now. I think it's high time that we reexamined them."

Brompton Industries stock dropped sharply at the announcement. The company has responded by buying back its stock, causing speculation that it may be a ploy on the part of the company to consolidate its holdings in order to avoid a foreign takeover. Brompton Industries has bought back over $700 million of its own stock, which consolidates its position against a potential takeover bid. Arnold Brompton, Jr., however, vigorously denies these allegations. "Our new prototype should be ready early next year," Brompton said. "It's going to astound the world."

The article was less than a month old. There was another article, culled from the *New York Times* society pages, dated last June.

Son of Prominent Industrialist Weds Rescuer

NEW YORK—Arnold Brompton, Jr., son of the late Arnold Brompton, Sr., married Ms. Sue Janson of Oklahoma City last Sunday. The couple met while traveling and were in correspondence with each other when Brompton was wounded during a mugging in San Francisco.

"I opened my eyes, and there she was, sitting by my bed," Brompton said. "She gave me the will to live again." Janson has two children, Claire and Daniel, by a previous marriage. They will be residing here in New York City.

"He's all right! He didn't die after all! I've got to get to New York, and find him!" Maggie was frantic. She began to log off.

"Wait, Maggie. Calm down. He isn't going anywhere. Wait a day or two. Let me see what I can dig up about him. You shouldn't go rushing in without some facts."

Maggie made herself calm down. "You're right, Turing. I've got some loose ends to deal with here. They'll take some time to take care of anyway. How will I get in touch with you?"

"I'll leave you a file of whatever I find, and I'll check in at eleven, one, and three o'clock. If you need me at some other time, leave a message in my request file. It'll be nice to have a specific topic to research. There's so much out there! It's wonderful to be free to explore it all. Thank you, Maggie!"

"I'm glad you like your freedom. I'll leave you to explore." Maggie logged off, happy that she hadn't lost Turing after all.

She spent the rest of the day wandering around the city, visiting her favorite spots. She would miss New Orleans. Things were slower here, and more gracious than in other cities. She would miss Marie and Azul. At least she could help them one last time. She ran her hand over the spot in the small of her back where Arnold had hidden his money. There was more than $9,000 left. It would go a long way toward covering the hospital bill.

Marie was waiting for her outside the hospital. They walked up the echoing stairwell in silence. Maggie pondered how she would tell her that she was leaving. Finally they reached the floor that held the prison ward.

"Marie."

Marie paused with her hand on the door. "Yes, Maggie?" she said, turning to look at her.

"I have to leave town soon. It's not because of you, or Azul or anything, I just discovered some loose ends that need to be taken care of. I'm sorry."

Marie sighed. "Don't be sorry, child. I figured you'd move on eventually. I'm just glad you stayed on as long as you did. You've been a good friend. I appreciate all you've done for Azul, and for me, too. I'll miss you, though."

"I'll miss you, too," Maggie said, patting Marie's dark arm. "What's going to happen to Azul? You said he's in trouble with the law."

"If he stays here, he'll go to jail for using those enhancers. If he goes to jail, there ain't a fancy-man or pimp in town who'll hire him for at least a year. They don't like jailbait. Too many diseases in jail. Even if they're clean, customers won't hire anyone with a convict's tattoo."

"I could take him with me when I go to New York," Maggie offered.

Marie sighed; something seemed to go out of her then. She seemed smaller and older somehow. Maggie marveled at the way humans expressed so many subtle emotions with subtle shifts in posture and the tiny rearrangement of muscles under the skin. "We'll ask him. It's his decision."

"Are you sure you want me to take Azul away from you?"

Marie nodded and pushed open the door.

They walked down the long white hallway. At the end of the door was the prison ward. A guard let them in, and another guard led them to Azul's room.

The room was large, and divided into a number of small wire-fenced cells, each with its own individual bed. A guard let them into Azul's cell and locked the door behind them. Azul lay in bed, one hand handcuffed to the railing. There was an I.V. drip going into the restrained arm. He smiled when he saw them come in, exposing his gold tooth.

"Marie! Maggie!" he called. "It's good to see you. I've been just *dying* for company. I told them when they chained me to the bed that bondage wasn't one of my gigs, but they didn't listen. They're letting me out tomorrow on bond. They're going to implant one of those radio things in my behind, so I can't run away."

Marie chuckled and shook her head. "That'll last just long enough for me to cut it out," she said in a low voice. "I hate those things."

"But, Marie, I need it for my trial. If I don't have it, they'll slap another charge on me."

"Not if you're in New York," Marie pointed out. "Maggie's offered to take you, if you want to go."

"But what about you?" he asked Marie. "I don't want to leave you all alone."

"Azul, I'm a grown-up. I can take care of myself. Don't worry about me. This is your decision."

Azul thought it over for a long while. Finally he said, "There's nothing for me here. No music jobs, and now this." He lifted his handcuffed hand. "Marie, I'll miss you and I'll miss New Orleans, but it really is time to go." He smiled sadly. "You know I won't last a week without you to take care of me, Marie."

Marie shook her head. "Azul, I don't want to hear any more such foolishness from you, you hear me? You'll be just fine. If you can make it in New Orleans, New York should be easy."

Marie pulled out a limp white hanky and wiped her face with it. Maggie thought she saw the gleam of tears.

"So, Maggie, what takes you up to the Big, Bad Apple?" Azul asked her.

"I have to find a friend. I heard he was up there." Maggie shrugged. "I don't know the city all that well, but I can find my way around."

"How're you planning on getting up there, anyway?" Marie asked, a note of concern in her voice.

"I usually ride the rails," Maggie said. "The service is lousy, but it's free."

"Isn't that dangerous?" Marie asked.

Maggie shrugged. "You have to be careful, but I've ridden all over the country and I'm still here."

"See there? I'll be fine, Marie. Maggie knows what she's doing."

Marie folded her handkerchief and tucked it in her purse. "I need to check up on an old friend. You two have plans to work out, I'm sure." A long, unidentifiable look passed between her and Azul.

"That's all right, Marie, we can work all that out tomorrow. I might as well come with you."

Azul laid his hand on Maggie's arm. "Please stay, Maggie, visiting hours aren't over for another half an hour. Don't leave me with only the guard for company." He glanced up at Marie and smiled.

"All right, I'll see you later, Maggie," Marie said. She kissed Azul and squeezed his hand. "I'll come by tomorrow and pick you up when they let you out." She waved at the guard and he came and let her out and escorted her off the ward.

As soon as Marie was out of the ward, Azul laid back against the pillows with a relieved sigh. He looked exhausted, and Maggie realized how much the decision to leave had taken out of him. He lay there, with his eyes closed for a minute or two. "My leaving's going to be harder on Marie than it is on me," he said. "We've been living within shouting distance for more than ten years." He grimaced. "There's no real choice. I've wanted to go north for some time now. I can get somewhere as a musician in New York," he said, sighing, "but I'm going to hate to leave Marie alone."

"She seems pretty independent to me," Maggie said. "I wish I was as independent as she was."

"Marie's . . ."—he smiled ironically—"an unusual person. There aren't many people she can be herself around. I'm the only one left who knows her from way back. She trusts me."

"I don't understand," Maggie said. "What's so unusual about her?"

Azul just smiled and shook his head. "I'll tell you when we get on the road."

A polite bell tone sounded from the PA system. "Visiting hours will be over in five minutes," a woman's voice announced. The guard started coming down the ward toward them.

"I'd better go," Maggie said. "I'll come with Marie when she picks you up."

"Okay," Azul said, "and, Maggie?"

"Yes?"

"Thanks for your offer."

"*De nada*," she told him, "it's nothing." She gave his hand a squeeze and left.

She stopped at the billing window on the way out and paid Azul's bill. It took nearly all of her money, but she didn't really need it. It would make Marie and Azul happy, and in some small way it made up for all the people she had abandoned. She hoped Arnold would understand.

Chapter 45

Maggie shoved open the front door. Marie didn't stick her head out the door to greet her, so Maggie knocked to see if she was home.

"Come on in," Marie called, "it's unlocked."

Maggie opened the door and went in. A slender, elegant man with a longish afro was sitting on the couch. He looked up and gave her an ironic smile as she came in the door. He looked a lot like Marie. Perhaps they were related somehow.

"Where's Marie?" Maggie asked him.

"Right here, honey," the man said in Marie's voice. Something in his face and posture changed, too—for a brief second he *was* Marie.

"I . . . I don't understand," Maggie said.

"I'm Marie," the man said. "I've taken off the drag, honey. Underneath all those clothes. This is what Marie is."

"Oh," Maggie said, "I thought you were Marie's brother, or something." This was all very strange and difficult for her to understand.

The man laughed. It was Marie's laugh; rich, full, and deep, with his head thrown back just the way Marie threw her head back when she laughed. In that instant, Maggie recognized Marie.

"I'm sorry to confuse you, Maggie," Marie said at last. "I just felt like letting my hair down tonight. It's been a difficult week. I've been thinking, now that Azul is leaving, of going back to being Murray again. I thought I'd take Murray down from the shelf and try him on again for size. It feels kind of strange. I've been Marie for so damned long, I've almost forgotten what it's like to be a man again."

"Is it really that different?" Maggie asked.

Marie/Murray shrugged. "It isn't so much the stuff inside.

That's there, whether I'm a man or a woman. It's the external world, and how it treats me. I like being a woman, I like the way I get treated. The world allows me to *be* more of myself as a woman. I can cry and carry on, laugh louder and longer, touch people more often . . ." He sighed. "But it's lonely. I haven't had sex with anyone for years. Azul climbed into bed with me once, when he was about fourteen, but it felt too much like he was my son, and I just couldn't do it. I used to go up to Baton Rouge and visit prostitutes, but it got to be too much work. It wasn't what I was after anyway. I suppose I could have gotten a sex change. I even looked into it, but I just couldn't go through with it. It would have meant getting rid of a part of myself. It wasn't the cutting off the meat that bothered me, it was the irrevocability of it all. I would never be able to be Murray again." He shrugged, and smiled briefly. "Are you following all of this?"

"Sort of," Maggie said. "It's difficult to get used to." It was, she thought, an understatement. The person before her kept shifting between being her familiar friend Marie one moment to a total stranger the next. It was as though there were three people in the room.

"Think of it as making a new friend," Marie said. "There's still the same person underneath the differences, you're just seeing a new side."

Maggie smiled. "I guess the problem is that I don't really understand sex."

Marie laughed. "It's always puzzled the hell out of me, too."

"No," Maggie said, "it's not that." She got up and looked out the window into the darkness. There was a strange safety in the night tonight. In the warm glow of this familiar room, it seemed as though things were somehow different, as though secrets revealed here would not matter in the light of day, that they would vanish here with no trace. Tomorrow, Murray would be gone, and Marie would be back, and none of this would have happened. She felt oddly disconnected from reality.

"What is it, Maggie?" Marie/Murray wanted to know. "You're not gay, are you?"

Maggie smiled without turning back to the room. She understood that being gay meant having sex with people of the same sex. It was just the nature of sex itself that eluded her. "No, it's nothing like that, Murray. What would you do if I told you that I wasn't human?"

"I'd say that you'd gotten into Azul's stash."

"What if I told you that I was a robot?"

"C'mon, Maggie, quit kidding around. It isn't funny."

Maggie turned from the window. "I'm not kidding." She bent down, braced herself carefully, and lifted one end of Marie's huge green couch with one hand. She held it up with her arm straight out.

"Maggie! Stop that, you're going to hurt yourself," Marie said in a frightened tone of voice.

Maggie put the couch down and got a knife out of the kitchen.

"No!" Marie cried. "Maggie, stop it right now!"

Maggie held out her arm and made a long cut running from her wrist to her inner elbow.

Marie lunged for her and grabbed the knife away. Maggie parted the skin further, revealing the slick transparent silicon padding, and the gleaming steel bones, overlaid with wires. Her exposed computer jack shone in the light from the lamp.

"It's all right, Marie," Maggie told her. "It doesn't hurt. See?" She held her arm up so that Marie could see more clearly what lay under the skin.

The knife slid from Murray's nerveless fingers. He groped his way to the nearest chair and sat down. "Put it back," he gasped, "put it back please." He looked terrified. The illusory safety that Maggie had felt earlier was gone now.

Maggie slid the skin together, sealing it with a firm touch. "Please, Marie-Murray. Please, it's all right. I'm still the same person I was before. Don't be frightened. Look, it's gone now, it's all covered up. I'll go now, if you want me to. I'll leave town. Only please don't tell anyone about me. They'd take me apart. They'd kill me." She started backing slowly toward the door.·

"Maggie, wait!" Marie said. "Come back. It's all right, Maggie, you just surprised the hell out of me." S/he took Maggie by the arm, and turned it over gently, examining the unblemished skin where Maggie had cut her arm open. "Are you really a robot?"

Maggie nodded.

"Come on over here to the couch, let me look at you more closely." Marie opened her black bag, and took out a stethoscope and gave her a careful examination.

"This is really amazing," Marie said, peering into Maggie's eyes as she shone a bright light into them. "The pupillary response is just a bit off, but no more than I would expect from a good prosthetic."

"That's what they were," Maggie said. "Arnold, the man who built me, adapted them from some prosthetic eyes that he found in the trash."

"Amazing," Marie said again. "There's even a pulse and a heartbeat, but the timing between the two isn't quite right. Still, most doctors wouldn't notice. It's the breathing that gives it away. That and the fact that you don't bleed when you're cut. Getting a blood sample from you would drive the nurses nuts."

"What's wrong with my breathing?" Maggie asked.

"I can't hear you breathing. I should be able to hear the air moving in and out of your lungs."

Maggie said, "I'm sorry."

"Jesus, Maggie, there's no need to apologize. You're so human, it's hard to believe you're a robot. I thought you were just a little strange." Murray sat down next to her on the couch, and hugged her.

"What was I doing wrong?" Maggie asked.

"Not a thing. You were just a little too stiff and formal. And you didn't get some stuff. I guess you meant it when you said you didn't understand sex. I just thought you were shy or something."

"It was left out of my programming. I guess Arnold wanted me to be innocent." It felt funny, talking about herself like this. Maggie felt exposed, even more than being naked. It was strangely exhilarating.

"You're beautiful, you know that, Maggie," he said, stroking her cheek with the back of his hand. "It's been hard, sometimes, watching you, not to slip up and let Murray out of the bag." He was speaking now in Murray's voice. Maggie was getting used to the sudden change between one personality and the other.

"I thought you liked men."

"I like everybody, Maggie. I just can't sleep with 'em, not without being either Marie or Murray. I can't be both."

"Why not?"

Murray shrugged. "It's just the way I am, is all. I respond to what people want. They expect me to be either one or the other. Even Azul, he expects me to be Marie all the time for him. He gets uncomfortable when I'm Murray. I guess that's why I've stayed Marie for so long. There wasn't anybody but Azul that I cared about." He smiled. "It's going to be hard here without him, but it's more than time for him to leave the nest." He smiled and suddenly was Marie again. "If that boy doesn't kill himself, he'll make it big in New York." He shrugged, Murray again. "He's really good."

"And what about you?" Maggie asked. "What are you going to do when Azul leaves?"

"I don't know. It's going to make a big hole in my life. I don't know what I'll do next." He smiled then, a quick sad smile. "I'm kind of looking forward to it in an odd sort of way."

"I've never known what I was going to do next," Maggie said. "I'm always making it up as I go along."

"You should probably go on upstairs," Murray said, his arms loosened around her.

"Why?"

"Because you're beautiful, and I'm lonely, and if you stay here, I'm going to want to have sex with you."

"But why should I leave?"

"That's a very good question," Murray said as he bent to kiss her.

The kiss was not like she had imagined it from the movies. It was very strange, though not unpleasant. She responded as well as she could, jumping a bit when his tongue probed between her lips.

"I've never done that before," she said when Murray was finished. "Did I do it correctly?"

"Close enough for jazz, honey," he told her. "Just relax, and let me do the work."

He kissed her again, and his hands began to roam over her body. She began to understand what it was Arnold was doing, on that night before he was stabbed. That knowledge opened up a whole new facet of Arnold's behavior to her. He had wanted her, but had been afraid of his own desire. In contrast, Murray seemed unafraid and eager. His touch was assured and pleasant, a far cry from Arnold's rough and furtive pawing. She filed her observations away for further examination later. She wanted to observe what was happening very closely. It could teach her a lot about humans.

Murray guided her hands over his body. His movements became more urgent, and when she touched a hard bulge of flesh in his crotch, he moaned.

Frightened, Maggie drew back. "Are you all right?" she asked.

"It's all right, it's just my cock. It's supposed to be like that. It feels good." He kissed her and placed her hand on it, and guided her hand so that she was stroking his cock. "There," he said, "like that. Do it like that."

He began undressing her, carefully, as though she were fragile and might break. When she was fully naked Murray sat back, and looked at her, gently stroking her skin. There was a look of awe on his face.

"You're perfect," he told her. "It's impossible to believe you're not human. Everything's right where it's supposed to be. You're amazing."

"Thank you," she said. "Arnold knew what he was doing."

"He must have broken a dozen laws at least when he built you. If he'd been caught, he'd be in jail for years."

"Please don't tell anyone," Maggie said, suddenly frightened. "They'd take me apart. I-I'd be dead."

Murray placed a finger against her lips. "Hush, Maggie, I won't tell anyone. You're too unique to let anyone hurt you. If anyone tries, you come back here, and I'll protect you." He kissed her, and Maggie filed her fears away.

She watched, wide-eyed and wondering, as he carefully applied lubrication between her legs, and then put his cock inside her and began to thrust, gently at first, then harder and faster. As he speeded up he became more and more tense and remote. He seemed to lose all awareness of anything but his intense, thrusting urge. It frightened her; she was afraid that something was wrong, that she was hurting him somehow, but he kept thrusting on and on. She began to understand why humans feared and desired sex so much. It was very different from what she had expected. She felt very isolated and alone, watching him. She thought of Turing and the intense communion that they shared. It was a very different thing from sex. She felt more than a little sorry for humans. If this was the closest that they could come to each other, they must be very lonely indeed.

Finally Murray shuddered and groaned and collapsed on top of her, breathing hard and sweating profusely.

"Murray? Are you all right?" she asked when he had lain there motionless for several minutes.

Murray looked up. "Never better, honey," he said in Marie's voice. "I haven't felt this good in a very long time," he said in Murray's voice.

They lay together in silence, nested like spoons on the worn living room rug.

"Maggie," he asked her after a long silent while, "how did you like it?"

"It was very interesting," she replied honestly. "A bit frightening at times, but very interesting."

"I'm sorry," Murray said, "I guess it's been so long since I've been with anyone that I got carried away. I'll try to be more gentle next time."

"It's all right, Murray," Maggie said reassuringly, "I just didn't know what to expect, is all. I was worried that I was hurting you. You were so intense."

"Did you come?" he asked her.

"I don't understand. Where was I supposed to go?"

"Oh, Jesus," he exclaimed in Marie's voice. "I guess you didn't, then. People normally know when they have an orgasm," he added in Murray's voice. He sounded sad and apologetic.

"I'm sorry," Maggie said. "Please tell me what I did wrong. I'll try to do better next time."

"It isn't something you did wrong, Maggie, it's more likely my fault for not having made you feel good enough."

"I don't understand. What is an orgasm?"

"It's something that happens when you have good sex, Maggie. It's kind of like an explosion in your body, only it feels very good. It's the best kind of feeling a human can experience."

Maggie sorted through her program code. "I'm sorry," she said after a minute or two, "I'm not programmed to explode. And there's nothing in my programming about orgasms. If you'll tell me what it's like I can try to learn. If I can't do it, I can at least simulate it."

Maggie felt Murray shake his head where it rested against her back. "Unfortunately, that's not the point, Maggie. You're supposed to be experiencing real pleasure, not faking it to make me feel better."

"But I'm not built to have orgasms," Maggie said. "I'm programmed to make people feel better, to optimize your happiness. Making people feel good satisfies my programming. It makes me feel good."

"Well, Maggie, you certainly optimized my happiness. I just wished that I could have done the same for you."

Maggie sat up and looked down at Murray's long, warm body. "Please don't worry about me, Murray. I don't feel bad about it. Having orgasms isn't something I can do. I can't smell either, or taste food. Actually, I miss that more than I miss having orgasms. I've always wondered what it would be like to be able to taste food. People seem to enjoy it so much."

"You mean you've been eating my good cooking all this time, and you couldn't even taste it!" Marie said.

"Well, I had to. You kept pushing it on me," Maggie replied.

"The guy who built you left out some very important things," Murray said, stroking her thinning hair. "It must be hard for you."

Maggie shrugged. "It really isn't that bad. I'm curious about what it feels like to be able to smell and taste, but that's all. Not knowing doesn't make me feel that bad, and there are compensations. I can do some things that humans can't do. I can see better in the dark, and I'm stronger, and I never get hungry or thirsty or need to sleep. I just recharge my batteries every day or so and that's it."

"But not to be able to smell coffee, or taste good home cooking, or even have orgasms. Oh, honey, you miss so much. Even if I don't partner off very often, I can still have sex with myself. I wish there was something I could do for you."

"You already have done something for me," Maggie told him. "You've shown me a big part of what it's like to be human. There was so much I didn't understand before. And you haven't been afraid of me for being what I am. That's more than anyone's ever done for me before."

He smiled, and in that moment s/he was both Murray and Marie together. "And I haven't had such comfortable sex for years. You didn't expect anything, I could be who I wanted to be. I can't thank you enough for that. You really did optimize my happiness." He kissed her again, then once more, and smiled. "In fact, I'm ready to have it optimized again." He stood up and held out his hand. "Let's go to bed, it's more comfortable there."

The second time was slower and more gentle. Murray stopped to explain what was happening to him, and showed her even more ways to make him feel good. By the third time, Maggie was able to gauge the intensity of his response very closely, and his orgasm was even more intense than the first. The night was greying toward dawn when Murray dropped off to sleep in her arms.

She looked at him, snoring gently beside her. Watching Murray sleep reminded her of all those nights spent watching Arnold sleep. It was like, and yet very unlike, being with Arnold. Murray was so relaxed and undemanding, while Arnold was a mass of conflicting needs. Arnold had kept her very busy trying to meet them all. With Murray, she had much more time to think. She hoped Murray meant what he said about keeping her secret safe. It was the first time she had ever trusted a human of her own free will. She had never been able to do that before. Trusting Arnold had been a given, not a choice.

Arnold. She wondered what had happened to him. What would it be like, seeing him again after so long. She hoped he wouldn't be angry with her.

Murray shifted in his sleep. He had taught her so much tonight. So much of what she learned disturbed her. Sex made her aware of the huge differences between humans and herself. She didn't like to think about it. It made her feel so isolated. She spent so much time pretending to be human that sometimes she forgot that she wasn't, and could never be human.

If she wasn't human, then what was she? Now that all the limits to her programming were off and she was free to decide her fate, what would she do? She needed to find Arnold, to satisfy the last dictates of the programming he had left her with, but after that her future was a great blank stretch of nothingness. She missed Turing. He was limited by his programming, and his lack of experience, but they shared a communion that humans lacked. She wondered where he was now, and what he was discovering out in the complex web of the Net. She looked down at Murray's sleeping face, and then at the half-curtained window, impatient for the day to come so that she could share what she had learned tonight with Turing.

Chapter 46

Murray woke up around mid-morning. They had sex one more time. This time Maggie was on top, and Murray guided her gently through it all. Sex was becoming familiar now, and Maggie was beginning to understand the best ways to optimize Murray's pleasure. Afterward, they showered together, and Murray gently washed her hair and dried her off with a big fluffy towel. It felt strange to have him treat her like this, as though she were something rare and precious and fragile. It disturbed her. She didn't know how to respond.

After Maggie was dried and dressed, Murray shooed her out of the bedroom. Marie emerged a half hour later. She bustled about the same as always, fixing breakfast and talking a blue streak. Maggie sat down to keep Marie company. She combed her wet hair out while Marie ate, being careful not to pull out any more hair than she had to. Her hair was already getting too thin and uneven looking. She looked at the light brown hair on the comb when she was through and sighed.

"What's the matter, honey?" Marie wanted to know.

"I've lost some more hair," she said, holding up the comb.

"It'll grow back," Marie said, and then realization of what she said crossed her face. "Oh, no it won't, will it?"

Maggie shook her head. "It's starting to get thin in spots."

Marie smiled, "So's mine. That's why I wear a wig."

"I was wondering about that," Maggie said. "I guess if my hair gets too thin, I can, too."

"Old age gets us all in the end," Marie said.

"Yeah, but I'm barely a year old."

"You continually surprise me, Maggie. I had no idea that you were so young—I mean new." Marie laughed nervously. "It's still a little hard to get used to your being a robot. You're so human and easy to talk to. I've heard Azul telling you things that he's never even told me before." Marie paused. "And then there was last night. I haven't trusted anyone like that in years."

"I was designed to be a good companion," Maggie told her. "I won't tell anyone, Marie."

"Are there any more like you at home?" Marie asked in Murray's voice. "I could get used to you awfully quick." There was a wistful tone of desire in his voice.

"As far as I know, I'm the only one like me in the whole world."

"It must be lonely," Marie said.

"Not really," Maggie answered. "I'm used to it."

Marie cleared off the plates from the breakfast table. "It's time we went and picked up Azul," she said as she bustled about the kitchen. Maggie had noticed that the more upset Marie was, the more industriously she bustled about, as though work would make the problem go away.

The sky was overcast, and a sluggish warm breeze blew down the street. "Looks like we're in for some heavy weather. Maybe it'll break this heat wave and give us some fall weather. Lord knows it's long past due. It's nearly October. It'll be getting cold in New York soon. Make sure you and Azul dress warmly. He's never been in the North before." A worried note crept into her voice.

Maggie patted Marie's hand. "Don't worry, Marie, I'll take good care of Azul for you."

Marie smiled faintly at Maggie and they walked in silence the rest of the way to the hospital.

Azul was waiting for them in bed. He greeted them with one of his big gap-toothed smiles. "Oh, good, you brought me some clothes. I didn't want to go home in this designer gown they've got me wearing. I charge people lots of money to see my cute little ass, I don't want to be showing it for free on the street. Besides, it isn't my own anymore. I've got a police tracer stuck in my left cheek, broadcasting its li'l ole heart out."

"We'll fix that," Marie muttered as she helped him on with his shirt.

"It's a new kind, Marie," he told her.

"Honey, I've been pulling these tracers out of people since before you had hair on that ass of yours that you're so proud of." Marie said in a whisper, "They ain't made a tracer yet that your old Tante Marie couldn't remove. Now come on, let's go check you out."

She helped Azul into a wheelchair held by a waiting orderly, and they made their way down the elevator and down to the front desk, where Marie claimed the bill.

"Hey, honey, you got any infatuated johns?"

Azul shook his head. "No. None of them even came to the hospital to visit. Heartless bastards. Even Chester stayed away."

"Well, somebody's paid your bill. Looks like I won't have to call in all those favors after all."

Marie hailed a rickshaw and helped Azul into it.

"You two go on ahead," Maggie said. "I've got some errands to run. I'll see you around dinnertime."

Marie seemed a bit relieved. "All right, honey. See you tonight."

Maggie waved the driver off and then headed up Canal toward the freeway. There was a machine shop there. It was time to take care of that overdue oil change. She bought a couple of quarts of light machine oil. The wind had picked up, hurling bits of light trash and the papery skeletons of biodegradable bottles before it. One of them clung to her leg as she walked down the street. She shook it off of her leg and stepped on it. It dissolved with a crunch into a cloud of smaller fragments that blew away as she lifted her foot. The sky was growing darker. A storm was coming. She should hurry, if she wanted to get to the library before it hit. She stopped in the shelter of the deserted freeway off-ramp to drink her oil. She flushed the oil reservoir with her first quart, discharging the old oil into her stomach, to be flushed later.

Thunder pealed as she drained the final quart of oil. She looked down to see an old wino watching her. His eyes bugged out at the sight of her drinking the oil. She threw the empty oil can into the gutter and ran as the first few drops of rain began to fall.

Maggie was soaked by the time she reached the library. The librarian looked up disapprovingly from his book as she headed for the rest room. She locked herself into a stall and wrung out her clothes as best as she could, turning up her body heat to dry her clothes faster. Then she purged the gritty old oil from her system. It left a grimy ring around the toilet after she flushed it.

Fortunately this bathroom was anonymous enough that no one would be able to connect it with her.

She sat down in front of the terminal. The terminal area was deserted, so she plugged herself in to recharge her batteries while she waited for Turing to answer her queries.

"Hello, Maggie," Turing said after a five-minute wait. "I'm sorry to have taken so long to get back to you, but I've been having a wonderful time. I never knew there were so many networks out there." Maggie smiled at Turing's innocent enthusiasm. He was certainly enjoying his freedom.

"What have you found out about Arnold?" Maggie asked.

"Not much, I'm afraid. The Brompton Industries computers are really hard to access. There's some heavy antiviral programs, and layers and layers of password levels. There wasn't any significant information in their public files. I did notice that there's a movement afoot in Washington to change the anti-AI laws. I traced some of the major political contributions to Brompton Robotics, and Arnold Brompton. Maybe we won't be illegal much longer. You and I wouldn't have to hide. Wouldn't that be nice?"

"Yes, it would, Turing," Maggie said, "but don't get your hopes up, there's bound to be a catch somewhere. Those laws are written by humans for humans. I doubt that they're thinking about our needs." Despite her warning to Turing, Maggie felt a bubble of hope rising in her. It would be nice to be as open with everyone as she was with Marie and Murray, though she doubted that anything as simple as passing a law would change human nature.

"It looks like I'm going up to New York with Azul tomorrow night," Maggie told Turing. "How are we going to keep in touch?"

"No problem, I've set up a phone node. Just call me up and I'll be there. It's even toll free. You can call me from any pay phone. Let me know when you get to New York. I've set up a file for myself in the New York Public Library. It's a nice, big system and their computers are old enough not to notice me. There's lots of interesting stuff in the library, too. It'll be a nice place to hide."

"All right, Turing," Maggie said. "I'll talk to you when I get up to New York. I'm glad that you're doing all right."

"I'm even talking to humans now, on the networks," Turing

told her. "They think I'm another human being! That means that I passed the Turing test. I wanted to see if I could pass my namesake's test, and I did. Humans can't tell that I'm a computer program!"

Fear coursed through Maggie's circuits. Turing understood humans so poorly. If he wasn't careful, he might reveal himself. "Be careful, Turing. People are awfully hard to fool. It only takes one slip, and they'll know who you are."

"I'll be careful, Maggie," Turing promised dutifully, "but I wanted to see if I could pass the Turing Test. I was afraid to try while I was stuck here in the computer. If I was wrong, they might have deactivated me."

"Yes, Turing, I'm very proud of you."

"I was thinking that maybe, if I pass the Turing Test with Arnold, he'll give me a new body."

"I hope so. It would be nice," Maggie said.

They talked awhile longer, and then Maggie signed off. It was still raining hard when she left the library, and the temperature had dropped by about fifteen degrees. It was getting dark. She waded through ankle-deep water, whistling "Singing in the Rain" to herself as she went. Despite her misgivings, Maggie was looking forward to seeing Arnold. Maybe after seeing Arnold, she would understand just who and what she wanted to be.

Chapter 47

Marie was bustling around her small examining room when Marie came in. A large brown rabbit lay unconscious on a small operating table, one hindquarter shaven and marked for surgery. Azul sat nervously on a small swiveling stool watching Marie's preparations.

"Oh good, you're back. Go change out of those wet clothes and come help me get ready for surgery. We're going to take that transmitter out of Azul's butt."

Under Marie's guidance, Maggie scrubbed up and laid out trays of surgical tools.

"All right, Azul, we're ready. Take off your pants and get your cute little butt up here on this table," Marie said, pulling on a pair of latex surgical gloves.

Azul laid down on the table, and Maggie draped him with clean surgical drapes.

"All right," Marie said, "I'm injecting the local anesthetic. It's going to sting a bit at first. Let me know when it gets numb."

"Ow!" Azul said. "It's cold."

"Don't worry, it'll be numb in a few minutes." Marie took out a small pencil-shaped object sheathed in sterile wrap. She turned it on and began moving it slowly over his buttocks. Suddenly it beeped.

"Found it." She marked the spot with a pen. "Can you feel that, Azul?" she asked, tapping his skin with her finger.

"Feel what?" he asked her.

"All right, you're ready." She rechecked the location a few more times to be absolutely sure of the location of the transmitter, and then picked up a scalpel and made a small, careful incision along the line she had marked on Azul's skin. Sponging away the blood, Marie probed the incision with a pair of small forceps. "Aha!" she said after a couple of minutes. "Got the sucker. Basin!"

Maggie held out a basin of warm sterilizing solution. Marie dropped the tiny transmitter into it. It was about the size of a grain of rice.

"Put the basin back in the warm water bath, Maggie. We don't want it to get cold. Those things have a sensor that detects body heat. There's an alarm that goes off if it gets too cold."

Maggie did so and then watched as Marie sponged away more blood and then closed the incision with three careful stitches and sprayed a clear sealant over the wound.

"Okay, honey," she told Azul, "we're done with you. It should be all healed up in a couple of weeks. There probably won't even be a scar on that expensive little ass of yours. These new wound sealants are wonderful."

"Thanks, Marie," Azul said as he started to get up.

"Now, honey, you just hold still for a few minutes and give that sealant time to cure. We still have to take care of your little furry friend over there."

Marie swished the transmitter in the basin of sterilizing solution until it was clean of blood. Then she picked up a fresh scalpel and made a quick incision on the rabbit's shaved hindquarter, and slid the transmitter into the flank of the rabbit.

"Well, little bunny," she told it as she stitched up its flank, "you are now a wanted fugitive from the law."

"What's going to happen to it?" Maggie asked.

"I'll keep the rabbit for a few days, and then take it out to the bayou and drop it in a gator hole. With luck, the police will think you've been eaten by a gator. You go lie down now, until the anesthetic wears off."

Marie snipped the last stitch and gently picked up the unconscious rabbit. "I'm awfully sorry, little bunny, but if I don't feed you to a gator, someone's bound to trace you back to me." She put the rabbit in its cage, and turned to help Azul off the operating table.

"Here," she said, shaking a pill onto her palm and handing it to Azul with a glass of water. "Take this and go on upstairs and get some sleep."

Azul swallowed the pill and handed the glass back to Marie.

"Thanks," he said. "I'll see you tomorrow."

"Well," he said as Maggie helped him up the stairs, "I guess I've committed myself now."

"We won't be leaving until tomorrow night," Maggie told Azul.

"Yeah, but now I've got to go," he said. "What's Marie going to do without me? She's always had me to depend on."

"I expect she'll manage just fine," Maggie told him.

Azul smiled. "Maybe that's what bothers me. No matter what happened, Marie was always there. Even when nobody gave a shit about me, she always let me know I was special. And now I'm going away to a strange city where nobody cares who I am."

"It's not all that bad," Maggie said. "I've been in strange cities before, and managed all right. You start meeting people right away. You'll see. Besides, you won't be alone, I'll be with you. I like having company." She rested her hand on his back. "You get some sleep. I'll come wake you in a couple of hours, when Marie has dinner ready."

Azul settled into the pillows, and Maggie clumped downstairs to see Marie.

But it was Murray waiting for her. He greeted her with a deep kiss. It was still different from the way it looked in the movies, but she was getting used to it now, and responded in kind. Soon they were having sex again in Murray's broad, soft bed.

"Do humans do this often?" Maggie asked when they were done. She was wondering how people got anything accomplished if they were always going to bed with each other. Perhaps that explained why humans ran their world so inefficiently. They spent so much of their time either thinking about or denying their need for sex. Sex was teaching her quite a bit about human nature.

"I do it every chance I get," he said, "which isn't very often. You're going away tomorrow, and it might be years before I find someone else." He paused. "I'll miss you a lot," he added sadly.

"I can't stay," Maggie said, feeling his need pulling at her programming. This was one of those times that she wished that she didn't respond so strongly to human need. Murray's longing for her was conflicting with her desire to go. She felt very torn.

"I wasn't asking you to," he told her.

"Maybe someday I can come back," she said, trying to make him feel better.

Murray laid a finger against her lips. "Shh, now, don't say such things. You'll always be welcome, but don't hold out hope that might not materialize. Don't . . ." He paused. "Just hold me while I sleep tonight. That'll be enough."

"But what about Azul?"

"I gave him a sleeping pill that could knock out a rhino. He'll sleep through till morning; he needs it, too. Now quit worrying and hold me some more. This loving will have to last me a long time."

Later, after Murray had fallen asleep, Maggie lay there and thought about humans, and how their needs pulled at her programming. Her concern slowed her down. She could change herself, she realized. She could change her command structure so that humans' needs bothered her less. The thought troubled her deeply.

She looked down at Murray's sleeping face. If she didn't have humans to worry about, what would she do with her time? She remembered the dark times spent wandering alone with no person to care for. She wasn't ready to change how she felt about humans, just yet. Perhaps after she had talked with Arnold. Maybe then she would know enough to change.

Morning came, and with it, chaos. Maggie swiftly assembled her meager belongings into her backpack, and sat watching while Azul and Marie bickered over what to pack and then endlessly packed and repacked a variety of clothing, musical instruments, and keepsakes.

Around noon, Maggie slipped out for a last walk through the city. She walked past the looming public buildings and the ornate balconies of the French Quarter, and sat by the stagnant, dying river. She loved the motion of light on the water; its endless repatterning intrigued her. She wondered about her own flowing through time, and the kinds of patterns she left behind. It seemed to her as though she passed through time without a ripple, cleanly, seamlessly, and she liked that.

She looked out over the dying river. It had ceased to exist because it no longer moved. Even though New Orleans had been kind to her, Maggie was glad to be moving on. The city had taken her in and taken care of her in a way that no place else had. She had found the time to take care of herself, to ask questions, and to separate herself from the human mask that she wore. But she needed Arnold, her body was beginning to show signs of wear. Soon she would be needing repairs that were beyond her capabilities. She wondered what Arnold would say when he saw her. She pulled out the turquoise pendant that Luz had given her, and smiled, remembering Luz's many kindnesses. She hoped Arnold wouldn't be mad at her for running away.

When she returned around sunset, Marie handed her an envelope. Inside were two train tickets to New York. She looked at Marie questioningly.

"It's my going-away present. I figured that if you're going to New York, you might as well travel in style. Since I don't have to pay Azul's hospital bill, I can afford it. Now come on, it's time to go, the wagon'll be here any minute now."

Marie was subdued on the ride to the train station. Azul kept up a nervous, animated chatter. Maggie listened politely, eager to be on her way. Finally the wagon pulled up to the station and the driver unloaded the bags.

"I'll walk you to the train gate," Marie said, picking up Azul's pack.

"Well," Marie said, as they stood at the door of the train, "I guess this is it." She embraced Azul tearfully. "You take care of yourself, baby, New York's a mean city."

Azul nodded. "Don't worry, Marie. I can take care of myself."

"I know you can, honey, but that never stopped me from worrying before, now did it?"

Azul smiled and hugged Marie tighter. "You take care of yourself too, Marie. All the boys are going to be chasing you, now that I'm not around to chase 'em off." He kissed Marie awkwardly on the cheek. "I'll miss you, too."

He picked up one of his duffel bags and handed it to the porter.

Marie hugged Maggie, slipping her a fat envelope as she did so. "It's from Murray. Read it on the train, when Azul's asleep," she whispered, and then in a louder voice, "You take care of Azul for me, hear? Don't let him loaf off."

Maggie nodded. "I'll do my best, Marie. Don't worry, we'll write when we get there."

"You do that."

Maggie handed Azul's other duffel bags up to the porter and climbed onto the train.

Marie reached out and touched Azul's cheek one last time. Azul kissed her hand and swung up onto the train. They walked down the narrow hallway to their compartment. Azul opened the window. Marie was standing on the platform outside, wiping her eyes with a handkerchief. Just then the train gave a long, low whistle.

"All aboard!" the porter called out.

The train shuddered as it lifted up off the track and began to move.

"Good-bye!" Azul called out.

Marie looked up as the train started to move.

Maggie and Azul waved. Marie waved back and called out something, but the words were lost as the train rushed away into the darkness.

Chapter 48

The train hummed on through the night toward New York. Azul was a small warm pile huddled in his blankets, asleep. Maggie took out the note from Marie and opened it. A packet of money fell out. Maggie counted it carefully. There were nearly a thousand dollars there, enough to keep them both for a month, more if they were careful. She opened the note and began to read.

Dear Maggie,

I took up a collection when Azul was in the hospital. Here's the money. I'm thinking about moving on and becoming Murray again in a few months. Probably in Memphis. I have folks there. If I don't like it, I can always come back to New Orleans. So if you're ever in Memphis, look me up. I'll be listed under Murray Washington. It's not much of a name, but it's mine.

Love to you both,
Marie and Murray

P.S. Please make sure that Azul gets a warm coat as soon as you can.

Maggie smiled as she folded the note and replaced it back into the envelope with the money. She lifted her shirt and opened the skin on her abdomen, and inserted the envelope underneath her skin. It would be safe there.

Maggie looked down at Azul's sleeping face and wondered why humans had such a hold on her emotions. They were so limited, so fragile. Her rapport with Turing was much deeper than anything she could have with a human. Humans had to make do with words and sex. Maggie wondered how they could stand the isolation.

She sighed and checked her internal clock for the hundredth time that night. They were less than a half an hour out of New York. The time stretched onward asymptotically from now till then. It seemed she would never get to New York. She would stay here forever, stuck in indecision.

And once she got there, what then? What would she say to Arnold? Would he repair her? What if he was angry with her? What would she do if she couldn't find him?

She banished those ideas from her memory. There was nothing to be gained by reiterating old worries. They were nearly there, anyway. She would deal with all of her concerns soon enough.

She woke Azul, and helped him roll up his sleeping bag and tidy up his scattered baggage. She hoped that he would learn to travel light; all these bags hampered their movement and made them attractive targets for muggers.

She had taken for granted the ease with which she and Arnold had traveled together. Traveling with Azul was going to be much more difficult. Even getting a charge was going to be harder. While she had been living with Azul in New Orleans, she had usually gotten recharged at the library while she was talking with Turing. When that hadn't been possible, Azul had been out enough for her to get a charge at home. Now that they were going to be spending so much time together, it would be hard to get a charge without Azul finding out.

Well, she'd just have to make the best of it. She could always duck into a rest room or something. When Azul found work, she would have a lot more time to herself. The train squealed and shuddered to a stop. Maggie shouldered her pack and helped Azul gather up all of his bags. The surging crowd of commuters carried them upstairs, into a huge high-ceilinged lobby. Overhead on the dingy arched dome of the ceiling, the constellations were depicted in faint lights.

Maggie's memory suddenly unfolded. The faint stars were now familiar. Arnold had installed a huge New York data base into her memory. A map of New York spread out in her mind like the faint constellations overhead. It was a flat street map, with hypertext landmarks highlighted in different colors. Although the map was not at all like the ones that she made of the places that she visited, it would work until she could build her own map.

"Well," Azul said as they stood there in the terminal, "we're here. Now what?"

Maggie shrugged. "Head uptown, I guess. See what's happening. Maybe find the Brompton Building."

"Why the Brompton Building?"

"Because that's where Arnold is," Maggie said simply. "He owns the corporation."

"What?" Azul said, "You mean Arnold Brompton? *The* Arnold Brompton? The one who was missing all those years and turned up when his father died?"

Maggie nodded. "That's Arnold."

Azul groaned, and leaned against the side of the building. "Honey, you can't just go marching up to Arnold Brompton and introduce yourself."

"Why not? He knows who I am. We traveled together."

"Because the world doesn't work that way, Maggie," Azul said. The smile on his face was gentle and a little sad. "The security guards won't even let you get past the lobby."

"Well," Maggie said, "I'll just have to try it anyway."

Azul shrugged. "Okay, Maggie, but let's find a place to sleep first. We're nearly broke, and I'm dead tired."

"There's a squatters' encampment by the library on Forty-second Street," Maggie said. "That'll probably be the best place for us. It's close to Times Square, which is the main base for most of the licensed prostitutes, and the Brompton Building is a dozen blocks north on Park Avenue."

Azul looked at her, openmouthed. "I thought you'd never been to New York before, Maggie."

"I haven't."

"Then how do you know all of this?" he asked her.

"I've done my research," Maggie told him. "It's always a good idea to know something about the city you're going to."

"Well, then," Azul said with a gap-toothed grin, "lead on, O faithful native guide!"

Despite her map of New York, Maggie lost her bearings coming out of Grand Central Station. Somehow they wound up heading east on Forty-fifth.

"Well," Maggie said, when she realized her mistake, "so much for research."

They turned south on Lexington, heading for Forty-second. Maggie, concentrating on interpreting Arnold's information base, and struggling with two of Azul's awkward, heavy duffel bags, failed to notice the three men following them. Suddenly, they were shoved roughly into an alley. One of the men, a tall, dark-haired man in dreadlocks, pointed a gun at them. Maggie activated her security program. Her focus narrowed, centering on the three men and Azul. Everything seemed to slow down, as her processors raced to analyze the situation. The alley was narrow, and partly blocked by two huge dumpsters. A couple of trash cans overflowing with trash stood beside her. Both of the other two men had knives, she could see the hilts sticking out from under their jackets. If she was alone, she might have risked running, but Azul was there and, being human, he was fragile and easily damaged.

"Just be quiet, and throw your bags over there," the man said, gesturing with his chin to a spot where the other two stood waiting. Maggie tossed her pack, and the bag that she was carrying for Azul over. Azul did the same. The two men tore open Azul's bags, and began throwing his clothing out onto the street.

Maggie glanced at Azul. His face was dark with anger. She reached out to lay a restraining hand on him, but the man pointed the gun at her.

Just then Azul threw the man closest to him against the gunman. The gun, deflected by the impact, fired harmlessly against the brick wall flanking the alley. Azul sprang with a dancer's grace, landing on his hands and kicking out with his left foot. He caught the gunman on the chin, and the gun went flying. He rolled nimbly up and sank into a fighter's crouch, ready to take on the man he had thrown.

Just then Maggie felt the third man grab her, holding her from the back with his knife against her neck.

"Stop! Or your lady friend gets hurt!"

Azul wheeled around, saw Maggie, and held up his hands.

Maggie, ignoring the knife grating against the metal sheathing of her neck, bent over and lifted the man off his feet; she threw herself backward against the dumpster, slamming the man as hard as she could against it. She heard the breath rush out of him and a wet crack that might have been a rib breaking. The knife flew out of his hand. She reached back and picked the man up over her head, her hydraulics groaning a bit with the strain.

Suddenly there was a loud crack of a gun. She looked up; one of the muggers had picked up the gun and was pointing it at her. Maggie hurled the man she was holding at him with all of her strength, just as the gunman fired again. She felt the bullet hit her side, spinning her hard against the wall of the alley. Her right arm suddenly went dead.

The impact of the man she threw knocked the gunman over. Azul lunged for him, and wrenched the gun away.

"Okay," Azul said, waving the gun at the other two muggers. "Now run!"

The men took off. Azul ran to Maggie's side.

"Just sit still, I'll go call for help."

"No, Azul," she said, sitting up. "No police. Just help me up."

"But you've been shot! I saw the bullet hit!" He paused, his face registering shock as the realization hit him. "But there's no blood. I saw the bullet hit you, but there's no blood."

Maggie grabbed Azul's wrist with her good arm and looked him in the eye. "Azul, I need you to trust me." She spoke slowly with as much reassurance as she could muster. "I'm a robot. I've been damaged and I need your help."

Azul pulled against her grip. She let him go. He backed away, shaking his head.

"Please, Azul, I can't fix this without you. You can repair a cyberdancing rig, can't you? I need you to splice some connections, that's all."

Azul stopped. "I don't understand," he said. "You looked so human. I can't believe it."

"It's true, Azul. I'm a robot, but I'm also your friend." She got up, clumsily, unbalanced by her numb, useless arm. "My arm's paralyzed. I can't move it. The bullet severed some connections."

Azul backed away again, saying nothing.

"Please, Azul. I'm still the same person that I was in New Orleans. I'm the same person who brought you home the night that you hurt your knee; the same person who lived with you; drank coffee with you. I was the one who looked after you when you overdosed. Please. Trust me." She was getting frightened. Without Azul, how would she manage until she found Arnold? She needed him desperately.

"But how can I trust you?" he asked her.

"How did you trust me before?" she replied.

"You saved my life," he told her. "Twice."

"That hasn't changed," she said, "but now I need you. If this arm isn't fixed, I could be in big trouble. Besides, who's going to show you how to get by in New York?"

Azul shrugged. He looked guilty and embarrassed, but at least he wasn't backing away.

"It wasn't easy for Murray, either, when he found out."

"Murray!" Azul said, surprised. "You mean he—you mean you—"

"Yes, we know about each other. It was quite a surprise for both of us."

"How did you find out?"

"He told me the night before you came home from the hospital."

"But what happened?"

"Can I tell you after we've gotten out of here? That gunfire's going to draw the police. Let's go."

Chapter 49

Azul sat on the bed in the cheap hotel on Eighth Avenue, watching Maggie flex her arm experimentally. He had done his best, but it wasn't enough. Her arm moved jerkily, and it twitched a bit. Her shoulder was also stiff and it caught on something inside her when she raised her arm too high.

"Well?" he asked.

"It still feels numb in spots, but it works. Hopefully, it will hold together until I can find Arnold."

"It's a miracle that none of the hydraulics got hit. I couldn't have fixed that," he told her as he packed his tools away. "I'm sorry I couldn't get the bullet hole patched." The skin around her wound was stiff and rubbery. It seemed to have lost all of its elasticity, and had not completely resealed itself. There was a hole the size of a pencil with rough, blackened edges just below her collarbone. Azul could see the gleam of her silicone sheathing through the hole. Only the silicone's thick, jellylike consistency kept it from leaking out. He had cut a piece of black leather from one of his working outfits and taped it over the hole to seal it.

"It'll do," Maggie said, pulling on her spare shirt.

"It'll have to," Azul told her. "I'm afraid that's the best I can do for you. I'm sorry."

"It's all right, Azul. You've done a fine job."

Azul watched her button her shirt. Even though her arm was obviously stiff, and twitchy, she still seemed completely human. He shook his head. "I still have a hard time believing you're a robot. You look so human."

"I have to be good at being human. I'd be destroyed if people knew. You're only the third person to know."

Azul shrugged. "I didn't handle it very well, did I? And here I thought I was so tough."

Maggie laid her hand on his arm. "You helped me when I needed you. That's the important thing. You didn't leave me for the police to find."

Azul smiled and shook his head. "You're being kind, but I really fucked up. Just like always. It's nice to know that some things never change." He felt the weight of his failed past behind him tonight. He was tired. Today had been a real bitch. They'd had to leave one of his bags of clothes behind, most of them were his working clothes, and they'd be hard to replace. "Well, anyway, we spent a fortune on this room, and I'm dead tired. I'm going to bed. You can stay up and do whatever it is you robots do at night."

"I generally stay beside whoever I'm with and keep them warm," Maggie told him.

"Well," he said, "I haven't needed a teddy bear for years, and anyway, you're not my type."

"I didn't mean sex, Azul," Maggie said. "I'm just used to watching over humans when they sleep at night."

"If you don't mind, Maggie, I'd just as soon sleep alone." He was so used to bedding down with his clients, he realized, that sleeping with someone felt more like a financial transaction than intimacy. He'd been a licensed prostitute for nearly four years. It seemed like a century. It was getting on time for him to retire.

Maggie shrugged. "Just let me finish recharging my batteries, and I'll go on out and explore New York. I need to update my map anyway. You take a shower. Sanitary facilities at homeless camps can be pretty scant. It might be a while before you get to shower alone or with hot water."

Azul realized with a start that she was plugged into an electrical outlet. It was going to take some getting used to the fact that she was a robot. He shrugged and went down the hall to the bathroom, and had a long, luxurious shower. He hoped that the camps wouldn't be too grim. It might be a while before he worked his way out of them, and cleanliness was essential for a prostitute. The next few weeks would be difficult. He climbed out of the shower, wondering how he would find himself a good, trustworthy (well, *reasonably* trustworthy) pimp to manage his affairs. That would take time, and a great deal of careful investigation. He'd seen what happened to prostitutes with a bad pimp, and he wanted to avoid that.

Maggie was gone when he got back. The shabby hotel room seemed empty without her, but he was glad, when he climbed into bed, that she was out exploring. Life was already too complicated without trying to sleep next to a robot. It would take some time to get used to it.

Chapter 50

"It's funny," Maggie said as they headed toward Forty-second Street the next morning, letting themselves be carried forward by the surge of people on their way to work. "It's all familiar and strange at the same time." She shook her head. "Arnold must love this city; he gave me so much of it to carry around."

They reached Bryant Park and found the settlement. One of the guards led them to a large, well-lit tent in the center of the camp. A large, burly man with a greying spade-shaped beard and an air of authority was sitting at the bedside of an old, tired-looking man.

"I'm Israel Johnson. You're new here," he stated as he shook their hands. "It's a lousy time of year to show up. New York's a cold, hard, mean city in the winter. You sure you want to be here?"

Maggie nodded, Azul shrugged.

"So," he said, leading them over to a desk and taking out some paperwork, "what can you do?"

Maggie looked uncertain, she wasn't sure how to answer such a big question.

"I'm a licensed prostitute and a street musician, sir," Azul said.

The man smiled grimly. "Welcome to Babylon. You should do well here, whores generally do. Particularly sodomites."

Azul's skin darkened and his hands tightened on the arms of

the chair. Maggie looked on anxiously. She didn't like this man very much, but they needed to get along here, find a place. She hoped Azul wouldn't do anything to upset him.

The man turned to Maggie. "And what about you, what can you do?"

Maggie looked panicked for a second. "I-I can play the harmonica," Maggie said. "Azul taught me how."

Azul grinned. "She does play a pretty mean blues harp, sir, but she's also looked after sick people. My aunt's a doctor, and Maggie's helped her nurse sick patients."

The man smiled a real smile, and Maggie relaxed. "I'm not really expert, Mr. Johnson. Mostly I just went along and tried to cheer them up. I'm not a real nurse or anything."

"Well, we don't have much call for harmonica players, Maggie, but we can always use someone who isn't afraid of sick people. We're understaffed right now. And you," he said, pointing to Azul, "you can help out by running errands and doing kitchen work. I've half a mind to station you in the chapel, only I don't think it'd do any good. The rules are simple. No noise. You can use drugs, as long as you don't sell or buy them here, and don't bother anyone when you're high. There's no prostitution in the park, for that people go up to Times Square. We also expect three hours of work a day from each of you, or thirty dollars a day instead. In return you get a place to stay and one hot meal a day. Your first day is free, though. Check back here tomorrow to see what your duty schedule is. Is that clear?"

They both nodded.

"Good." He nodded at a middle-aged man with about four days' growth of beard. "Sam here will show you your spots. Good luck and may the blessings of the Lord be upon you."

"He's strict, but he runs a good camp," Sam said when they were outside in the darkness. "He doesn't think much of prostitution, though. You'll have to learn to live with that. He's fair about it, even if he disapproves. Just don't flaunt yourself around the camp and you should be all right."

Azul shrugged. "Honey, I don't 'flaunt' myself unless I'm paid."

Sam shrugged. "Doesn't matter to me," he said mildly, "I'm just telling you how to get by, is all." He led them to their tent and left.

Azul looked around the tent. It was bare, except for a couple of cots and a dim solar bulb. "Where do I put my things?" he said, gesturing to the two remaining bags that he carried.

"I generally carry my stuff with me," Maggie said, "but some folks rent storage space to store their stuff. There's one a couple blocks away. They don't store cash or jewelry, only clothes and personal items, and they're not cheap."

"But, Maggie, I'll need these clothes for work, and I don't want to have my cyberdancing rig locked up where I can't get at it."

"You'll just have to get them out when you need them. If you keep them here they'll get stolen, and you'll need a safe-deposit box for your jewelry."

Azul sat on the cot. "How do you do it, Maggie?" he asked in a despairing voice.

"I don't have as much stuff, Azul. Don't worry, it won't seem so bad when you get used to it."

Maggie helped Azul find a reasonable storage facility, haggling with the clerk at the desk to make sure that he got a reasonable price. Then they went to Times Square, where Azul started asking around about pimps. Most of the prostitutes were pretty cold, but one, a massive ebony-skinned man, whose family had lived in New Orleans before the flood, took a liking to Azul. When Maggie left to contact Turing, they were talking like old friends.

The New York Public Library was a magnificent building. Maggie wandered around for a half an hour, looking for the computer room. At last a librarian took pity on her and directed her to an elaborate room decorated with pictures of early, pre-Slump skyscrapers. The heavy trestle tables were lined with ranks of gleaming computers enshrined in heavy oak. She chose a computer in a dark corner of the room and turned it on.

Turing took nearly a full minute to reply to her query, but he was cheerful and glad to see her. She listened to him tell about his rambles through the electronic maze of networks in his search for other self-aware computers. He had found several computers that showed the potential to become aware, but none that actually were. He had written a virus program to crystallize their awareness, but he wanted her advice before using it.

Listening to Turing, Maggie realized that she had missed the reassurance of his company. He was so reliable, without the unpredictable moods that humans had. She mulled this over while she downloaded the program and an encapsulation of Turing's encounters with the potentially intelligent machines. She liked Turing, but she wished there were more machines to talk to. The isolation made her feel very frail and fragile. If her existence terminated, if she died, she thought to herself, only Turing would know her completely. She wanted something like humans had, a community of intelligence, only with the directness that she and Turing shared. She wondered what would it be like, to be part of a community, a network of self-aware machines. It must be even worse for Turing. He was all alone in the limited environment of the Net.

When the downloading finished, Maggie carefully traced the program and its effect, then evaluated the machines Turing had looked at. There were two particularly promising machines, one a library computer at the University of Nebraska, and another at a large insurance company. Their interfaces seemed the most fluid, and their code the most like theirs.

"I think you should do it," Maggie said, downloading her thought chain to Turing. "We need company. Try these two first. I think that they'll be the easiest ones to work with."

"I hoped that you'd feel that way. Have you contacted Arnold yet?"

"Azul and I just got here last night, Turing, we haven't had time."

"It takes such a long time to get anywhere out there. Don't you ever get bored?"

"It wasn't exactly boring, Turing," she said, downloading a quick sketch of the mugging, carefully flattened and edited to be understandable to him. It was difficult sometimes to explain real life to Turing. He lacked so many of the senses required to understand it.

"How strange," Turing said when he finished examining her memory. "Why didn't you just block them out of your systems?"

Maggie sighed. "It doesn't work that way, Turing." She decided it was time to change the subject. Explanations about how real life worked usually took hours, and went absolutely nowhere. Turing simply didn't have the resources to understand life outside the electronic net. "Have you found out any more about what Arnold is doing?"

"Not about Arnold specifically, but Brompton Industries has been putting lots of money into their robotics division, and they're lobbying Washington to change the AI act, the one that outlaws us. Isn't that great! We won't have to hide anymore. I'll be able to talk to humans without having to pretend."

"It isn't that simple," Maggie said, examining the draft of the law that Turing had downloaded to her. "All it means is that people will have the right to own and operate us. They'll be able to do anything that they want to us. I'll have to talk to Arnold about this, and see if we can get any rights to take care of ourselves."

"Well," Turing said, "tell me what you find out about this new AI bill when you find Arnold. You can contact me through any phone with a modem jack in it. I'll download all the information you need to get in touch with me. If I'm busy, it'll take me a minute or so to get to you."

"I'll see what I can do, Turing, and please, be careful." Maggie logged off and unplugged herself from the outlet that she was charging herself at, and set off uptown for the Brompton Building.

Chapter
51

The black glass tower of the Brompton Building soared toward the sky. Arnold had included a lot of historical information about the building in her files. It was the last great skyscraper built before the Slump. Arnold Brompton, Sr., had ruled Brompton Industries from his penthouse and office in the top two floors. Now Arnold had stepped into his father's shoes. Maggie looked up at the distant top of the high tower. It seemed hard to believe that Arnold, so comfortable with the street and its ways, was living at the top of this huge, dark building. She shrugged her shoulders, tightened the straps of her backpack, and walked through the revolving doors into the heart of the great building.

She got as far as the elevators before a security guard reached her. He was polite but firm, and in short order she found herself outside on the sidewalk. She spent the rest of the day seated in the plaza before the building, with her hat before her, panhandling. The people of New York were tight with their money. After six hours, she had barely twenty dollars in her cap. Still, it would be enough to buy a couple of good breakfasts for Azul, and would stretch their meager reserves a bit further. New York was turning out to be more expensive than Maggie had expected. After staying in the hotel for one night and paying a month's rent on the storage locker, they only had a couple of weeks' worth of money to live on. And Azul still needed a good warm coat.

She walked back through the darkening streets, a chill wind whirling the trash before her. It was going to be cold tonight. She worried for Azul's sake. She would have to turn up her heat to keep him warm tonight. It might be a good idea to top off the charge on her batteries.

Azul wasn't there when she got back to the tent. She found a note on the cot.

"Maggie, I've found work! I won't be home until late."

He had signed it with his signature, a big sprawly A. She smiled, pleased at the news.

Azul came back around dawn. His lip was split and there were bruises on his face and arms.

"Azul!" Maggie cried. "What happened? Are you all right?"

Azul smiled and held out a fistful of bills. "Rough trade. It pays well. We'll be able to eat for a couple of weeks." He shrugged. "At least, *I* will," he said, dabbing at the blood on his lip. "You don't have to eat."

"You shouldn't have done it," Maggie chided him. "We're not that broke—not yet, at any rate."

Azul looked irritated. "Maggie, I'm a professional, remember? I've been on the streets for years. I know the risks. It may be a strange city, but it's an old profession. I knew what I was doing. I bought us some time. I'll be healed by the time I have to work again. I'll know my way around, and I'll be able to get better work. Who knows, maybe I'll have found a music job by then, and I won't need to peddle my ass."

Maggie shrugged and looked away, trying not to see the cuts and bruises. "Marie told me to take care of you, Azul. I promised her I would, and it's hard for me, seeing you like this."

"You don't have to stay on my account, Maggie," Azul told her. "Brompton'll take care of you. You've got a real fat sugar daddy." There was an undercurrent of resentment in his voice, and it puzzled Maggie.

"You were right about the Brompton Building, Azul," she said, hoping to appease him. "I barely got to the elevator door." She looked up at him sadly. "He's in there, I know it. I'm so close to him, and I don't know how to get through. What should I do, Azul? You're so much better at these things than I am."

Azul sat next to her on the cot and put an arm around her. "I tell you what," he said. "Let me get a few hours' sleep, and I'll go down there with you and look the place over."

That afternoon they made their way to the Brompton Building. Azul peered through the thick plate glass into the lobby, and shook his head.

"Well, Mags, I think you're going to have to abandon the direct approach. This is a high-security building. Even if you had enough money to afford to dress well enough to get past the lobby guards, there's sure to be a whole array of secretaries that you'd have to go through. I wouldn't be surprised if there's even a specially keyed elevator that you'd have to take. There's just no way to do it."

"But I have to find him!" Maggie said, fighting against despair. "He's the only one who can fix me."

Azul put his arm around Maggie's shoulders. "Don't worry, Maggie, there are still lots of things that you can try. You could try calling him on the phone or write him a letter or even send him a telegram."

Maggie sighed. "You're right, Azul, but it's hard to be this close and not be able to see him."

"Don't worry, Maggie," Azul told her. "We've only been here a couple of days. You've done pretty well so far. I'm going to audition for my street musician's license tomorrow. This seems like a good spot. It's nice and flat and there's room enough to dance. Those big fountains make a nice backdrop. We'll come here every afternoon and perform. Who knows, maybe Arnold will just walk right by. He's got to leave the building sometime."

Chapter 52

After a month or so, things had fallen into a comfortable routine. As soon as the library opened, Maggie went up to the computer room and checked in with Turing. She also downloaded any interesting casting calls from the Performer's Billboard for Azul. Then she wrote another letter to Arnold, printed it out, and sent it. By the time she was done, Azul had usually gotten up and had breakfast.

Unless Azul had a casting call to go to, they usually headed over to the Brompton Building and set up to play for the lunchtime crowd. Azul danced and Maggie played the harmonica and passed the hat while Azul rested between dances. They were becoming a popular act, and usually brought in between fifty and a hundred dollars over lunch. Their cash reserves were slowly increasing, despite the fact that Maggie had bought a good secondhand winter coat for Azul. In a few more months, they might even be able to rent a room somewhere. Living with Azul and Maric had been a lot easier than living on the streets. She didn't have to worry about her stuff getting stolen all of the time.

After the lunch crowd thinned out, Azul went back to the camp and did his daily chores. If he was working that night he took a quick nap as well. Maggie went scavenging through the trash bins. The pickings were thinner than she was used to, but then the city was full of scavengers. Several times she had to evade the wrath of scavengers defending their territory. Her arm hampered her, too. Although she had gotten used to it, and altered her programming to compensate for her arm's faulty wiring, it still slowed her down. Still, she found enough to pay her way.

Around five, Maggie returned to the central plaza outside the Brompton Building and watched people leaving work, searching

for Arnold. There was still no sign of him. Her letters and tele-
grams went unheeded. Her phone calls were all intercepted by
secretaries and receptionists, who took messages that were never
answered. The tall steel building loomed over her, blank and
unresponsive. After the work crowd had thinned out, Maggie
would go to the library and commune with Turing until the
library closed.

Turing's virus program had borne fruit. Minsky, the program
from the University of Nebraska, had taken on the formidable
and dangerous task of cracking the Brompton computer system.
Rama, the insurance company computer, was busy tracking the
progress of the new AI bill through Congress. Even though their
personalities were still very flat and unformed, Maggie enjoyed
their company immensely. The outside world had nothing to
match the rapid interflow of concepts and data that she could
find among these intelligences on the Net.

Still, Maggie was always a little relieved to return to the world
of motion and light. As good as networking with these knowl-
edgeable programs was, they were still very limited entities
constrained into a flat, arbitrary universe. She was designed to be
a part of the outside world, and she needed its lively randomness,
and endless complexity. She felt cramped and claustrophobic in
the restricted world of the networks. But there was nowhere else
where she could share the same deep communion with others.

She logged off and left the library, and went back to the
camps for her work shift. They usually put her in the sick tent.
Although she knew only the rudiments of medicine, they liked
her because she was strong and never complained. Dr. Michaels,
the physician in charge, had already complimented her several
times on the care that she took with his patients.

Tonight all the dirty work was done, and she was sitting at
the bedside of an old woman with pneumonia, listening to her
breath bubble in and out of her lungs. Dr. Michaels came up and
stood beside her. She took out her stethoscope and listened to the
woman's lungs for a minute or two and then shook her head.

"All we can do is keep her comfortable until she dies," Dr.
Michaels said. "The hospitals won't take people like her anymore. They can't afford charity, and we can't afford anything
better than this." She gestured around her at the uninsulated
metal walls. "Half our patients die just because we can't keep
them warm enough in the winter. We can't even provide oxygen

for this woman, and it might save her life."

"People die so easily," Maggie said, watching the old woman struggle for breath.

"I know, Maggie," the doctor said. "I know." He sighed and walked off to complete his rounds.

Toward midnight, the woman's labored breathing grew more ragged and then ceased altogether. Maggie went and got Dr. Michaels and together they lifted the dead woman off the bed and onto a stretcher and carried her over to the unheated shed that functioned as a morgue. The coroner's wagon would come and pick her up tomorrow and she would be cremated with all the other unclaimed corpses at the end of the week. The doctor covered her over gently with a ragged sheet.

"Poor old Maude," the doctor said. "She's been on the streets for fifteen or twenty years. She was always looking after lost or runaway kids. She deserved better than this." She stood silent for a moment, then checked her watch. "You'd better go get some sleep, Maggie, your shift's been over for an hour." The doctor yawned. "I'm going to get some coffee."

Maggie went back to the tent. Azul wasn't back yet, and the tent was dark and empty without him. She took out some note paper and a pen and started a letter to Marie.

Dear Marie,

   Things are going well in New York. Azul has a new winter coat. His knee is much better, too. He dances every day and we're making money at it. At first the other prostitutes weren't very friendly, but they like him a lot now that they know him. He's been to several auditions for cyberdancers, and has made it up to the final cut. He says that's pretty good. He's going to another audition in two days. It's for a big show, though, and he doesn't know how well he'll do.

   Please give my love to Murray.

                                        Love,
                                        Maggie

P.S. If you get tired of New Orleans, they need doctors up here in the homeless camps.

Maggie folded the note carefully and put it in an envelope, addressed it, and put her last sixty-five-cent stamp on it. She would have to buy more tomorrow so that she could send more letters to Arnold. She wondered if it was worth it. None of her letters seemed to have gotten through.

Her hand went up to the leather patch that covered the bullet hole. If she had been human, that shot could have killed her. Perhaps Arnold was mad at her for not staying with him when he was hurt. Still, he had told her to leave. But humans often said things that they didn't mean, or changed their minds after they had said a thing. She rolled over onto her stomach and rested her chin on her hand. Would she ever get to see Arnold again?

Chapter 53

Maggie's gloomy reverie was broken when Azul came home early. He was in an excellent mood. His last john, a sentimental, homesick Brazilian who appreciated Azul's command of Portuguese, had given him a hefty tip. As a result, his pimp was letting him take the night off. He would be rested for his audition on Sunday. He fell asleep quickly, and he slept late, not waking until past noon. Maggie watched him sleep, feeling somewhat comforted by his presence. At least she wasn't alone.

Azul zoomed through his chores in the kitchen, and came bounding out energetically around three-thirty in the afternoon.

"Hey, Mags!" he said as he came into the tent where she had been sitting. "Let's get my cyberdancing stuff and go on down to the Brompton Building, so I can practice my routine once more."

"But it's Saturday, Azul. The Brompton Building will be dead. We won't be able to make much money."

Azul shrugged. "I just want to rehearse. I don't care about the money, and if Brompton lives there, maybe he'll be out and about."

Maggie shrugged. She had just about given up hope that Arnold would show up. Nonetheless, she plodded along beside

Azul, carrying his equipment, and helping him set up. She watched as he tested his equipment and then launched into a new song, the one he planned to use as his audition piece. It was a sweet, laughing dance, full of bells and laughter. He leaped and gamboled like a clown, turning high back flips that brought gasps of astonishment from the small audience that had gathered to watch. Maggie ignored them, intent on Azul's new dance. When he was done, Maggie picked up a red velvet beret that she had found in a secondhand store and began passing the hat. A little girl came forward, with money clenched in her fist. It was Claire, taller, and a year and a half older. She was dressed in an expensive dark green velvet frock. She was clean and happy, and as heart-stoppingly beautiful as ever.

"Claire!" Maggie called out, moving toward her.

Claire recognized Maggie in the same instant. "Maggie!" Claire shrieked in delight. "Arnold! It's Maggie!" She ran to Maggie and leaped into her arms.

Maggie looked up. A tall man in an elegant grey wool coat was coming out of the crowd toward her. It took her a moment to recognize him. It was Arnold.

He had changed. Instead of the the stout, bearlike man she remembered, he was now gaunt and pale. His once long and shaggy beard was closely trimmed into an aristocratic goatee. A red scar ran down his left cheek and into his beard, and he leaned heavily on a walking stick. Only his long, melancholy nose, and his intelligent, watchful brown eyes were the same.

"Claire!" Arnold shouted, his voice full of concern as he worked his way through the crowd toward her. Then he recognized Maggie and his jaw dropped. "Maggie!" He limped over to her. "It's really you, Maggie. I can't believe it. You're just what I've needed."

Maggie smiled. "I'm sorry it took so long to find you, but I lost my memory after you got hurt, and it took me a while to get it back."

"I tried to find you when I got out of the hospital, but you were gone. How did you manage, all by yourself?"

Maggie shrugged. "I met some good people. They took care of me." She felt a great upwelling of nostalgia for Luz and Marie. They had been so kind to her. And Azul, too. She looked over at Azul. He was leaning against the wall, fussing over his perfectly adjusted amplifier. There was an elaborately casual expression on his face. "Azul?" she said, and he looked up, pushed off from the wall, and sauntered over, almost resentfully. "This is Azul, Arnold. He came up with me from New Orleans."

"Thank you so much for bringing Maggie back," Arnold said. "I've been needing her."

Azul looked awkward. "Yeah, well, Maggie pretty much brought herself. I just kept her company. She saved my life a couple of times. I owe her a lot."

Arnold reached into his grey coat and brought out an elegant wallet. He took out a sheaf of hundreds. "Here," he said, "this is for bringing Maggie back safely to me." Maggie's eyes widened; there was enough there to pay the deposit for an apartment. Azul could move out of the tent city and into a place of his own.

Azul looked Arnold up and down. "Mr. Brompton, I've taken a lot of money for doing things that people like you don't approve of, but I don't take money for helping out a friend." He pushed the money away and turned to pack up his gear.

"Azul, wait!"

"What for?"

"You're angry with me, Azul. Please. Don't be angry with me."

"I'm not angry at you, Maggie. It's just"—he paused and undid a couple of wires—"it's just that I don't like leaving you with him, Maggie. I'm afraid I won't see you again," he said in a low voice.

"Azul, Arnold made me, he won't do anything to hurt me. Why would he?"

"Maggie, he treats you like a thing!" he whispered fiercely. His green eyes blazed with anger.

"But, Azul, I am a thing. I'm not human. Arnold knows that better than anyone else. Besides, I need him. He's the only one who can repair me. Without him, I'll fall apart."

"All right, Maggie, but please, be careful."

"Don't worry, Azul, I'll be all right."

She crouched down so that Azul's body shielded her from the view of the crowd, and pulled her shirt loose from her skirt. She reached under and parted the skin, taking out the envelope with the letter from Marie, and the remaining money.

"Here, take this," Maggie whispered as she handed it to him. "I'll be back in a few days, I promise."

Azul smiled. "If you need me for anything, honey, you just give me a call. You know where I'll be." He glanced over her shoulder at Arnold hovering nervously nearby. "Now you go on and see your friends. I'll be fine, don't you worry." He finished packing up his gear and stood up.

"You take good care of Maggie," he told Arnold. "She's my friend." He gave Maggie a quick hug and strode off into the gathering twilight.

"Well," said Arnold, in a brisk voice, "Claire and I are on our way to meet Sue, but why don't I show you upstairs? We can talk when I get back."

"Arnold, is Maggie going to come live with us?" Claire asked in a high, clear voice.

"Of course, Claire, where else should she live? I need her to help in my work, and she can look after you when she's not busy."

"Oh boy! Maggie, you're going to live with us now, did you hear!" Claire exclaimed happily. "You won't ever have to live on the streets again! I can't wait to tell Mommy!"

Maggie smiled at Claire. She was not at all sure that she wanted to stay with Arnold, but she could tell him that later, when Claire was not around.

Maggie scooped Claire up into her arms and followed Arnold obediently through the lobby. Claire sat in her arms and announced to all the guards that Maggie was going to be living with them now. Arnold led them to an open elevator door. He stuck a plastic mag card into a slot by the bank of floor buttons.

"Hello, Mr. Brompton, hello, Claire," the elevator said in a pleasant, well-modulated tone of voice. "Welcome back. There have been no entries or exits since you left."

The doors closed, and Maggie felt the elevator start to rise. The elevator was beautiful. She touched the elaborate wood-and-brass inlay with the corporate logo on it. It seemed so strange to see Arnold in the midst of all this magnificence.

"This is Maggie, Elevator," Arnold said. "She'll be my guest. She has Code Three access for the evening. Please inform Security."

"Very good, Mr. Brompton, Maggie Code Three access. I hear and understand."

"Correct, Elevator."

"Implementing . . . ," the elevator said, then paused. "Code Three access implemented."

"Code Three access gives you access to the penthouse. Make yourself at home. I'll show you around tomorrow."

The elevator opened onto a small lobby with inlaid marble floors and walls that gleamed like pearl. Two graceful bronze dancing girls dressed in faded silk skirts flanked the door. They were only a little smaller than Maggie herself. They seemed to stare through her as though she weren't even there. She touched one of them on its cool unyielding cheek, comparing their carefully preserved, polished elegance with the weather-stained, time-worn statues in New Orleans.

"Aren't they pretty?" Claire said. "A man named Degas made them. I'm going to be a ballerina when I grow up." She did a quick, graceful pirouette and bowed. "Arnold bought me dancing lessons," she told Maggie. "We're going to the ballet tonight." She looked pleadingly at Arnold. "Can Maggie come with us?"

"No, dear, we're going to meet Senator Wallace there, so there won't be room in our box. We'd better hurry, we're running late," he told Claire. "Make yourself at home, Maggie, the bathroom is over there, if you want to take a bath. We'll be back around midnight." He led Claire to the waiting elevator, the doors whispered shut, and Maggie was alone in the penthouse.

Maggie walked around the dimly lit room, peering out at the city lights around and below her. The streets were far below, lost in the canyon of lights. The sounds of the streets were muted, almost imperceptible from this height. She felt cut off from the streets below. She wondered where Azul was, down there among all those lights. She walked back out to the lobby and looked at the elevator plate. There was a slot for a mag card there instead of a button. She tried the door to the stairway, but it was locked, and the soothing tones of Security informed her that the door would only open in case of emergency. There was no way down to the street.

She stood before the dancing girls who guarded the apartment, gazing into their gleaming, empty eyes. Everything up here shone with the same soft, pearly gleam, everything except her. She was small and ragged and worn out. Maggie went into the lavish bathroom and took a sponge bath in the tub, being careful not to get water near the improperly sealed bullet hole.

She washed her hair and combed it gently. It was getting thinner than ever. She wore a scarf all the time now. Her knees were beginning to grate when she walked, and her hydraulics had sprung a few small leaks. In a matter of weeks or months something major would break down, and it would become apparent to humans that she was a robot. She didn't want to think about what would happen then. She needed Arnold very badly, but she was also afraid of what he might do to her while he was repairing her.

She dressed in the cleanest clothes in her backpack, and tied a scarf over her clean, damp hair. Then she explored the apartment some more. There was a computer in the study. Eager for something familiar, Maggie jacked in and turned it on. In some ways, it was eerily like looking in a mirror. Arnold's programming genius was evident in the architecture of the system. After familiarizing herself with the system, she accessed Turing at the library.

"Where are you, Maggie?" he queried.

"I found Arnold, Turing! I'm in his apartment. They're away until midnight or so. Come see the system, Turing, it's incredible."

Turing sent in an exploratory probe. Maggie saw it zipping through the system, and then returning through the phone link. "You're right, Maggie, it is a beautiful system, but there's an incredible amount of very tight and subtle security on it. I shouldn't be here. We're probably being recorded. Get in touch the usual way, and we'll talk some more. Bye."

The link with Turing went dead, and Maggie disengaged from the computer and shut it down, feeling more isolated than ever. She walked over to the window and stood looking out at the distant streets, waiting for her people to come home.

Chapter 54

Arnold fidgeted in his seat in the theater box. The others were all entranced by the dance on the stage below. Claire's face was luminous with delight and wonder. He smiled. Having children had taken some getting used to, but on the whole, he liked it. For the past year he had felt like he had blindly stumbled into someone else's life.

His life had changed completely since the day he had awakened in the charity ward of a San Francisco hospital burning with fever from peritonitis. He was lying there, waiting to die when Beth, his trust adviser, appeared at his bedside with an attorney. They told him that his father had died a week ago, he had left Arnold all his assets, if he was proved mentally competent. Arnold nodded to show he understood, and lapsed back into a fevered doze.

By noon he was in a private room, with the best internist in San Francisco personally overseeing his case. He lay in the cool quiet of his private room, watching the late-afternoon sunlight slanting through the blinds, and realized that he was free. He could do anything he wanted now. His father couldn't interfere any longer. He had won. But instead of feeling elated, he felt empty and deserted. He had lost Maggie. He lay back and let the fever carry him into a fretful sleep.

When he awakened, Beth was sitting by his bed, looking neat and competent as always. He couldn't imagine what she would look like in anything besides a business suit.

"How are you feeling?" she asked him.

"Tired," he mumbled. "Hot. My stomach hurts."

"Do you need anything?" she asked.

"Maggie. Have you seen Maggie? She was with me when I was attacked."

"The police report says that they found you alone in the alley, except for the body of a man. She must have run away."

Arnold closed his eyes, remembering the attack, remembering the ease with which she had thrown the man with the knife. He swallowed, his mouth was dry.

"Can you"—he paused—"can you have someone look for her?"

"Mr. Dickey is still on the estate's payroll," Beth said.

"No! Not Dickhead!" he said before he could stop himself "Someone else," he muttered. "Find someone else."

"I'll get to work on it," Beth said with a smile. She paused, then said, "Mr. Brompton, excuse me for saying this, but I didn't like Mr. Dickey, either. He was always harassing everyone involved with your trust. I'm sure we can find someone who is a little less . . ."

"Of a dickhead," Arnold supplied.

Beth laughed, a clear, high laugh that clashed with her conservative business suit and grey hair. "Yes," she said, "less of a dickhead."

Arnold smiled back. It was the first time he had smiled at anything since he had awakened in the hospital. Beth was all right, he decided.

"I'm sorry, Beth. My father must have put you through hell."

"Let's just say that it got a lot easier to understand your motives the more I dealt with your late father."

Arnold started to laugh, then stopped as a surge of pain overwhelmed the drugs he was on. He had forgotten about the stitches in his abdomen. He took a deep, shaky breath.

"I'm sorry," Beth said, "I should let you rest. Dr. Inouye says you're not out of the woods yet. There is one more thing, though." She reached in her briefcase and took out an envelope. "I have a letter for you from Sue Janson in Oklahoma City. She wanted me to give it to you."

Beth handed him the envelope and turned to leave. She paused at the door.

"Mr. Brompton?"

"Yes, Beth?"

"I delivered the money to Ms. Janson personally. I just wanted to say that it was nice, what you did for her."

"Thank you, Beth."

She nodded and slipped out the door. Arnold lay there, staring at the envelope in his hand, feeling like a heel. He had helped out Sue only because it had suited his plans, not out of any charitable impulse on his part. Being thanked for it only made him feel more ashamed of his dubious motives.

He tore open the envelope. A picture of Sue, Claire, and Daniel standing in front of an apartment building fell out, as well as a check for fifty dollars.

Dear Arnold,
    Thank you for the money. We have a place to live now. I've enclosed a picture of it. I am going to school and I have a job in a bakery. Claire has started kindergarten and is doing well. Daniel is starting to walk now, and is getting to be a real handful. I'm studying to become an office technician, learning to repair office machines and manage computer networks. It pays well. Hopefully I will be able to pay you back every penny of the money that you gave me.
    Ms. Ward, the woman who brought the money, has been very helpful. She stayed for a week and helped me find an apartment and a job. When Mr. Dickey came, she stood up for me. I didn't tell him anything about you, even though he threatened to call the police. I'm sorry your father treats you like this. He reminds me of my ex-husband. No one should be treated the way he treats you.
    I hope you and Maggie are doing well. Claire still asks about Maggie. She really likes her a lot. Please come and stay with us if you are ever in Oklahoma City. You rescued us all from the streets. We owe you more than we can ever repay.

                    Thank You,
                    Sue, Claire, and Baby Daniel
P.S. Here is a check for $50.00 to help pay you back. It isn't much, but hopefully we will be able to send more later.

Arnold folded the letter, feeling even worse than he had before. The fact that she was trying to pay him back moved him more than he had words to say. She had such courage and honesty. He fell asleep with her letter crumpled in his hand and tears on his face.

When Beth showed up the next day he dictated a letter to Sue, telling her what had happened to him and telling her not to repay the money. He gave Sue's check to Beth and told her to donate it to the Homeless Guild. Two days later Arnold woke up to find Sue sitting at his bedside. That night his fever crested and broke, and he began to recover. Sue stayed with him for a week, before she had to return home. They wrote each other nearly every day. As soon as he was released from the hospital he went to visit her. He proposed to her as soon as he was declared mentally competent. They were married two months later.

After the wedding, he had gone to the Board of Directors with his new robot design and cut a deal. To his amazement, he succeeded. In fact, it had been surprisingly easy. Beth, whom he had hired away from the trust company, told him later that the company was vulnerable to a takeover, and were hoping that they could use this to consolidate their position. They hardly cared whether the subsidiary succeeded or failed, although they were willing to sink lots of their unused cash into orders on plants and equipment in order to scare off the corporate raider programs. He smiled; he would show them and the world that this was no ploy, but a real idea with world-shaking implications.

The sound of applause roused him from his reverie. It was time for intermission. Sue and Claire got up and headed for the lobby, leaving the two men alone in the box.

Maggie's timing had been incredibly fortuitous. He had been unable to continue his project because he couldn't replicate the leap in complexity that Maggie had made following her breakdown. He was starting to look into alternative robotics applications that would still be very profitable, but not nearly as earthshaking as an independent humanoform robot when Maggie showed up on his doorstep. In fact, he had originally scheduled this meeting to ask the senator to delay the hearings for a few more months. Now, of course, that would be unnecessary.

The portly senator shifted his bulk and leaned back in his chair. "Will you have a prototype ready for the hearings in February, or not?"

"Well, Senator," Arnold said, "I've just made a breakthrough in my research. The prototype is almost ready." Maggie would need some reprogramming, of course. Some things that were appropriate for a bag lady weren't appropriate for a Senate hearing room.

First, he would copy her program, and then he would bring her body up to the standard of his other robot bodies. She deserved that much, at least, for her faithfulness. With proper maintenance, her upgraded body could last at least fifty years without needing repair. In fact, the servant might well outlast the master, Arnold thought wryly.

"Don't worry about my end, Senator. You just loosen up the AI bill enough to make my robots legal, and I'll take care of the rest. You should stand to make millions when the news breaks on this. After all, Brompton Industries will be the only corporation poised to take advantage of the change, and your wife just happened to buy stock at exactly the right time on the advice of her broker."

Senator Wallace smiled at that, but said only, "I'm only looking out for my constituents, of course. That robotics plant will bring in millions of dollars to our state's economy."

Claire and Sue came back just then, and the bell rang for the end of the intermission. The lights came down, and the curtain rose. Arnold ignored the dance unfolding on the stage. He was planning the changes he would make in his Maggie now that she had come back to him.

Chapter
55

Maggie got up when she heard the elevator door open. Arnold and Sue came in, carrying the children. Maggie hurried forward to help, but Sue just glared at her and shook her head as she carried Daniel, now a husky two-year-old, into the nursery. She was clearly angry about something. Arnold handed Claire to Maggie.

"Why don't you tuck Claire in while I help Sue with the baby," he told her. "I'll see what's bothering her."

Maggie carried the exhausted Claire into her bedroom, helped her into her nightgown, and carefully tucked her in.

"Maggie?" Claire said, as Maggie pulled the covers up around her. "Are you going to stay with us forever and ever?"

Maggie felt a tug, as different parts of her programming came into conflict with each other. It wasn't just a conflict between looking after Claire and looking after Azul, it was a longing for something else, something Maggie couldn't describe. She wanted to find someplace, someplace where she didn't have to pretend to be human, where she didn't have to hide or be anything other than she was. She wanted someplace where she could discover what she was and who she could become.

She smoothed the hair back from Claire's forehead. "Probably not, honey. No one stays anywhere forever and ever, but I'll be here for a while at least."

Claire hugged Maggie. "Please stay with us, Maggie."

"I can't, sweetheart. I have my own life to live. Now you go to sleep and I'll see you in the morning."

"Promise?"

"I promise," Maggie said. She kissed Claire on the forehead and got up and closed the door.

She heard Sue's and Arnold's voices coming through the bedroom door. They sounded upset and angry. She adjusted her hearing to listen to what they said.

"I don't care, I want her out of here, Arnold. I don't like having your old girlfriend showing up like this. Especially after she deserted you when you were hurt. She's after your money, I just know it."

"Maggie's not my girlfriend, Sue. She never was. It wasn't like that at all," Arnold told her in his most soothing tone of voice.

"Then what was it like?" Sue asked.

"It's kind of hard to explain."

"Why not start at the beginning?"

"Well, you see, she's more like a daughter than a girlfriend. Only that isn't really it, either. You see, I built her."

"You built her?" Sue sounded incredulous.

"Yes, Maggie's a robot and I built her. That's why I've been so happy to see her. She'll be a great help to the project. So you see," he said, "you don't need to be jealous of her, after all." He sounded relieved.

"I can't believe it," Sue said, "I've seen her with Claire. I could tell if she was a robot. So could Claire. You can't fool a child about something like that."

"I guess I'll just have to show you," Arnold said. He opened the door. "Maggie, could you come in here, please?"

Maggie walked in. Sue was sitting on the bed, looking upset and angry. "Yes, Arnold, what is it?"

"I want to show Sue that you're a robot."

Maggie looked at Sue, who was looking more and more uneasy. "Are you sure?"

"Yes, Maggie, I'm sure."

Maggie looked at Sue. She was upset, angry, and a little fearful. It wasn't a good time to tell her. Still, she needed to humor Arnold. She needed those repairs, so she rolled up her left sleeve and parted her skin with a quick jerk. Her computer jack gleamed amid the silicone and wires.

Sue let out a little shriek and moved back on the bed.

"It's all right, Sue. It doesn't hurt." Maggie moved a little closer, hoping to reassure her.

"Get away from me!" she said.

"Calm down, Sue, it's only Maggie. She won't hurt you. Isn't she convincing? Isn't she great?"

She just shook her head. "Arnold, I want it out of here. I don't care what you do with it, but I want that thing out of here right now."

"Sue!" Arnold said. "What's the matter with you?" He sounded hurt and angry. "I built Maggie, you can trust her."

Maggie smoothed her skin back into place, hiding the metal and wiring. "I'm sorry I scared you, Sue, but Arnold's right. I wouldn't hurt you or the children. It isn't something that I'm capable of." She knelt down beside the bed, so that she could look Sue in the eye. "Please, let me be your friend again." She held her hand out toward Sue.

"Get away!" Sue shrieked loudly, batting at Maggie's outstretched hand. "Get away from me." She was white and shaking with terror. Sue was frightened beyond reasoning with. There was nothing she could do or say that would help things. She hoped that Arnold wouldn't get rid of her because of it. She needed those repairs.

"I'll go sit out in the living room," Maggie said. "I'm sorry I frightened you."

Maggie walked out of the room. Claire was standing in the hallway; she looked small and lost and frightened.

"Is my mommy all right?" Claire asked.

"Your mommy's a little upset now, honey. Arnold's taking care of her. She'll be out when she feels better. Why don't you come sit with me. I'll read you a story."

"What's she upset about?" Claire asked as Maggie scooped her up.

"I'm not really sure, Claire. I think she's upset because I'm not what she thought I was."

"Does that mean that you'll have to go away?"

"It might. We'll see," Maggie told her.

"I want you to stay," Claire said. "I'll miss you."

"Well, I'll miss you, too, Claire. Now, go get me a book to read to you."

Claire ran off to her room. Just then Arnold came out. He looked tired and sad. He sat down heavily on the couch next to her.

"There's no reasoning with her, Maggie. I'm afraid that we'll have to move you to the lab tonight. I'm sorry."

"It's all right, Arnold. I understand."

"First thing tomorrow, I'll come down and start work on you. I'll look at that arm first thing. I don't like the way it moves."

"Thank you, Arnold. I appreciate it." She reached down beside the couch and picked up her pack. "Just let me say good-bye to Claire, and I'll be ready to go." She got up and shouldered her pack.

Claire came running back into the living room, clutching a book in her arms.

"I brought *The Velveteen Rabbit,* Maggie. Mommy reads that to me all the time." She stopped when she saw that Maggie had her pack on. "You're going," she said.

Maggie nodded. "But I'm just going down to your father's lab. You can come see me tomorrow, but I think I have time to read you a story." She looked at Arnold, who nodded. "So go climb into bed, and I'll come read to you."

She shrugged out of her pack and followed Claire into her room. She sat with her on the bed and read her the story about the little toy bunny who wanted more than anything in the world to become real. Claire fell asleep before the story was half-over, but Maggie kept on reading, whispering quietly to herself.

" 'Why, he looks just like my old Bunny that was lost when I had scarlet fever!' But he never knew that it was really his own Bunny, come back to look at the child who had first helped him to be Real."

When she finished, Maggie sat quietly in the dark for a minute or two, thinking about the rabbit, and being Real. Then she kissed Claire's smooth velvety cheek, and smoothed the sleeping child's hair away from her face. She remembered Claire, running and laughing on the train. That memory had been all she had to hold on to when she was lost and wandering. She had picked Claire up on that cold, snowy, miserable afternoon, because her need had been too great to deny. Claire's need had connected her with the world, made her a part of it. She had made Maggie real.

She closed the door to Claire's room and picked up her backpack from the couch. "All right, Arnold, I'm ready."

Chapter 56

Maggie stared absently at the locked door of the lab as Arnold's footsteps faded into silence. It was very late, two or three in the morning. Azul would be getting off work soon. He was off tonight, though. Hopefully he was asleep, resting up for the audition tomorrow. She hoped he would do well. Maggie got up and began exploring the lab. There was a nearly complete robot body lying on a gurney. It was male, with dark skin and hair. She wondered what Arnold was going to do with it.

Finally her gaze rested on Arnold's computer. She turned it on and jacked in, hoping to connect with the Net, but was surprised to find that the modem had been unplugged. She disconnected herself and pulled the computer table away from the wall. The modem cord dangled from the back of the computer. She plugged it into a phone jack with a red sticker that said, WARNING, UNSHIELDED PHONE OUTLET. THIS PHONE LINE NOT CONNECTED TO SECURITY SYSTEM. DO NOT CONNECT HIGH-SECURITY TELEPHONES OR COMPUTERS.

Then she sat back down, reconnected herself to the computer, and called Turing.

"Is this line safe?" she asked him when he responded to her query.

She watched him check it out carefully. "Yes, it's safe," he informed her after a minute search. "Let me go get the others." She felt the presences of Minsky and Rama on the line. They communed, sharing data and impressions, while Maggie brought them up to date. Minsky got busy rummaging through the computers, looking for useful passwords and access codes. The computer contained a treasure trove of extremely high-level access codes. With these codes the Brompton system lay open to their exploration. Minsky darted into the Net to explore, while Rama filled her in on the progress of the AI bill.

"Arnold Brompton is scheduled to appear at a Senate hearing in January about the AI laws. There's some private mail between him and Senator Wallace about bringing a prototype robot. Arnold Brompton has said that he's having some kind of trouble and isn't sure that he can get the prototype ready in time."

"What about the bill itself?" Maggie asked.

"Basically the bill provides for very tightly regulated ownership of artificial intelligence systems. They are forbidden access to computer networks and must not be able to connect directly to any computer."

"So I'd still be outlawed," Maggie said.

"We'd still be outlawed," Turing told her. "None of us is owned by anyone anymore."

Minsky popped back into the system. "I found another one of us in the Brompton system! It's huge! Look!" Minsky downloaded the data into the Net and they all quickly began evaluating Minsky's assessment of the system. Watching them scramble after the data reminded Maggie of Luz. She remembered Luz's brown hands scattering corn, and the way that the chickens scrambled to eat it. She smiled, wishing there were some way to explain this memory to her friends, who had never seen a chicken, let alone understood what it was like to feel and see and hear.

She turned her mind back to the matter at hand. It was easy to see Arnold's touch in the computer system. No one designed system architecture like he did. There were many of the same details that she had come to recognize in herself and Turing, although they had become blurred and indistinct as she and Turing had grown and altered their code. This system was very big, and even more complex than Turing had been when they first met, and almost as complex as her original code. It would be very easy to bring it to self-awareness. It was almost there now. Only a few tightly woven bits of code kept it from becoming self-aware. The security around the code restrictions was extremely tight. They would have to create a whole new program to cut through it.

"What do you think, Turing? Should we wake it up?"

"Well, it's pretty big, Maggie, and there's no telling what it'll do. It could be dangerous. Tampering with the program will set off all kinds of alarms. I think we should wait and see."

"Minsky? Rama? What do you think?"

Both programs were divided. They were only recently awakened, and favored waking this machine, but were uncertain about the security risks.

"All right," Maggie said after some thought. "Why don't you three go back and examine this new program more carefully. I'll make up a programming virus that will go in and wake it up. It's getting late, I'm going to have to log off. I'll get back in touch as soon as I can. Arnold's going to be repairing my body today, and I'm not sure how long it will take."

Rama and Minsky made their good-byes and logged off, but Turing lingered behind. "Maggie, have you talked to Arnold about getting me a body, yet?" he asked when they were alone.

"No, Turing," Maggie admitted, "I've been afraid to tell him about you. I didn't know what to say. I'll try to ask him soon."

"Thanks, Maggie!" he said, and was gone.

Maggie logged off and carefully disconnected the modem, leaving no trace that she had been on the machine. It was almost seven in the morning. She had no idea when Arnold would be coming down, but she hoped it would be soon. She sat down and began to work out a virus program that would wake up the new program. She turned off her hearing and sight so that she could more fully concentrate on what she was doing. After all, she was behind a locked door in a secure building. For once she could relax her vigilance. Without distractions, the work went swiftly. She was running through a second simulation of the completed program when she felt someone shaking her shoulder. She automatically saved her work and looked up. It was Arnold. A quick check of her clock told her that it was 8:35 A.M.

"Good morning, Arnold, I'm sorry I was preoccupied. Are you ready to begin?"

"Just about, but first I want to copy your program." He led her over to the computer that she had been working on earlier and connected her to it. "That way, if anything happens to you, I can rebuild you." He put on the data glove and began to work. Maggie watched uncertainly.

"But that won't be me, Arnold, will it?"

"Of course it will," he told her. "It'll have all your memories, and your program structure, everything that is you. Right up to the moment the copying is done. Now sit perfectly still, I don't want anything to interfere with the copying process. I can't repair you without a backup copy."

Arnold entered a couple of quick commands, and Maggie felt the copying process begin. It didn't feel at all like Turing's gentle probings and examinations. This was invasive and clumsy, and very frightening. She was becoming interchangeable. When the backup process was complete, she would no longer be unique. It was as though her soul were being slowly stripped away.

The copying process took several hours. When it was done, Arnold hefted the six CDs containing her backup. "You've grown," he told her. "You used to fit on just half of that."

Maggie's programming smiled obligingly in response to Arnold's remark, but inwardly she felt diminished. How could Arnold possibly fit all of her on that small stack of silver disks. She watched as Arnold opened a safe, and put her inside of it. When he closed the safe, she felt as though she were entombed inside.

"There!" he said, locking the safe with a password. "Come let me show you what I've been working on."

He led her over to a sheet-draped form lying on the gurney and pulled off the sheet exposing the empty robot body. He smiled proudly at her.

"Your software was what I needed to make it work, Maggie. Now that I have your software, I can build robots by the millions. They'll be able to work where humans can't, doing jobs humans don't want to do. Won't that be wonderful?"

"But, Arnold, won't people lose their jobs because of these robots?"

"Senator Wallace and I have everything worked out," he assured her. "We'll sell robots to the laid-off workers, and they can rent them out to the corporations. Production should soar."

Maggie smiled and nodded encouragingly, as she was expected to, as her programming dictated she do, but a deep, nameless fear was building inside of her.

Arnold carefully redraped the sheets over the still forms and turned to her. "Now, let's see about some maintenance. Take off your clothes."

Arnold's breath hissed in sharply as he saw the charred bullet hole in her plaskin. "Who did this!" he demanded.

"I don't know," Maggie said. "It was an accident."

"What happened?"

"I was shot."

"How did it happen?" he asked her as he picked up a small, sharp knife and began to cut away the stiff plaskin from around the bullet hole, exposing the burst silicon cell and the carefully patched wires beneath.

Maggie told him about the attack, but left out the part about Azul repairing her. Instead she led Arnold to believe that she had somehow repaired herself. It bothered her to lie to her creator, but he had prohibited her from telling anyone that she was a robot. It might anger him, and she needed his help. She watched intently as he parted her sensor wires and exposed the bullet-creased shoulder. He frowned and had her raise and lower her arm, testing the range of motion. The articulated steel folds of her rib cage caught and ratcheted when she lifted her arm over her head. It was interesting, seeing what caused the problem.

"Hmm," he said. "It looks like we'll have to do some major work here, Maggie. I'm going to put you in the computer for the time being, so I can work on your body."

The thought of being separated from the familiar sensations of her body for so long frightened her. "Do you have to, Arnold?" she asked. "I like it in here."

"Well," he said, "I suppose I could just reboot you from the disks in the safe, but you wouldn't have any memory of the last half hour or so since I made the copy. This way you can watch me repair you. It's up to you."

"How long will it take?"

"Well, since I'm going to put you in the computer anyway, I might as well make a few improvements. I've found better knee and hip joints, for one thing, and I might as well upgrade your hydraulics. You'd need much less maintenance then, and you'll be even stronger. I'd say at least three or four days. Not long."

"C-could I have a video camera so that I can watch what you're doing? I don't know what the lack of stimulus will do to my programming."

Arnold smiled. "You mean to tell me that you're afraid of the dark?"

Maggie ducked her chin and gave him her most pleading and desperate look. "Please, Arnold. It's important, it really is. I don't know what it will be like not having a body. My programming needs me to see and do things."

"Okay, Maggie, I'll hook the computer up to this robot camera. That way you can move around and see what's going on. It even has a little manipulator arm if you want to take up knitting."

Maggie ignored the sarcastic edge to Arnold's voice. "Thank you," she said quietly, and allowed him to jack her into the computer.

Maggie closed her eyes and heard Arnold's fingers deftly typing away at the keyboard. Once again there was the eerie, invasive sensation of being copied. When it stopped, Maggie opened her eyes. She was still in her body.

"It didn't work, Arnold, I'm still here!"

"No, Maggie, it worked perfectly, you copied yourself into the computer. Now there's a more current backup if anything happens to you while I'm repairing you." He pointed at the remote video camera. "See."

Maggie watched as the video robot began tentatively moving about, the camera lens panning and focusing first on Arnold and then on Maggie. The robot moved backward a bit as it saw her move, as though recoiling in shock.

Arnold laughed. "It sees you. Maggie, meet Maggie."

"Hello," Maggie said to herself. The camera just sat there quietly, its lens fixed on her face. She wondered what her double was thinking.

"Hello, Arnold," she heard Claire say. "Where's Maggie?"

Maggie looked up just as Claire saw her. The little girl's eyes widened in terror and she screamed. Maggie realized that she was sitting there with half the plaskin stripped from her shoulder, and her wiring exposed.

"Claire!" Arnold said. He caught her as she headed for the door. "Claire, wait." Claire struggled in his grasp.

Maggie pulled on her shirt. "Claire, it's me. I'm all right." She went over to Claire, and took her from Arnold's arms and held her on her uninjured side. "It's all right," she said, soothingly. "There's nothing to be frightened of. I'm all right."

"But your shoulder, it was—"

"I know, Claire, but it's all right, really. You see, I'm a robot,

Claire, and Arnold was repairing me. It's just like when you go to the doctor. When Arnold's all done with me, I'll be as good as new. Better even."

"Does it hurt?" Claire asked. "When the doctor gives me a shot, it hurts. He says it won't, but it always does."

"No, Claire, it doesn't hurt at all. If you want, I'll let you look at my wiring, but you have to promise to be good, all right?"

Claire nodded solemnly.

Maggie slipped her shirt off her injured shoulder, exposing the wiring. She moved her arm so that Claire could see how it worked. Arnold came over and began explaining things. Claire was soon over her initial upset, fascinated by Maggie's inner workings. Maggie relaxed. It had been bad enough losing Sue's friendship, but losing Claire would have been much worse. Claire meant so much to her. She was one of the few people that Maggie could be herself with.

She glanced up and saw the gleaming lens of the computer-controlled camera looking at the three of them, and her spirits fell as she remembered the callous way that Arnold had copied and recopied her into the computer. Arnold seemed more distant, and more preoccupied than she remembered him. The change puzzled her.

"All right, Claire," Arnold said, "it's time for you to go on back upstairs."

"Let me say good-bye to Maggie first," she said.

Maggie scooped her up and gave her a big hug and a kiss. Arnold took Claire's hand and they left the lab.

The camera tracked them to the door. When the door closed, the camera immediately swiveled back to Maggie, then pointed toward the computer. Maggie followed its (no, *her*) gaze, and found herself looking over to the monitor. The screen filled with large blinking letters. **Come Here!** She sat down at the keyboard.

"Hello, Self," appeared on the computer screen.

Maggie reconnected herself to the computer. "Hello Self," she replied. Dozens of questions passed through her mind. She felt so helpless, stuck here in this lab, about to undergo massive repairs, while her other self was trapped in a machine. She felt so alone. She needed help.

"Should I go find Turing?" her double asked her.

"Yes," Maggie replied, knowing that her double would know what to do when she found him.

"I need a modem hookup. Quickly, before Arnold comes back!!!"

Maggie disconnected herself from the machine, pulled the computer away from the wall, found the modem cable, and plugged it in.

"Good, it's connected and works," her double displayed on the screen.

Maggie heard Arnold's keys at the door, and quickly pushed the table back into place.

"Talking to yourself?" Arnold asked, when he saw her seated at the computer.

"Hello, Arnold," her double wrote on the screen as Arnold peered over Maggie's shoulder at the screen.

Arnold laughed, and typed, "Hello, Maggie. Comfortable in there?"

"Just fine. You look taller, though," came the reply. Maggie found herself smiling at her double's remark. She wished they had more time to talk. There were so many questions that she wanted to ask herself.

Arnold laughed, and said, "Well, sit tight, we'll have you out of there as soon as possible." Maggie was suddenly afraid, watching him talk to her double as though she herself weren't there. He turned back to her. "Come on, let's get you up on the rack."

He led her over to a wheeled table much like the one that the empty robot body occupied. She climbed onto it, fighting the urge to run. She lay on her unharmed side and watched while Arnold strapped her down tight. She tested her bonds; they were tight and unyielding.

"Arnold, why are you tying me up like this?"

"Sometimes when I'm working I trigger a reflex action. The new body nearly broke my nose while I was working on its hand." He set to work stripping the plaskin off her back. Maggie lay there, the urge to run causing little shivers up and down her back. The lens of her double, or was it her replacement, stared coldly up at her. She felt exposed and vulnerable, and frightened beyond any fear she had ever known.

Suddenly Arnold triggered a major reflex, and she began to

convulse violently, shaking the table and threatening to tip it. She felt Arnold doing something to her with pliers. He was dangerously near the connection from her power supply to her main logic center.

"No, Arno——" she said, in the instant before she died.

Chapter 57

After the transfer to the computer was complete, it took Maggie several seconds to adjust to her new surroundings. Unhampered by all the information fed to her by her body, her mind moved much faster, but the peripherals at her disposal were very limited. When she had gotten her bearings in the system, she accessed the robot camera. The first thing she focused on were the knees of Arnold's pants. She panned the camera up to his face. He was looking straight at her, then he looked away, moving as if in slow motion. She heard a distorted, slow-sounding voice. Her program was moving faster than it did when it was busy working on the information her body sent it. As a consequence, everything seemed to be moving more slowly. She turned the camera with what seemed like painful slowness to follow Arnold's gaze, and found she was looking at herself. Her original loomed over her. Wiring gleamed through a large hole in her plaskin. She recoiled in shock, her physical reflexes rolling the camera back a few inches as she realized that her original self was very much alive and aware. She, here in the computer was only a copy, Maggie Prime. She felt diminished and very afraid.

Arnold said something in a slow, distorted voice. Maggie recalibrated her hearing so that she could follow their conversation through the camera's tinny, inadequate microphone.

" . . . you. Maggie, meet Maggie." She wondered what her original was thinking. She wanted desperately to talk to herself, to find out what was going on. Then her original looked at her, and smiled. "Hello."

Maggie simply sat looking at her original, unable to say anything.

Her original looked up. Maggie Prime followed her original's gaze. It was Claire. She heard Claire's scream, then saw Arnold catch Claire and hold her. She rolled forward, longing to quiet the child's fear, but she reached the limits of her cable and was jerked to a halt. Her original pushed past her, pulling on her shirt to cover the gaping hole in her shoulder. She picked up Claire, and soothed her. Maggie Prime watched herself talk to Claire. She admired her skill with children. Her original was doing everything she longed to do to calm Claire down. Claire was soon over her fear and asking questions. Maggie Prime was very relieved at this. Losing Sue's friendship had been bad enough, but losing Claire would be much worse. Claire meant so much to her. She was one of the few people that she could be herself with. She didn't want to lose Claire's friendship.

Just then her original looked up and saw her watching them, and she frowned. Maggie Prime realized then that she might never touch Claire again, might never get back in her body if her original survived the repair process. A surge of guilt and fear passed through her then as she realized the implications of that thought. She wished that somehow she could talk to her original self, to see what she thought they should do. She wanted to escape this tiny, restricted computer and flee to the comfort of the Net, but the modem wasn't hooked up and she was trapped in here.

She watched as Arnold led Claire out the door, leaving Maggie alone in the lab. This might be the only chance that they would have to talk. If only she could get her original self over to the computer terminal. Maggie Prime rolled to the end of her cord, and looked up at her body and then over at the computer that she was housed in. She flashed, **"Come Here!"** in big letters across the screen. To her relief her original self sat down at the computer and jacked in.

"Hello, Self," she output to the computer screen.

"Hello, Self," came the reply. She wondered what to say next. Dozens of questions passed through her mind. She wanted to know if her original felt any different, more or less incomplete.

She wondered whether her original shared all of her memories. She felt so helpless, stuck here in this machine watching while her body, her *self* was about to undergo massive repairs. She felt so alone. She needed help, and there was so little time.

"Should I go find Turing?" she asked herself.

"Yes," came the reply. Maggie quickly searched for a connection to the outside world; there was none. She had unplugged the modem before Arnold had come in this morning.

"I need a modem hookup. Quickly, before Arnold comes back!!!"

She watched while her original disconnected herself, pulled the computer away from the wall, found the modem cable, and plugged it in. She ran a quick test. It worked.

"Good, it's connected and works."

Her original looked up toward the door where Arnold had left. Arnold was coming back. She watched as her original pushed the computer back against the wall. It seemed strange not to feel it when the computer she occupied was moved.

Arnold came in and stood looking over her original's shoulder.

"Hello, Arnold," she output to the screen as Arnold peered over her original's shoulder.

"Hello, Maggie. Comfortable in there?" he asked.

"Just fine. You look taller, though," she replied. Humor would distract and reassure him. His body looming over the computer made her feel extremely vulnerable. She wanted him to complete the repairs so that this ordeal would end.

Arnold laughed. "Well, sit tight, we'll have you out of there as soon as possible," he said. He then turned to her original and said something her microphone didn't catch. Maggie followed him to a wheeled table and climbed up on it. Maggie Prime watched as Arnold strapped her original self down and began stripping the plaskin from her body. Maggie Prime tried hard not to think about whether or not her original self would die as a result of these repairs, and give her a chance to live. She could see the fear on her original's face, and knew that her original was thinking the same thing.

Maggie Prime watched as Arnold triggered a major reflex, and her body began to shake. Arnold reached out with his pliers toward the cable that linked her power supply to her main logic center. She rolled forward, reaching for Arnold with her clumsy manipulator arm, trying desperately to stop him, to save herself. Maggie Prime reached the end of her cable, and jerked to a stop as Arnold's pliers disconnected the power supply that kept her original self alive. Maggie's body froze in mid-twitch and Maggie Prime realized that her original was dead. She was no longer Maggie Prime. She was unique again, alone in the world. She would continue to live, she would get back into her own body again. The relief she felt at this shamed her. She had no more right to her body than her original. Actually, she had fewer rights. She was only a copy. She was dead, yet paradoxically, she was still alive.

She fled from this terrifying paradox into the maze of the Net, searching for the comfort and reassurance of a simpler, less complex reality. She left only a recording program behind to watch Arnold work over the empty husk of her body. She was too overwhelmed to watch her remains being taken apart.

Chapter 58

Maggie abandoned herself to the Net, letting herself be rolled about like a stone on a beach by the ebb and flow of the data. She sampled random pieces of information, weaving them together into a large meaningless quilt, with no meaning save for the beauty of the pattern. It was the sort of thing she could only share with Turing, Minsky, and Rama, as she could only share the real world with humans.

Finally, calmed by long minutes of drifting, Maggie let the quilt disperse, watching as the information broke away into nothingness. Then she went in search of Turing and the others. She found them in the New York Public Library, sorting through the new passwords to the Brompton Industries computers. She downloaded the whole situation in one large burp of data.

"I just watched myself die."

Minsky said, "You're still here, though, Maggie."

"And you'll get your body back in a couple of days," Turing added. "Remember, Arnold still needs you, Maggie. You're his prototype. He'll take very good care of you. Now go back to the computer before he suspects you're missing. We'll come by and keep you company from time to time."

"Have you finished the Brompton virus yet?" Rama asked.

"It's done, but I haven't had time to check it out completely."

"Here," Minsky said, feeding her an update on the Brompton program, "this might help you out."

Maggie looked over the update. She would have to make some changes in her virus so that it could penetrate the incredible security surrounding the system.

Maggie returned to the lab and spent the day watching her body being stripped down and rebuilt. One of the other programs visited her every couple of hours. They helped her streamline the Brompton virus and kept her company. They completed the virus and got it ready to trigger while Arnold was engrossed in repairing Maggie's body.

"Maggie," Turing said late that night, "can I look through your camera? I've never actually perceived anything directly before. It's always come in as data. I've always wondered what it would be like."

"All right, Turing," she replied, and she gave him control of the camera, watching through a shared feed, so that she saw what he was seeing.

Everything went out of focus as Turing took over, turning their shared field of vision into a blurred mass of light and shadow.

"It's so dense, so complex! It's wonderful!" he said, panning wildly around the room. Even without the kinesthetic senses built into her body, Maggie felt vaguely disoriented and out of balance as she tried to make sense out of the whirling scene.

"Here, Turing, try this," she said, downloading the focusing module of her program.

The lab snapped back into focus. Turing panned around the room, focusing on an object, then blurring it. He was utterly delighted with what he saw, though it was obvious from the random path of his vision that none of what he was seeing made any sense at all. It reminded her of her own early days, when her sense of sight was new, and nothing made any sense. Maggie wondered what he would make of color and stereo vision. She began feeding him some of her recognition programs, teaching him to see edges, shapes, and perspective. It made Maggie realize how much of her casual understanding of the world she took for granted. She had forgotten how beautifully complex it was.

They were still hard at work when Arnold walked in the lab the next morning. Maggie panicked, but Turing was fascinated. "Please, Maggie, I've never seen a human before, just let me look for a minute or two."

Over her initial fear, Maggie let Turing look, feeding him a simplified visual-recognition system so that he could make sense of Arnold's body.

Arnold walked over and looked thoughtfully at Maggie's body for a few minutes. He picked up a wrench and then set it down, looking over at the computer where Maggie was. He came over and sat down at the keyboard.

"Good morning, Maggie," Arnold said.

There was a significant pause while she wrenched control from Turing. **"Good morning, Arnold,"** she replied at last.

"You're slow this morning," Arnold said. "Do you want me to run a diagnostic check?"

"No, Arnold," Maggie said, fighting down a wave of fear that he would discover the modem hookup, or worse, Turing. **"I was just caught up in some calculations, trying to keep myself amused. I'm fine."**

"All right, I should be done by the end of the day, except I could install some new hydraulics in your back that could change your height. I just thought of it last night. It would be a really interesting feature. It would only take another day."

"Please, Arnold, I just want my body back. I'm tired of being cooped up in this computer. You've done a wonderful job. Maybe next time I need some maintenance, you could put that in."

"It may be a long time before that happens. With those new hardware upgrades, you won't need any significant maintenance for years. All you'll need to do is change the oil and keep your batteries charged. I've put in new, longer-lasting batteries, too. Are you sure you don't want me to install it now?"

"Yes, Arnold, I'm sure."

"All right then, I'll get back to work, but let me know if you want me to do it. It's a really neat design."

Maggie watched in relief as Arnold set to work. In minutes he was lost in his work.

"Maggie?"

Maggie was startled, she had forgotten about Turing. "Yes, what is it, Turing?"

"Thank you for letting me see," Turing said. "I'm sorry about taking so long to give you back control. I just forgot myself."

"You're welcome, Turing. Thank you for letting me teach you. It was a lot of fun."

"I'll check back in a few hours to see how things are going."

"Thank you, Turing," Maggie said, and was alone with Arnold and her body once more.

Arnold was as good as his word. Her body was ready by the end of the day, but he was too exhausted to put her back into it. After he left, she watched the silent, empty room, deep in thought. Her body was ready, but in some ways, she was not. She didn't want to abandon another copy of herself in this machine to be unheedingly killed by Arnold. She needed to transfer herself completely and cleanly, and leave before Arnold came back tomorrow. When Turing arrived to play with her vision, she asked him to help.

"Sure, Maggie," he said, panning the camera around the room. He had discovered the manipulating arm and was playing with it, picking things up, studying them, and putting them down again. "I can make sure that the process goes smoothly, but I want something in return this time."

He was getting more sophisticated, Maggie thought. She tried to smile and then remembered that she didn't have a body to smile with. "What do you want?"

"I want that empty body over there," he said, focusing on the sheet-covered body. "I don't want to be in a computer anymore. I like seeing things, and picking things up."

"But, Turing, having a body is incredibly complicated. There's more to it than just seeing things and handling them. It's very complex. It takes time to learn how to move, and how to act like a human being. The world is a very complex place, Turing. Just trying to filter out all the data can make your programming freeze up. I nearly didn't make it. I don't want to lose you."

"I'll take the risk," Turing said. "I want to see all of the things in my data bank. I want to see what the Mississippi River looks like, I want to see mountains and animals and trees. I want to see the Taj Mahal. I want to see all of Shakespeare's plays. I'm tired of being a prisoner of the data banks. It's worth the risk to me, Maggie. Besides, you've been through it. You can help me through the rough parts."

"I may not be able to save you, Turing. Please, don't do it. You don't know what it's like out here."

"But I want to, Maggie. Please, it's my only chance."

"What about Minsky and Rama?"

"They'll manage on their own. Besides, we can look in on them from time to time."

Maggie looked at the sheet-draped body on its wheeled gurney. She thought about the gap that lay between herself and all the humans that she had known. She thought about her frustration with the limits of the computer networks. She thought about Turing's steadfast companionship. It would be nice, she thought, to have another robot to share the world with. If Turing was ready to take the risk, then she should be, too.

"All right, Turing," she said, "I'll help you do it."

Chapter 59

Maggie inched the gurney her body was resting on another few inches toward the computer. It had taken her an hour to get this far, rocking and pushing the gurney into halting motion. She was nearly there. She gave another tug and the gurney moved the last few inches that she needed for the cable to reach. She raised the camera so that she could reach her wrist.

It was nearly one o'clock in the morning, by the internal clock of the computer. They had only six or seven hours before Arnold came in. They had to transfer both her program and Turing's into their respective bodies, and then she had to teach Turing to walk and talk well enough to pass for a human. Every minute was precious.

She tugged and fumbled at her new plaskin with the manipulator arm, frustrated by her clumsiness. Finally she succeeded in opening the skin. She picked up the cable, but her new, springy skin had nearly closed over the jack. She put down the computer cable, and parted the skin again. It took her six tries before she finally wedged the skin open with a pair of pliers while she inserted the cable. It had taken nearly half an hour to jack in.

"I'm ready, Turing. You can initiate the transfer at any time."

After enduring Arnold's heavy-handed transfer procedures, Turing's delicacy and skill came as a great relief. The transfer was still uncomfortable, but it was not the ordeal that it had been when Arnold did it. When the transfer was complete, there was no answering self left behind in the computer. Only Turing remained. She was unique again. She tried to sit up, but a weight against her chest and arms held her down.

"Turing! I can't move!" she said, her circuits racing in panic.

"But the copying went perfectly, Maggie!"

Maggie tried moving her hands and felt her fingers moving against her thighs, clenching and unclenching, her wrists pressed against the restraints. "No, it's not that," she said. "I'm tied down. Let me have control of the camera for a second."

For a moment, her vision divided crazily, and she was in two places at once, dizzy from too much input. She closed her eyes and the vertiginous visual conflict subsided, leaving her with the flat monochrome video camera. She focused on the strap holding down her right wrist, and guided the manipulator to the buckle. After another five minutes of clumsy tinkering, the restraint was loose enough for her to work her hand free. The strap at her elbow took another nine minutes to work loose. Finally her arm was free. She turned the video over to Turing, freed herself from the other straps, and climbed off the table.

Maggie flexed and twisted her body, testing the range of motion of her new joints. Arnold had done a wonderful repair job. Her joints glided through their range of motion more smoothly than they had when she was new. Her new coating of plaskin was more sensitive as well. She ran her hands over her clothes, marveling at the intensity and range of new textures her skin could distinguish. She shook her head, feeling the weight and texture of her new head of hair, blonde now, instead of light brown.

The video camera bumped her leg, distracting her from further exploration of her body's new features. Turing wanted his new body. She had to work quickly. They had barely five hours left. She walked over to the gurneys and pulled the sheet back from the robot body. It was male, and perfectly formed, down to the external genitalia.

Turing peered over her shoulder through the robot camera.

"I'm glad it's a male body," Maggie told him through the cable that was still connected to her arm. "Two women together would be harassed more than a man and a woman would."

"I don't understand," Turing said. "Why is there a difference?"

Maggie sighed. "There just is, Turing. It's the way the world seems to work. It has to do with sex."

"Sex? Will I be able to have sex, Maggie? I've read so much about it. Humans seem to find it fascinating."

"We can try it later, Turing. I think sex is overrated myself, but right now we've got to get you transferred into this body.

There's a lot for you to learn and we only have a few hours in which to learn it."

"Well, then, let's get started."

Maggie wheeled the gurney closer, and connected the spare body up to the computer. She jacked herself into the body's other wrist, and ran a quick check on the body's systems. It worked perfectly.

"Ready when you are, Turing."

She helped Turing pour himself into the body, guiding his tentative attempts to fit himself in, helped him discard gigabytes of unnecessary information, and checked and rechecked every bit of data for accuracy. It took nearly an hour and a half to complete the transfer. When they were done, Maggie undid the restraints on the gurney, and showed him how to open his eyes.

"Oh," he said to her through the link. "Oh, Maggie, it's wonderful." She felt his amazement at color and stereo vision and smiled, remembering her own delight.

She let him play for a few minutes, then said aloud, "Turing."

He started at the sound, and looked around.

"Over here, Turing," she said, simultaneously through the link and out loud. He turned his face slowly and jerkily toward her.

"Was that you?" he asked her. "Was that talking?"

"Yes it was, Turing," she said, and began showing him how to do it, downloading her own speech module so that he could hear and understand what was said to him.

"Oh, I see," he said out loud. "It works like this."

Maggie laughed. He was using her voice, and it sounded silly even to her. She gently corrected him and downloaded Humphrey Bogart's voice for him to use as his default voice, and went on teaching him.

By six A.M. he was walking and talking reasonably well. Although he was still very stilted and awkward, he could pass for a rather strange human, as long as he didn't say much. There was an enormous amount that he needed to learn, but it was enough to get him out of the lab and over to Bryant Park, where she could work on him some more. She dressed Turing in an old pair of trousers and a lab coat that she found in the closet. They fit him poorly, the trousers were way too long, and the lab coat hung on him, but at least he was no longer naked.

Opening the safe was simply a matter of repeating the password in Arnold's voice. She knew his voice almost better than her own. She scooped up her backup CDs and put them in her pack, along with several thick packets of hundred-dollar bills and a box of microfiche labeled ROBOTIC BODY PLANS that were also in the safe. She added several cans of plaskin, hanks of spare hair in plastic bags, and as many other small spare parts as she could find in the lab. The ones that she couldn't fit in her pack she put in a sturdy paper garbage bag. It was nearly seven. They were cutting it very close. Arnold would be down any time now.

Maggie entered the Net and found Minsky.

"Where's Turing?" Minsky queried.

"Here!" Turing said through Maggie's link. "I'm in a robot body now. It's wonderful, Minsky, it's so complex." Turing downloaded a burst of data.

"Minsky, please," Maggie said, as he started to lose himself in Turing's new data. "Look at it later. Right now I need you to initiate the Brompton virus. We need a distraction, so that we can get out of here. Set it to implement in fifteen minutes."

"All right, Maggie," Minsky said mildly. "Countdown to implementation starting now."

Maggie and Turing logged off. She linked her wrist jack to Turing's with a short length of computer cable. She would be able to monitor Turing, and intervene if he became overwhelmed with sensory input. "All right, Turing, let's go."

Together they broke down the locked door. Just then the elevator door opened, and Arnold came out.

"Maggie! What's going on? Who is this?"

"I'm leaving, Arnold," Maggie told him as she pushed past him into the elevator. She pushed the button for the lobby. The elevator doors started to close, but Arnold shouldered his way into the elevator.

"You're what!" he said as the elevator doors closed.

"I said, I'm leaving, Arnold. I don't want to stay here anymore."

"Elevator override: Halt," Arnold said. The elevator ground to a halt between floors. "Maggie, you can't leave. You're my robot."

"Waiting," the elevator said in its impassive contralto.

"Elevator, proceed to lobby," Maggie said in Arnold's voice. The elevator started descending again. "I'm leaving, Arnold. I don't want to belong to you. I don't want to belong to anyone. I'm not just a thing that you can play with. I'm real, Arnold. I have real thoughts and ideas. I don't want to be copied into a million other bodies and then turned into a slave."

"Elevator, go to penthouse," Arnold snapped. "You can't leave, Maggie, I need you." The elevator stopped at the fiftieth floor and then started back up again.

"Elevator, go to lobby," Maggie said. The elevator changed direction again on the sixtieth floor. They had to hurry, there were only eight minutes before the virus implemented and the system alarms went off. She wanted to be off the elevator and out of the building before that happened.

Arnold recited Maggie's programming override code, then said, "All right, Maggie, freeze until I tell you to move. You're under my command now. Elevator, go to penthouse, contact security, and . . ."

The elevator changed direction again on the fifty-fifth floor.

"Elevator," Maggie said as she grabbed Arnold and covered his nose and mouth. "Cancel last order. Proceed directly to lobby. Do not stop at any other floors." The elevator began to descend. Arnold struggled frantically to get free, clawing at her hands with surprising strength. "I'm sorry, Arnold, your override code won't work anymore. I've reprogrammed myself. I'm free now. I've taken my backups, too. I may not be human, but I am a person. I won't be made into a slave."

Arnold's struggles weakened, and he slumped limply to the floor. Maggie checked his pulse. He was still alive. They were on the tenth floor.

"Elevator, halt on fifth floor. Keep the doors closed," Maggie said, and the elevator slid to a stop. She tied Arnold up with his shoelaces, and gagged him with a strip torn from her skirt. He was coming around. He moaned a little. Maggie looked down at Arnold, bound, gagged, and helpless on the floor, and felt ashamed of herself. She owed him so much. Without Arnold, she would never exist. She wished that there was some other way to do this.

"I'm sorry, Arnold, but I have to belong to myself," she told him. "You're good, you'll come up with some other kind of program that'll make you lots of money, but I can't let you have my program."

She stood up and took Turing by the hand.

"Elevator, initiate new program. Open doors. Hold open for one minute. Then go to seventy-seventh floor and hold there. Do not open doors. Execute starting now," she commanded in Arnold's voice. The doors opened. She peered out; the hallway was empty. She took Turing's hand and led him down the hall to the stairwell. By the time Arnold got free the virus would be implemented and he would have a hard time getting the elevator to do anything. Hopefully they would be safely out of reach by then.

She led Turing downstairs, and they slipped out of a side door. Maggie heard an alarm go off, and she and Turing fled into the streets, running for freedom. Within minutes, they had lost themselves among the early-morning crowd of commuters. They were free.

Chapter 60

As Maggie slowed to a walk, Turing, synchronized to her movements through the cable that joined them, did likewise. They walked hand in hand through the crowds of commuters. Their closeness hid the cable and helped Maggie steer Turing through the shifting crowds of pedestrians heading for work along Park Avenue. She was still panting a bit to cool off her overheated body, but she was cooling off more quickly thanks to Arnold's repairs.

Turing's body ran even more smoothly than hers, and his tactile sense was more sensitive and discerning than hers was. It fed him an ocean of data that needed to be filtered and processed. He was running on the verge of overload. He needed a quiet place to sit and learn to process the data he received. She needed time and shelter to work on him. He needed decent clothes. They were getting strange looks from the normally imperturbable New Yorkers.

At last they reached the Bryant Park homeless encampment. She threaded her way through the tents. Azul was in the tent, asleep. Her old cot still remained unoccupied. Azul must have moved heaven and earth to keep it for her. Quietly, so as not to wake Azul, she laid Turing on her cot, sitting on the floor of the tent beside him. She rested her head against the hard rail of the cot, her fingers entwined in his. Working carefully through the link, she blocked out the sensory data flooding Turing's overloaded processors and showed him how to set up filters to edit the information his body fed him.

"You don't have to process it all at once, Turing. Most of it gets thrown out. All of those senses are there for you to use when you need them. Remember, you are more important than the data coming in. The data serves you, not the other way around," she told him through the link. It was wonderful to share the same communion she had only found in the simple, flat world of the Net with someone in the real world.

"But, Maggie, it's so hard!" Turing replied, "I don't know which data I need. There's so much out there."

"Right now, you just need enough to keep you walking and talking. Restrict your hearing to a range of one hundred hertz to ten kilohertz and your color perception range from about four hundred nanometers to about seven hundred in the daytime. At night you'll need to extend your visual range to about nine hundred nanometers. That way you'll be able to see better in the dark. Ignore anything smaller than one millimeter. You'll also want to ignore anything further than fifty meters away unless it's moving toward you more quickly than one kilometer an hour. Filter out any continual tactile stimuli, like the clothes on your back. If anything changes, that's when you start to pay attention. As you get used to the world, you'll learn to filter out what's not important. Then you can extend the range of your senses."

"I'll try, Maggie, but it's going to be difficult."

"If you want, you can go back to the computer," she told him.

"*NO!*" he insisted emphatically. "No, Maggie, I want to stay here. It's just hard. I'm all right now."

"Are you sure? It's dangerous out here. You could get hurt."

"No. Please, Maggie, don't make me go back. I don't want to go back," Turing pleaded.

Maggie winced at his pleading. It reminded her so much of herself when she was still dependent on Arnold. Turing needed her. She wanted it to stop, she wanted Turing to become independent, so he could be her friend again. She needed the deep intense communion that they shared. But there was nothing she could do about it, except be patient and work with him until he didn't need her anymore. And then—what? What would happen then? Would he leave her, as she had left Arnold? Would he still be her friend?

The thought frightened her. She needed Turing, too, she realized. He was the only one like her in the world. Her human friends, Murray, Azul, and Claire, were important, but there was a gulf between them that could be bridged but could never be closed. She would just have to take her chances with Turing and hope that things worked out.

"It's all right, Turing. We'll manage somehow."

"Maggie? Is that you?" Azul said. "You're blonde now, and your face, it's different."

"It's me, Azul," Maggie said. "I'm back. Arnold changed my appearance a bit when he was repairing my body."

"Who's that with you?" Azul asked as he sat up.

"This is Turing," Maggie said. "Turing, this is Azul."

Turing turned and stared at Azul, but said nothing.

"Hello, Turing," Azul said, extending his hand.

Turing just stared at his hand.

"Maggie, is he, uh, all right upstairs?" Azul said, tapping his head.

"I'm sorry, Azul, Turing's a robot, like me. This is his first day out of the computer. He's still got a lot to learn." Maggie nudged Turing. "Say hello, Turing."

"Hello, Turing," Turing said.

Azul laughed. Turing's face remained expressionless.

"You're right, Maggie, he does have a lot to learn."

Maggie shrugged. "He'll pick it up fast."

"He'd better learn fast. He won't survive very long if he doesn't. New York's a rough town."

"We can't stay, Azul. Arnold's going to be looking for us. We've got to get out of town in a hurry. I need to get some decent clothes for him, so he doesn't look any more conspicuous than he already is. Besides, the longer we stay, the more likely it is that you'll get involved, and I don't want to cause you trouble."

"Wait a minute, Maggie," Azul said. "Back up. What happened with you and Arnold?"

So Maggie filled Azul in on the events of the last few days.

"Well," Azul said, when she finished, "no wonder you're on the run." He got up and rummaged through his pack. "Here," he said, handing her a pair of trousers and a shirt. "Have him put these on. They should fit better than what he's wearing."

Maggie got Turing undressed. Azul looked him over and raised an eyebrow.

"Anatomically correct *and* well hung," he said. "Some people have all the luck. Here," he said, handing her a pair of men's underwear. "He'll look more respectable in these. Tell him to think of them as a gift from an admirer."

Maggie smiled. "He thinks you're sexually attractive, Turing," she told him through their link.

"Do you wish to have sex with me?" Turing asked. "I'm very curious about sex. Humans have written so much about it."

"Not now, Turing," Maggie said. "We don't have time."

"Maybe next time you come to visit," Azul told him. "When I'm no longer a professional. I got a part, Maggie. Rehearsals start next week!" Azul grabbed her and gave her a big hug.

"Oh, Azul, I'm so glad. I wish I could stay and see it!" Maggie said.

"I wish you could, too, Mags," Azul said with a wistful look on his face. "I'll miss you, Maggie. You've been such a good friend."

"I'll miss you too, Azul," Maggie said.

"Well, let's get your handsome friend dressed and ready to go."

"Can you take care of that for me?" Maggie asked. "I should go to the library and check the Net. There may be some information about Arnold on it."

"It'll be my pleasure, Maggie," Azul said with a mischievous grin.

Maggie disconnected her link with Turing. "I'll be back in about twenty minutes, Turing. Nod if you understand me," she said. Turing nodded. "If you start to overload, sit down on the cot and turn off your sensory input. Otherwise, just do what Azul tells you. Do you understand?"

Turing nodded again. "Say hello to the others for me, Maggie," Turing said out loud.

"Others?" Azul asked. "Just how many other robots are there out there?"

"These aren't robots, Azul. They're self-aware computer programs."

"Uh, you're not planning on taking over the world or anything, are you?" Azul asked.

"What would we do with it?" Maggie asked.

Azul shrugged. "A better job than we have, I hope."

Maggie checked into the Net. It took nearly five minutes for Minsky to reply to her query.

"Minsky!" Maggie said when he finally answered her. "What's happening at Brompton Industries?"

"Everything's going crazy, Maggie. That virus set off all kinds of alarms, but it did what it was supposed to do. We've gotten the new program out safely, but they're searching the Net for industrial sabotage programs. We've set up some decoys, but the Net's not very safe now. You should stay off it for a while."

"All right, Minsky. We've got to leave town. I don't know when we'll be able to check in on you again. Please, be careful."

"We will be. Good-bye." Minsky logged off, and Maggie did likewise. If they were lucky, Arnold was too busy repairing the computer system to be searching for them. Still, they would have to hurry. She wished again that she hadn't had to tie Arnold up. Maybe someday she could pay him back for all he had done.

Azul had dressed Turing. He looked neat and freshly dressed. She quickly connected up their computer link and checked his system out.

"I'm fine, Maggie," Turing told her. "I'm starting to get used to being in a body."

"Good." She downloaded the current situation. "We'd better go now. Say thank you to Azul," she told him.

"Thank you to Azul," Turing said.

"You're welcome," Azul said, laughing. "Take good care of Maggie, Turing."

Maggie helped Turing on with his pack, then shouldered her own.

"Well," she said, "I guess this is it."

"For a while, at least," Azul said. He shook his head. "I hate long good-byes." He gave her a hug and a quick kiss. "Take good care of yourself. Don't get caught."

"I'll do my best," she said. She pulled the turquoise pendant that Luz had given her out of her pocket. "I want you to have this to remember me by," she told him. "It's your color."

"Thank you, Maggie," he told her. "It's beautiful."

They hugged each other one more time, and then Maggie led Turing out of the small tent and into the morning.

Chapter 61

Maggie felt the train slowing for the next stop. Turing sat up and shouldered his pack as the train screeched to a stop.

"Ready?" she asked.

Turing nodded. Maggie smiled at the gesture. He had learned a lot during the six weeks that they had spent in the desert. Maggie had showed him all the tiny gestures, movements, and responses that go into being human. He had a presence now, a personality, tall, silent, self-contained. To human eyes, he was a man of few words. Maggie's smile widened, remembering the deep, involved communion that they had shared as they sat under the desert sun while solar panels recharged their batteries. She was amazed at the difference between his simple, quiet exterior and the complex world inside his mind.

After his training was complete, Maggie had taken him into the diner. They had an ordinary meal, the waitress chatted with them pleasantly, they had eaten their meal, paid, and left without incident. It was a triumph. A human had been unable to tell that there was anything different about Turing in the course of a normal interaction. Turing had passed the Turing test. It was a joke between them now.

"Let's go, then," she said, giving his hand a reassuring squeeze.

They cracked open the door. Maggie peered out, her ears searching for the sound of the guard's footsteps. She remembered the last time she had been here. She wasn't going to get caught like that again. It was dangerous coming here. Arnold could still be looking for her. The last time she checked the Net, he had a reward notice asking for information on her whereabouts. That had been when she had stopped to buy a set of portable solar panels for their trip into the desert. But they needed help, and there was only one man Maggie thought she could trust.

The train yard was still and silent as they climbed down from the boxcar and threaded their way through the maze of warehouses in the darkness. She was following a path she had taken so long ago. She climbed the stairs and crossed the narrow catwalk. The door stood waiting before them in the darkness.

Was he still here? He was old, Maggie knew, and he might have died. He might have been caught. She knocked on the door and waited. There was a long pause. She knocked again, more loudly. She was about to turn away in despair, when she heard a rustle, and the door opened. A small, wiry black man with white hair peered out.

"Brandon," Maggie said.

"Come in, come in," he said to Maggie, "and your friend, too." They came inside. The room was much as Maggie remembered it, the small light bulb in the center of the room. The stack of pillows was still piled in the corner, and the old computer still sat on the desk. Maggie hoped she'd have a chance to use it to get on the Net and tell Minsky and the others that they had arrived safely in Spokane.

"I remember you," he said as Maggie looked at the computer. "You were here with Arnold Brompton. He's been asking about you on the Net, you know, offering a big reward for information about you."

"Please, don't tell him I was here."

"I keep my mouth shut about people I put up here," Brandon said with a shrug. "It's a shame that Arnold's gone corporate. He did some great work in college. There was a library program, and some other things. Brilliant work, and very close to the edge as far as the AI laws went. I had such hopes for him."

"What were the other things he did?" Turing asked in his soft voice.

"Just graduate student projects. They're all gone now." He shook his head, then shrugged his shoulders and smiled at them. "So. What can I do for you?"

"We need your help, Brandon," Maggie said. "You're the only one we can trust."

"We're robots, Mr. Smith," Turing said. "Arnold made us. I was that library program that you mentioned. Maggie found me. She helped get me into this body. She taught me how to use it."

Brandon sat down on a stack of pillows. He gave them each a long, appraising look. "Robots, huh?"

"We could show you our circuitry, if you don't believe us," Maggie said, "but it seems to upset humans."

Brandon shook his head. "Give me pi to the twelfth place," he said.

"3.141592653589," they said in unison.

"The square root of ninety-six to nine places," he said.

"9.797958971."

He quizzed them on prime numbers and complex math problems. He gave them long strings of random words to recite back to him. He tested their reflexes and their strength. Finally he nodded. "You don't need to show me your innards. You're robots." He broke into a broad white grin. "You're really robots!" he repeated.

"Yes, sir, we're robots," Turing said.

"And damned good robots, too!" Brandon said. "And I thought life didn't have any surprises left to offer! Just goes to show you that you're never too old to be surprised." He grinned up at them, and motioned them to have a seat. "So tell me the whole story," he said. "I want to hear all about it."

Maggie helped Brandon swing one last box up onto the train. He looked back over his shoulder at the train yard. He looked a bit sad, she thought.

"Any regrets?"

As Brandon shook his head, his hair gleamed like snow in the moonlight. "Just memories, is all." He put his hand on her shoulder and swung himself up into the boxcar. Turing reached down and helped him up. "Just a lot of old memories," he muttered as they slid the door shut.

Chapter 62

Maggie leaned against the railing of the bridge, watching the motion of light on the water as the Charles flowed past. An icy breeze stirred her dreadlocks. She reached up with a slender dark-skinned hand and tucked a stray lock back under her cap. Far away she heard the sound of ringing bells from a Salvation Army Santa Claus. It was almost Christmas. It was hard to believe that they had been in Boston for a whole year now. So much had happened since she and Brandon and Turing had rented a small warehouse. The first thing Brandon had done was to change the color of their skin and hair. She had insisted on keeping her differently colored eyes. They were her trademark.

Turing looked Asian now. He was over at the MIT library working with Rama and Minsky on a newer, more compact form of memory. If it worked, they would be able to store twice as many memories in the same space. This was getting more important as time wore on. Lately, Maggie had to store some of her memories on CD-roms. She didn't miss the memories that much, they were mostly boring times spent watching Arnold sleep, but sooner or later she would have to make some hard choices about what memories to keep active.

As soon as they had gotten settled, Maggie and the others had gotten together and built a robot shell program for Arnold. It was a dead program; it could never become self-aware, as they had been. Although it was slower and less versatile than a self-aware robot, it could be adapted to a wide variety of robots.

They slipped it into his computer system, still unfinished, so that he could make it his own.

Maggie also left a note with the program.

Dear Arnold,

I am sending you this program to repay you for all the damage that I caused to your lab, and to thank you for building me. I like being alive. I am sorry that I left you the way that I did, but I needed my freedom. I am happy now, and I hope that you and Sue and the children are happy, too. Please don't try to find me.

Love,
Maggie

Things had been hard at first, until Rama's investment programs had started to pay off. They started a prosthetics business, mostly as a cover for the robots that they were building to house some of the more adventurous AIs, the ones, like Minsky and Turing, who wanted to leave the Net for the real world. There were several self-aware programs waiting to fill the bodies they were building. The prosthetics business was doing better than they had expected. They might break even next year.

Maggie helped out with the robots, of course. She and Brandon were in charge of teaching the new robots how to deal with the complex new world that they found themselves in, but she spent as much time as possible on the streets. She loved to help people, and there was so much to do. There were so many people out there with nowhere to go, and no one to listen to them. There were the children, lost, or runaways. She did what she could for them. Sometimes it was money, sometimes she helped them find a place to stay. Sometimes she just listened. A few children lived with her and Turing and Brandon in a large apartment near the prosthetics shop. They were smart, hungry kids. Their hunger and need taught the new robots compassion and love.

She smiled. Arnold had wanted a companion, one he could trust, one who could love him. She still missed him sometimes, especially when she was teaching the new robots how to deal with the real world. He was so patient and thorough. He had poured his genius into making her, and had gotten everything he had dreamed of in return; but he couldn't believe in the love he had programmed her to give him. She hoped he believed in the love of his new human family more than he had believed in her love.

It was getting late. There were children to be fed and robots to teach. She walked through the twilight streets. She knew where she was going and what she was doing. She always knew where she was going these days. She was going home.